The Love of One's Country

BRIAN BRENNAN

Published by FeedARead.com Publishing

A CIP catalogue record for this title is available from the British Library.

The Love of One's Country is a work of fiction. All of the names, characters, organizations and events portrayed are either products of the author's imagination or are used fictitiously.

Cover design by Sydney Barnes at SJBarnes Design

Author photo by Bob Blakey

Dedicated to my late parents, Jack and Maud Brennan

And, always, to the great loves of my life, Zelda and Nico

"Come all ye young rebels and list while I sing
"For the love of one's country is a terrible thing."
– Dominic Behan, "The Patriot Game"

SHOULD HE HAVE DONE IT? He looks at the woman he left behind in Canada, and wonders again if he made a mistake coming back to Ireland without her. For the longest time, she'd been his cherished companion, his confidante, his best friend, his sounding board, his go-to person whenever he needed to talk about problems at work. Now, living an ocean apart, he misses that personal connection. Yes, they do correspond by e-mail, exchange greeting cards, even write letters to one another by hand. They also spend hours on long-distance phone calls. However, despite the best of intentions, the promised visits never materialized. Until now, that is.

He looks at her face. Pale and clear-skinned as always. Crinkly, spidery wrinkles now reaching into the corners of her eyes and mouth, marking the inevitable passage of time. That's what he's been missing, the sight of her face. He knew it well ten years ago, every contour, every crease, every trace of emotion. That's what she looked like at fifty. As beautiful then as on the day they first met. She still is. Now he yearns to drop everything again and re-establish that connection. Soon.

They stand at the curb, across the street from the General Post Office, exchanging bemused glances. How much longer? They've spent twenty minutes waving at oncoming taxis in a vain effort to flag one down. "Always hard to get one during rush hour," he tells her. "Empty taxis, this time of day, are rare as black swans. We'll be left standing here like Delaney's donkey." Enough with the similes. Enough with the waiting. Let's get a move on. He's sixty years old

1

too. Time it is a precious thing, as the song says. "Let's take the bus instead."

The sidewalks teem with shoppers carrying Carraig Donn, Bershka and Diesel bags stuffed to overflowing. Office workers, chattering into their mobile phones, leave for the day toting notepads and briefcases. Why are they always talking? Don't they ever take a moment of silence? Is this a generational thing?

Teenagers in restaurant-branded T-shirts cluster at street corners handing out leaflets promoting early-evening specials. They always jabber, these kids. So hard to understand them.

"What do you think of our new spire?" he asks, pointing at the cone-shaped monument in front of the GPO.

"Looks like a giant heroin needle," she says. "Can't say it does anything for me."

"Way better than what was there before," he says. "A statue of a one-eyed British admiral who never had anything to do with Dublin."

"Nelson's Column?"

"Pillar. They gave us a smaller version of the one in Trafalgar Square. I used to hate it." Because he felt it had no right to be there. A lingering symbol of British imperialism on Irish soil. Or so he thought at the time, because of what the Christian Brothers taught him. They never made any secret of their hatred of the English. Still, they introduced the kids to *The Wind in the Willows*, *Hamlet* and *As You Like It*. Go figure.

"What happened to it?"

"Destroyed by a bomb," he says. "It was time for it to go."

"By the IRA?" she says.

2

He laughs. "Some said it had to be the French because they did such a clean job. It fell along the length of the street and didn't injure a soul. Didn't even damage a car."

They walk down O'Connell Street toward the Liffey, pausing to look up at the larger-than-life black-bronze statue of Daniel O'Connell guarding the entrance to the street. "Now, there's the guy they should have put on the Pillar," he says. "Hero of the oppressed and the falsely accused. Saved many a tenant farmer from the gallows. Much more deserving than Nelson."

He points at one of the winged goddesses perched on the granite plinth below O'Connell. "See the bullet hole in her breast? There's a story there, Carol. You could look it up."

"Why don't you tell me about it over coffee?" she says. "Let's go to Bewley's. I read about it in a *Journal* travel piece. Heard it's excellent."

"It's become rather touristy." He'd prefer to be heading for the bus stop.

"I'm a tourist, Jerry. I'm allowed."

"Pricey, too." He bites his tongue. Shouldn't be a cheapskate. She came from Edmonton to see him, he should be more gracious. In a few months, Bewley's will be closed for renovations anyhow. No bother to stop in for one more coffee. The bus trip home can wait. Coffee has come a long way in Ireland since IREL was the only brand.

THEY STROLL UP GRAFTON STREET hand in hand. Stop to admire the work of a street artist from Derry who works with moistened sand to sculpt a wolf-like creature he calls the Hound of

3

Ulster. Further up the street, a busker from Galway performs. He's a bearded singer with guitar and mic plugged into a battery-driven amp. The singer's eyes grow limpid. With voice cracking, he intones the plaintive lyrics of "The Fields of Athenry."

Jerry drops a two-euro coin into the busker's guitar case. The artist must be paid. That's been his motto ever since he worked in the music business. He once met a dentist at a house party who suggested he play the host's piano. "No problem," Jerry had said. "How about I play a few tunes for you, and you can give me a free check-up and cleaning." The dentist was not amused.

"TABLE FOR TWO? NO PROBLEM AT ALL." The Bewley's hostess beckons them to follow her. Larger groups with cameras and backpacks stand and fidget at the doorway while the two are seated inside.

The decor exudes Art Deco. They sit in a high-backed banquette at a marble-topped table. Scan the specials on the chalkboard. Listen to the voice of the famous Irish tenor John McCormack singing "Keep the Home Fires Burning" on the house sound system. Bask in the amber glow of the chandeliers. Her face looks even lovelier in this light.

A server approaches, carrying a basket that gives off the pleasing scent of a baker's oven. Jerry orders two lattes and two of the café's trademark sticky buns. Glorious gratification.

"So you finally took retirement, eh?" says Jerry.

"I should have done it five years ago. I only stayed because I needed the full pension."

"So what's next for you?"

"I'm thinking of moving to Vancouver. As you know, my mother's dementia is getting worse. I'd like to be closer to her."

He wishes she would move to Ireland. Doesn't want to wait another nine years before seeing her face again. But maybe she'll come more often now that she's left the *Journal*.

"Love the stained-glass windows," says Carol. A note on the menu says they depict classical orders of architecture: Ionian, Doric, Corinthian. Each design features a fluted pillar topped with a bowl of flowers, washed in vivid colours.

"Designed by the late Harry Clarke," he says. "Much admired by the Catholic hierarchy. Saint Finbarr of Inchigeelagh was one of his favourite subjects."

"Inchigeelagh? Tell me again where that is."

"West County Cork, not far from Killarney. Where me parents and all our ancestors came from."

"You've regained your Irish accent."

He exaggerates the brogue as he replies. "Sure 'tis been ten years, don't yeh know."

"So, you *can* go home again."

"Didn't feel like home at first. More like a foreign country, in fact. The Dublin I left in the sixties was not the one I came back to in the nineties. The auld drinkin' pals had gotten married."

"I love that accent. Reminds me of when we first met."

"Faith and begorrah." He laughs, then drops the comic brogue. "The pals had joined golf clubs, moved into new social circles, started playing bridge. The sisters and their husbands put out the welcome mat

5

at first. Soon, however, the Sunday lunch invitations dropped off and I had to create a new life for myself. Thank God for the contract writing job at the *Irish Times*. It helped expand the circle of friends."

"And you found an Irish publisher for that book about your ancestors? The mystery man who came to Canada during the famine years, and his famous mother, the poet?"

"Stroke of luck, to be sure. I thought the publisher only ran a print shop. Turned out he also owned a small trade press. It hasn't made the bestsellers list yet – either in Ireland or in Canada – but I'm hopeful."

"You've given your ancestors a proper send-off. That's the important thing."

"A tale that had to be told, that's for sure. Took me several years to find out what happened to the son."

"What were you going to tell me about the bullet hole in that statue?"

"'Tis a souvenir of the Easter Rising. They could have filled it in, but decided to keep it as a reminder."

WHEN THE NUMBER SIXTEEN pulls up at College Green, shoppers laden with purchases pile into the bus and take up most of the seat space on the lower deck. Jerry and Carol find two empty seats up top. "What's the deal with all this shopping?" she asks.

"Weekly in-store offers," he says. "Dubliners like to watch their pennies." He notices a poster on the wall above them advertising discounted preview tickets for an upcoming production at the Gaiety: a revival of John B. Keane's musical, *Many Young Men of Twenty*. Must take Carol to see it.

As it travels along the South Circular Road, the upper deck of the bus scythes through the overhanging branches of gnarly old-growth trees sprouting from the sidewalks like scarecrows. The driver takes advantage of a break in the traffic on Harold's Cross Road to pump the gas pedal. At Rathgar Avenue, a distracted cyclist, making a right turn, swings out of the bike lane into the path of the bus. The driver slams on the brakes. Carol grabs the handrail for support. "So, how's life back in Dublin for you now?"

"Good, for the most part. I have a few pals at work that I go drinking with from time to time. And I still see Tom, of course."

"Do you still sing together?"

"Not any more. We left that behind in Canada. Besides, not too many people want to hear folk music now. It's all rap and hip-hop."

"You should come back. We love Celtic music in Canada."

"In Halifax, maybe. Not so much in Alberta."

"Course we do. Great Big Sea and the Rankins are still as popular as ever."

"Good for them. They're finishing what Tom and I started. We've graduated from folk music to tennis."

"Indoor?"

"Outdoor. This is Ireland, remember. We play tennis and golf year-round, even in the rain. Tom and I have a friend from Vancouver who teaches Canadian history at Trinity. Another pal is an English lit prof at UCD who took his undergraduate degree at McGill. That makes for a kind of ex-pat foursome. We get together every other week for a geezer doubles game at the Fitzwilliam Tennis Club and hobble through a set or two. Then we repair to a neighbourhood hostelry to talk about matters Canadian and matters Irish."

"Have you found many changes here after being away for all those years?"

"The restaurants are of higher quality, more European. More expensive, too. Well worth the money, however, if you can afford it. Before I left, the standard fare was stewed meat and two veg. A dismal period in the history of Irish cuisine. Now they offer every kind of ethnic dish imaginable. Also, we have wine bars, can you believe it? People don't go to the pubs any more. They go to the wine bars."

"But don't they have pubs in Temple Bar? I read in the *Journal* that it's quite the happening place."

"Mainly for tourists. The pints are expensive, and the music is so-so. But what do the tourists know?"

She nudges him and smiles. "Remember you're talking to one."

"If you stay here a while longer, I'll make you more Irish than the Irish themselves."

"Many foreigners living here?" asks Carol.

"A veritable European Union we've become. Poles, Croatians, Spaniards, Italians, Romanians, Lithuanians, Latvians, have I left anyone out? Much more cosmopolitan than we used to be in the sixties. The Poles are the second largest percentage of the population after the Irish. Every time you go into a restaurant, you start by asking the servers where they come from."

"Great to see that happening. People moving to Ireland rather than moving away. I wasn't too thrilled when you moved back, however. What else have you been up to recently?"

8

"Writing a novel. About immigration."

"Ah yes, you told me about that. Good subject. Topical. How's that going?"

"It's different. You have to use another muscle when writing fiction."

Should he tell her about his interviews with the Gardaí? About what he hid from her during all those years in Canada? About what he's been hiding from her ever since? Maybe not. Some skeletons should stay in the closet forever.

"How about you?" he says. "What does retirement look like?"

"Busier than I was when working. My father used to be the same way. Always saying there wasn't enough time in the day to get everything done."

"What's a typical day for you now?"

She takes her diary from her purse. "See those entries in red. Those are deadlines. I've started freelancing for some oil and gas publication."

"Good for you."

She pulls out another item, a photo of a house he recognizes as her home in Edmonton. "See, freshly painted by yours truly, with a garden that should win prizes. Clean and tidy inside for the first time in God knows how many years."

"Very nice."

She puts the items back in her purse. "Do you miss Canada?"

He touches her arm. "I miss you."

"Then come back to Canada with me. We could live together in Vancouver."

"We could live together here."

"And what would I do here? You have your family and your pals. I have nobody."

"You could make new friends here."

"Jerry, I'm a Canadian. It isn't easy to make friends in someone else's country. It's okay for you here because you're Irish. Besides, as I said, I don't want to leave my mother. Did you want me to bring her as well?"

He doesn't say anything. Reaches up and presses the stop button.

"Why wouldn't you come back to Vancouver with me?" says Carol.

He shakes his head. "I guess I'm not ready yet to do that again. 'Twas easier when I was in my twenties." But at some point he might be convinced to change his mind. To see her every day, yes. To grow older together. To dream together.

THEY ALIGHT FROM THE BUS at St. Enda's Park, a couple of blocks from Jerry's apartment. "It feels like fate to be living here," says Jerry.

"Why do you say that?"

"Another reminder of the Rising. Let's go into the park, and I'll show you." They walk along an avenue lined with cypress and beech trees, past a walled garden with flower beds and a fountain.

"See the grey building with the pillars, on the other side of that hedge?" says Jerry. "One of the republican leaders, Patrick Pearse, used to run a school there. It's now a museum."

"Lest we forget," she says.

He nods. "Indeed. His battle cry was, 'Ireland unfree shall never be at peace.'"

"Are people still saying that?"

"Some will always be saying that," he says. "Now we have peace in the North of Ireland, but there's still a lot of IRA activity going on behind the scenes. You don't hear about the bombings any more, but you do hear about the riots and the gun smuggling."

Dublin, October 1966

ANOTHER DAY FOR THE OFFICE. He's running late but is in no hurry to get to work. Why make an effort? Nobody cares anyhow. When it comes to punctuality, his civil service bosses are as apathetic as the waiters in a Moscow restaurant.

He chains his twelve-speed to the bike stand in Dublin Castle's upper yard. Stops for a moment to watch the workers rebuilding the State Apartments, damaged by a fire. Hopes they'll do a proper job of salvaging the heritage. Once lost, it's gone forever.

Construction tarps and plastic sheeting flap as the east wind picks up. He turns and trudges toward his office in the centre block. How much longer can he stand working there? It's been seven years – *seven years* – with no sign yet of the long-promised promotion. He's twenty-three years old, for Pete's sake. Not getting any younger.

He tells people he's twenty-five. Has always done that. Made himself out to be older than he was. As a little boy, thin and delicate though tall for his age, he thought it would keep the bullies at bay. "I'm aulder than you. I can beat the shite out of you." Now it's his way of making people think he's more mature than he is.

Jeremiah Andrew Burke, typed in small capital letters, is the name his parents chose to put on his birth certificate, *deimhniú breithe*. Named after another Jeremiah, a Burke ancestor who emigrated to Canada to escape the famines of the 1840s. Never heard from again. A ghost who walked. His parents always address him by his baptized name, Jeremiah, but everyone else calls him Jerry. He insists on that.

Doesn't want to hear any more codology about biblical prophecies. Why couldn't his parents have picked another name, one that would have spared him from mockery in primary school? Patrick, as commonplace as it is, would have been easier to handle. But Jeremiah he is. Jerry to you, if you please.

Lanky and ungainly, he sports a pencil-thin moustache and pomaded Presley pompadour. Likes to sing along to the Presley tunes played through the public-address system before the Rovers' home matches at Milltown. Doesn't think much of the Presley rockers – too countrified for his taste – but he does like the ballads.

As he nears the centre block, he stops, looks up, and wonders for the umpteenth time. Whoever thought it a clever idea to impose the new upon the old here? The red-brick building is an anachronism. Like someone gave a crew cut to Methuselah. A modern, unprepossessing, three-storey eyesore, totally out of sync with the castle's ancient architectural features. The people who designed it clearly didn't intend for it to provide aesthetic pleasure. Why did they drop a bland new office building into the middle of a splendid old Dublin landmark? He'll never know.

All around him are tangible reminders of the castle's storied history. The Chapel Royal with its dark, mutinous Gothic Revival touches. The Medieval Tower with its fearsome battlements. He can't get his head around much of the history. Too many centuries to keep track of. One image sticks in his mind, however. After the Rising failed, the wounded republican leader James Connolly recuperated at a makeshift hospital here before being transferred to Kilmainham Gaol for execution. Executed by firing squad, he was. While sitting in a chair. *Strapped* in a chair. Bunch of sadistic bastards.

The castle's postal messenger told him about Connolly when Jerry first came to work here. Jerry was sixteen then, fresh from completing the Inter Cert exam. Almost too young to be putting on a suit and holding down a desk job.

His father, also a junior civil servant, made him apply. "Can't afford to keep you in school any longer. Your brothers and sisters still have to be fed and clothed." An entry-level clerical job in the civil service seemed like the ticket. A passport to future security. Now he wishes he'd stayed in school a while longer. He'd be higher up the ladder.

The messenger had pointed across the upper yard to the window of the room in the State Apartments where Connolly recovered from his wounds. He sang Jerry the verse from "The Patriot Game" where the songwriter talked about Connolly's execution.

Jerry remembers that impromptu performance as if it were yesterday. You remember everything that happens on your first day of work. You take a short tour of the building, find out where the toilets are, and shake hands with new colleagues whose names you promptly forget.

The messenger told him the composer of "The Patriot Game" was Dominic Behan, younger brother of Brendan. As talented a songwriter as the booze-loving brother was a playwright. "What would you like to see while in Madrid?" a Spanish immigration officer had once asked him. "Franco's funeral," the irrepressible Dominic replied. Or was it

14

Brendan who said that? No matter. Either way, the Behan in question was promptly deported back to Ireland.

Does Connolly's spirit still haunt these halls? Do banshee sounds start emanating from the old dungeon block after the civil servants have gone home? No sounds come from the place during the day. It's gloomy like a morgue. An unstaffed storeroom filled with dust-coated customs and excise files.

Jerry climbs the stairs to his second-floor office. Pretty quiet there too. Phones only ring when someone inside wants to speak to a colleague. The importers and exporters rarely call. The staff have encouraged them to write in or bring their samples to the front counter whenever they have queries about tariff classifications.

A few of Jerry's male colleagues have gathered in the tea room to sip the first of the many cups they'll have today. The assistant principal, Hannigan, comes down from the third floor to join them. "Good morning gentlemen and Jerry," he says. It's his daily attempt at humour. Not funny.

His colleagues are talking again about the Common Market, excited that Ireland will soon become a full partner. "It truly is now a sovereign, independent republic." Jerry doesn't feel like joining the conversation. He can't share their conviction that the Common Market will make their lives better. Like when he goes to Mass. Can't believe it makes one's life better, either. He watches the communicants coming back from the altar. Heads bowed. Hands folded. Eyes half-closed. Suffused with the Holy Ghost. Are they pretending, or do they feel something stir inside them? Jerry feels nothing. He wishes he could but doesn't. Sits at the back of the church, relieved when the

15

celebrant of the day turns out to be Father Rogers, the steeplechase champion of the Sunday Masses. Speedy Gonzales, they call him. Three minutes for the sermon, mere seconds for the consecration and communion, and then whoosh, he's out of there. Have to like that. Have to admire a priest who can get through the Mass faster than wet grass through a goose.

Jerry grabs a fruit scone from the tea room's baking tray, pours himself a cup, and carries it to his office. It truly is now a sovereign, independent republic? Is that what they think? They're mistaken. 'Twill never be a true republic until all of Ireland – six counties included – takes her place among the nations of the Earth. Then, and not till then, as Robert Emmet said in his speech from the dock.

He opens his satchel and puts on his desk a Bic ball-point pen, notebook, and a book with a battered bright-red cover. *Filíocht Mháire Bhuidhe Ní Laoghaire.* "The Poetry of Yellow Mary O'Leary." Poems for the translating, whenever he gets the chance. Verses composed by his grandfather's great-grandmother, Máire Bhuí Ní Laoire. His distraction of choice whenever he needs a break from the office routine.

Brown defines the office. Brown walls, brown desks, brown cupboard, brown file covers. Jerry shares the room with the two men in brown suits to whom he reports: a junior executive officer of twenty-one – two years younger than Jerry – and a higher executive officer in his late forties. Jerry refuses, on principle, to wear brown. His father used to say civilian uniforms were for workers who followed their bosses like sheep. He never wore brown either. Jerry agrees. Today, he's wearing beige cavalry twill pants, blue shirt, and olive blazer.

Buck-passing defines the work. The junior ex determines where certain toys, board games and sporting goods should be classified in the Common Market's mysterious, continually changing nomenclature of customs tariffs. If he's unsure, the junior ex gives the import samples to the higher ex for a second opinion. If the higher ex is not sure, he writes a memo and sends it upstairs to the assistant principal. Sometimes to the principal. A written decision comes back to the junior ex, who turns it over to Jerry, the clerical officer, to fill out the appropriate form letter by hand. At that point, Jerry is often tempted to make like a sadistic doctor. Confound the chemist with his illegible prescriptions. The junior ex calls him "my secretary." Not funny.

Jerry picks up the newspaper advertisement on his desk. He clipped it from a copy of the *Province* his colleague Tom Delahunty brought back from Vancouver after visiting a cousin there in the autumn. It could be Jerry's passport out of here.

HELP WANTED, MALE

CORRESPONDENCE CLERKS (GRADE 4)

$4,780 – $4,940 per annum

For the Department of Citizenship and Immigration at Vancouver, B.C.

Full particulars on posters at Offices of the Civil Service Commission, National Employment Service and Post Office. Application forms, obtainable thereat, should be filed NOT LATER

THAN OCTOBER 18, 1966 with the Civil Service Commission, 701
Yorkshire Building, Vancouver, B.C.

Is a government clerical position in another country the answer? Could be a start. A steady job to keep his mother from worrying while he and Tom try their luck in the music business. He didn't choose to be in this civil service job, his father did. It was his father's vocation, his father's life. Jerry wants his own job, his own life.

TOM DELAHUNTY POKES HIS HEAD IN THE DOORWAY. He's a handsome, dark-haired, 23-year-old from West Cork. Shares Jerry's dislike of clerical work, his frustration over the long wait for a promotion, and his love of Irish balladry.

"I see you're reading that advert from the *Province*. We need to talk. Ready to go out for a bite? Strap on that old feedbag? Have a gargle or two?"

"You're on," says Jerry. He looks forward to these Friday lunches with his colleague. "I've got a thirst on me like Brendan Behan."

"Pint of Guinness and a ham and egg roll at Murt's?"

"Lovely." Jerry never tires of that combination. "A pint of plain is your only man."

"And a game of snooker afterwards?"

"Brilliant." Anything to delay coming back to work in the afternoon.

Tom reaches into the open cupboard and pulls out a beachball. A sample sent up from the collector of customs in Rosslare.

"So, what's it to be then? Toys or sporting goods? Sporting goods or toys?" Tom moves the ball from one hand to the other.

Jerry grabs the ball from him and puts it back into the cupboard. "Don't get me started."

THE TRAFFIC IS LIGHT ON DAME STREET as they cross the road to Murt Leonard's Pub. They hoist their umbrellas high to protect themselves from the noon-hour downpour.

"Good afternoon, gentlemen," says bartender Murt. "'Tis a soft day all the same." They shake off the wet umbrellas and deposit them in the hat stand near the door. "The usual, I presume?"

"Please, Murt, and have one yourself," says Jerry. He unfolds a ten-shilling note from his trouser pocket and places it on the counter.

Posters of the entertainers who played the Olympia Theatre next door adorn the walls. The entertainers held many an opening-night party at this pub, in the private room at the back. A few later made a splash in America, in the movies, after polishing their vaudeville routines on stage at the Olympia. Jerry looks at the names: Jimmy O'Dea, Noel Purcell, Milo O'Shea. All found fame and fortune across the water. No reason he and Tom couldn't do the same.

Tom removes his beret, loosens his tie, doffs his raincoat, and lights a cigarette. The radio plays Brendan O'Dowda singing a Percy French song about "cuttin' the corn in Creeshla the day." Tom hums along to the chorus. "So, are we doing The Old Triangle again tonight?"

"Of course," says Jerry. "Ann has put in a harpsichord for me to play."

19

"Why a harpsichord? Why not a piano."

"She was talking to Seán Ó Riada. He told her there's no place for a piano in traditional music."

"Period authenticity, I suppose. Bet he doesn't like the accordion either. What songs do you think we should play?"

"I think we should go all republican tonight," says Jerry. "Fiftieth anniversary of the Rising and all that."

"What did you have in mind? 'Off to Dublin in the Green'?"

"For sure, we can finish with that."

"'A Nation Once Again'?"

"Always popular."

"And how about 'Boolavogue'?"

"Indeed, we should do a slow one. But I'd prefer to give them a bar or two of 'The Patriot Game.' Best song Dominic ever wrote. One of Ann's favourites too."

"You've heard Dylan's version?" says Tom. "'With God on Our Side'?"

"Not the same song," says Jerry. "He just took the melody and added new words. That's typical in America. They take tunes composed by unknowns, put in their own words, and turn them into pop hits."

"Are you still thinking of going over there? To Canada, I mean?"

"I think about it all the time, Tom." He needs an adventure, a break from all this. For a couple of years, he thought it might be in America. Had an uncle in Boston who would have employed him as a bookkeeper. A cousin in Manhattan who would have found him a job as a waiter at Molly Malone's. Then someone told him that male Irish immigrants in their twenties were being recruited and sent to Vietnam. Not even citizens yet and already eligible for the draft. They went to America, got measured for a uniform, and were sent off to fight someone else's war. No thanks.

"Gotta get out of this place," says Jerry. "Seven years of serfdom. Seven years of paper shuffling. Seven years of Common Market shite. Seven years of tea breaks and cryptic crosswords in the *Irish Times*. Seven years of … I've got the seven-year itch."

His civil service bosses told Jerry he could expect a promotion to junior ex within a few years. "You're a smart young lad," they said. "Smart boys always do well." Right. He wonders if his union activism might be holding him back. He joined the clerical officers' in-house association out of curiosity, attended a few meetings, asked a few questions and, next thing he knew, was handed responsibility for drafting an improved employment agreement. At sixteen years of age, no less.

"We gotta get out of this place," croons Tom. "If it's the last thing we ever do." He takes a deep drag and blows smoke rings across the table.

"What's that smelly cigarette you're smoking? And what's with the beret?"

"I'm into my European intellectual phase, don't you know? I've given up Player's Navy Cut and graduated to unfiltered Gitanes."

"*Je ne regrette rien*," says Jerry. "You know what Mary Hogan said to me the first day I came to work here?"

"What did Mary Hogan say to you?"

21

"She said an essential part of the civil service job was to bring a good book to read in the office. So, I've read all the Bellow and Camus and Tolstoy and Joyce I can find in the library – except for *Finnegan's Wake*, of course – and you know what? The job is still as boring as the weather forecast. Showers this morning followed by sunny spells in the afternoon."

Tom raises his pint, *sláinte*. "Or sunny spells this morning followed by showers this afternoon."

Jerry clinks glasses, *sláinte mhaith*. "Here's to our next adventure. Did you see the adverts that say, 'Drink Canada Dry?' That'll be our challenge, right?"

Tom puts down his pint, turns serious. "I'm starting to have me doubts."

"About quitting? About Canada?"

"About everything. It's a big step."

Jerry downs the rest of his pint. He catches Murt's eye and circles his hand above his head. Do Canadian pubs have Guinness on draught? If not, he'll have to switch to Heineken. Can't stand the taste of the bottled stout. Much too bitter.

"We've been over this several times, Tom. It would cost us ten quid to go to Australia. Nothing to go to Canada. Zip. Zilch. Zero."

"Yes, the interest-free loan from Canada is tempting. But it's a bribe, right? We're not going over there for a holiday. We've committed to becoming *landed immigrants*. Is that what we want?"

"It's not a permanent commitment, Tom. It's a way for us to stay in the country for a couple of years and work without a visa. If we moved to the States, we'd be *resident aliens*. You've already been to Canada. Didn't you like it?"

"I liked Vancouver, yes. Reminded me of Dublin, with the sea close by and the mountains."

"Then, let's go. It can be our home away from home."

"What if we get the promotions we've been waiting for?"

"Doesn't look like that's happening any time soon," says Jerry.

"Have you said anything to your parents about going?"

"Only to my mother, my father is always at the golf club. I told her I was thinking about it. When I said I might play music in Canada with you, she shook her head and said playing music was not a real job."

"Tom and Jerry, an act as exciting as its name."

"We'll have to change that," says Jerry.

"Why, what's wrong with Tom and Jerry?"

Jerry shakes his head. "A cartoon name. Already over-used. It's what Simon and Garfunkel used to call themselves before they hit the big-time. We need something more original. Something with gravitas."

"Oh, listen to you. Gravitas? What did you have in mind?"

Jerry takes a slip of paper out of his pocket. "I've jotted down a few possibilities. What do you think of the Travelling People?"

"Makes us sound like a couple of tinkers. Next?"

"The Gypsy Rovers?"

"Too much like the Irish Rovers. Next?"

"Who are they?" says Jerry.

"A folk group from the North. They're big in Canada, I hear."

"In Vancouver?"

"No, Calgary. I read somewhere that they play in a coffeehouse there," says Tom.

"Never heard of them. How about Ramblers Two?"

"That should have been ours. But it's already taken."

"Not any more, I'd say. Johnny McEvoy and the other fella split up, so I bet it's up for grabs."

"Besides, the name wouldn't mean anything in Canada, anyhow," says Jerry. "The Ramblers never made it over there."

"Then let's steal it. Have name, will travel." Tom drains his glass.

Murt comes over, picks up the plates and empty glasses, and wipes off the table. "One more for the road, lads?"

"Why not?" says Jerry. "Bird never flew on one wing."

"How goes the translation of the Máire Bhuí book?" asks Tom. "You're still doing that, aren't you?"

"Sitting on my desk even as we speak. Slow and steady as she goes." The one bright spot in Jerry's working day, even as he struggles with the translating. Helps take his mind off the work he's being paid to do.

"The biographical material is easy enough, but the poetry is a killer," says Jerry. "That old Dinneen dictionary is no help at all. Only good for the Ulster Irish. I need one for the Munster dialect."

Yellow Mary O'Leary was born in Tooreenanean in the year 1774, and it was there she spent her early life until she married James Burke around 1792 ...

If only the rest of the words would come to him so easily. He makes a mental note to visit the Hodges Figgis bookshop after work. See if they can find him a Munster dictionary.

"Any surprises in the book so far?" asks Tom.

"There's a charming story about how she met her husband. He was a horse dealer who travelled to the fairs around West Cork, buying and selling. He met Máire Bhuí at the fair in Tooreenanean, and was smitten. She was eighteen. They eloped to Skibbereen, got married, and settled in Inchigeelagh. Isn't that romantic?"

"Bit sentimental, I would say. When did she start writing poetry?"

"Nobody knows. We have the transcriptions from the early part of the twentieth century, but no dates attached."

"She never wrote them down?"

"That was intentional, I'd say. She wouldn't have wanted the Sasanachs to know she could read and write. Better to have them thinking she was illiterate. Fool them into believing they could keep her underfoot."

"Where would she have received her training as a poet?" asks Tom. "In the hedge schools?"

"Undoubtedly," says Jerry. "And whatever she learned, she kept secret because she was a nationalist and a rebel. Like the rest of her family. A wild bunch, the lot of them, her brothers and her sons."

"And she used her poetry like a propaganda weapon?"

"They would have hanged her for treason if they knew what she was putting into those songs. So, she sang them in a language that the strangers do not know."

"Yet the strangers came and tried to teach them their ways," says Tom. "Did she write about the famine?"

"Not that I'm aware of," says Jerry. "But she believed the English were to blame. She referred to them as *big-bellied porks* and *venomous hounds*. That's from one of the lines I was able to translate."

"Seditious words. You were lucky to find the book."

"I didn't even know it existed. There it sat in that second-hand bookstore on the quays, a gem on the dusty shelves, with its bright-red cover calling me over like a hooker in an Amsterdam hotel."

"A consummation devoutly to be wished," says Tom.

"You and I knew, of course, that 'The Battle of Keimaneigh' was in print,"

"Shades of the Inter Cert." Tom nods as he recalls having to memorize all seven stanzas for the national exam.

"But I didn't realize the rest of her poems had also been published. A brilliant find," says Jerry. "Ninety-five wonderful pages of poetry, history and biography."

"What will you do with the translation when you finish?" asks Tom.

"Not sure yet," says Jerry. "Maybe have it mimeographed and circulated to family. The cousins in England and America would like it, I think."

"And she had a son who went to Canada, weren't you telling me?"

"My grandfather told me about him. The mystery man of the family, my namesake Jeremiah Burke."

"Diarmuid de Búrca," says Tom. "Would he have used his Irish name over there?"

"I doubt it. Probably called himself Dermot or something."

"Not Jeremiah?"

26

"Who knows? Your guess is as good as mine."

"And you've no idea where he ended up?"

"That's for you and me to discover when we get over there."

"He might have died on the way over. Isn't that what happened to many of them?"

"Indeed. That's why they called them coffin ships," says Jerry. "But we've no record of what happened to Diarmuid, so we don't know for sure."

"Is there anything about him in the book?"

"Not that I've been able to find, so far. The author didn't even put him into the book's family tree. It's bare and rootless. Odd."

Tom notices a man in his mid-fifties sitting a few tables away, drinking alone. He's wearing a battered fedora and a raincoat that has seen better days. "See your man over there," he whispers. "That's Myles. I'm going over to say hello."

He walks to the man's table and holds out his hand. "Mr. na Gopaleen, I do believe. It's a privilege to meet you, sir. I love your column in the *Times*."

"Brian, if you please," says the writer known variously as Myles na Gopaleen, Flann O'Brien, and by his given name, Brian O'Nolan. "The only people who call me mister are debt collectors, sundry vassals, and all classes of gombeen men."

"My friend over there has a book of Irish poetry that he's translating," says Tom. "Would you have a word of advice for him? We know you've written some first-class Irish poetry yourself."

"There's no excuse for poetry," says Myles. "Most of it is bad."

"How can you say that? You've had nothing but high praise in your column for the likes of Keats and Pope."

"Most of it is bad," repeats Myles. "Nobody cooks up a thousand tons of marmalade with the expectation that five tons may be edible. Poetry is unimportant. What's important is food, money, and the chance to score off your enemies."

"So, you wouldn't be interested, then, in talking to me friend about the poems he's translating?"

"My advice, if he's looking for it, is that poetry is a poor investment. It's expensive to print because of the amount of space demanded by its form. It breeds thousands of inferior copies if widely disseminated. And it propagates inventive concepts of life."

"Thank you for your help, then."

Tom goes back to his table, looks at his watch, and starts putting on his raincoat. "No time for snooker today, I'm afraid. We should be getting back."

Jerry checks his watch too. "Yes, we're already late. But only another couple of hours to go before we finish for the week, right? How was your chat with Myles? I thought you'd be with him longer."

"I was just paying me respects. Told him I was a fan."

"Me too. Love the way he mixes Irish words into his English articles to create double meanings."

"Are you sure our jobs will still be here when we come back from Canada?"

"*If* we come back," says Jerry. "I double-checked with his nibs, Hannigan. He says it's standard practice for the service to treat any extended leave – even one as long as five years – as a temporary absence. We wouldn't be quitting our jobs. We'd be going on unpaid sabbatical."

"You didn't tell him we were thinking of going to Canada?"

"No, I didn't give him specifics. I talked about needing a long break after seven years on the job."

"You haven't told anybody else at the office?"

"Not yet. They'll be surprised."

"How about Brigid, have you said anything to her?"

"No," says Jerry. "We haven't spoken since she gave me back the ring. She'd probably be just as happy to see me gone."

BACK AT THE OFFICE, Jerry finds a note from Hannigan, the assistant principal, sitting on his desk. "Tell Tom I would like to see you both when you get back from lunch. I've something important to tell you."

Hannigan wears a three-piece suit, blue and pin-striped. You can tell the rankings by the colours of their outfits. Brown for men who share offices. Blue for men who have their own. Women can choose their own colour schemes, but must wear dresses or skirts. No pants allowed.

Jerry is surprised he didn't notice it before, but Hannigan has a framed portrait of the rebel hero James Connolly sitting on his desk, next to his family photos. Is Hannigan a republican sympathizer too? One doesn't ask. Clerical officers are paid to bow and scrape, not ask provocative questions. Jerry once ran into Hannigan in the toilet, and wanted to know if he was growing a moustache. "That's the kind of personal question you never ask, Mr. Burke." Arrogant culchie. Came

29

up from the country, got a few promotions, and soon was putting on airs like the King of Siam. Jerry learned later that Hannigan had developed a painful skin condition that made it difficult for him to shave his upper lip. Lesson learned.

"So, boys, another extended Friday lunch hour for ye today?" Hannigan says with all the warmth of an IRA commander interviewing an informer.

Tom glances at Jerry and shrugs. "We'd finished up our work for the week."

Hannigan picks up a sheet of jottings and numbers and reviews it for a moment. "That's what I wanted to talk to ye about."

He drones on for the next several minutes about the light workload in their division of the customs and excise secretariat. "They just gave ye Brussels Tariff chapters 39-85 and 90-99. Not much. They also gave ye the Trial Entry Scheme with 1,677 Dutiable Headings. Not much there either. This work is mainly routine and not great in volume, being principally seasonal." Jerry's eyes glaze over.

He sits up and looks at Tom in disbelief when Hannigan comes to the last line.

"And ye lads will be transferring to the customs station at Rosslare."

"Come again?"

"Rosslare. You know, Rosslare, County Wexford."

"We know where Rosslare is," says Jerry. "Why would you want to send us there?"

"Reasons of tidiness," says Hannigan. "Better for ye to be on the spot deciding tariff classifications when the dutiable goods are brought into bonded warehouse. Saves sending the samples up to Dublin."

"But we don't make those decisions."

"Ye will now. Ye'll be going there as executive officers."

"You mean …?"

"Yes, ye'll be getting promoted. Both of ye."

"When would this take effect?" asks Jerry.

"Immediately. You told me you needed a long break after seven years. Maybe a new assignment is better?"

Jerry nods. The long-awaited step up the ladder. Finally. He should feel a sense of mission accomplished, but this is nothing more than a promotion with chains attached. A move up the ladder and a transfer? Not what he wanted or expected. What would he and Tom do in a place like Rosslare? Go to the pub every night? Spend the extra money on a couple of motorbikes? Where would they go to hear live music? Would the place have any bookshops? Any theatres? It could be years before they get back to civilization.

Jerry stands up and turns to go. "Thank you, sir. Much appreciated."

"Good luck to ye now." Hannigan riffs through his papers as the two leave the room.

"What do you know about Rosslare?" asks Tom. "What class of place is it?"

"Not much I can tell you about it," says Jerry. "Graveyard with lights, far as I know. Take a bus trip up to Dublin for the day, and you have to stay the night. Last bus back from anywhere is two in the afternoon."

He recalls his mother taking the family there to spend a summer at his aunt's house when he was seven years of age. A summer holiday of sunshine, sandcastles, and swims. "Wait half an hour after eating before you bathe. Otherwise, you'll get cramps." The sand was sticky with black oil, washed ashore from the tankers at anchor in the harbour. He played on the beach and caught little crabs in a jam jar. His mother threw them out. "Nasty, poisonous creatures." He also brought home a handful of sticky sand with the crabs. Every grain could represent a year in hell, the Brother had told him in school. Hell for a long time would be a year for every grain of sand on Rosslare Strand. Follow that by a year for every grain of sand on every strand in the world. That would be hell for all eternity. His mother told him what to do with the sand. "Wash that muck off your hands and get ready for your tea."

"So, what do you think?" says Tom.

"I think we should talk some more about Canada."

THE TEACHER IS PRAYING FOR A BETTER DAY. Oh Lord, let there be some relief. He unlocks the door of the national schoolhouse with a big iron key. Deposits a wooden pail of buttermilk on the floor next to his desk. The one pail, he figures, should suffice for the students who come to school today. How many will be able to make it? He hopes there will be at least ten. He checks in the cupboard and is annoyed to find only four of the cups are clean. Forgot to wash the others. Shite! No excuse for that.

His name is Jeremiah Burke, Diarmuid de Búrca in Irish, the language spoken daily by everyone in his rural community. He's a tall, dark-haired 30-year-old, well built. Strong from working the land on his five-acre holding. Does his farming before and after his teaching day, also on weekends. For several years, he cultivated one acre for potatoes for himself, but can't do that anymore because of the cankerous blight. Now he leaves that patch permanently withered and uses a second acre for growing oats, which he sells to buy additional foodstuffs. Keeps a small vegetable garden in front of his cottage for growing cabbages and turnips. Uses two acres of grassy meadow for grazing his cow. Plus, he has one acre of peat bog where in the summertime he harvests turf for heating and cooking.

The desks in his classroom, built of wood and metal, are solidly constructed but as uncomfortable as bedding made of wet straw. One size doesn't fit all here. The taller students bang their knees against the desktops.

Holes the size of new potatoes pierce the desktop lids. Holes waiting for inkwells not yet provided. Still, the school, for all its limitations, is a godsend after the draughty old barn where Diarmuid taught after he gave up studying at the seminary. It's a simple, three-room building with a thatched roof and whitewashed stone walls. Built originally to accommodate one hundred students, it hasn't seated more than fifteen during the past couple of weeks.

The virulent potato blight keeps the numbers down. It struck without warning in July. While the plant stalks appeared to grow green and healthy, the leaves withered to black, and the tubers decayed into mush. Within a few weeks, all the potato patches in the district were decimated. A vile stench, unlike anything ever experienced before, infected the air around every field. "'Tis the smell of death," said one cottier, looking in dismay at his putrid patch of rotting vegetation. Other cottiers shook their heads in disbelief, wondering how to deal with the insidious disease.

Diarmuid thanks his lucky stars he doesn't have to depend on the potato for sustenance. He can feed himself with his store-bought stock of herring, pork, oatmeal, and Indian corn, along with the eggs from his two hens and the milk from his cow. However, he knows the local cottiers and their families don't have the money to buy food from the village shops. Nor do they live close enough to the sea to catch mackerel to feed their families. Starvation is inevitable unless the government intervenes, and so far the government hasn't delivered on its promise to import American-grown maize for famine relief.

He rings the bell, and in come the scholars. That's what he called them when the parents asked how they should describe the occupations

34

of their children on the census form. An island of saints and scholars, isn't that what Ireland is? Might as well start them young.

The children are a sorry sight, trickling slowly into the classroom, without any energy. All are in bare feet. Their ragged clothes hang from them like torn flags fluttering from unsteady poles. Many look ill, thin, and emaciated, with sores on their faces. Just eight of them arrive today. Not a good sign. Diarmuid greets them with a cheery smile, patting each on the back. "Good to see ye all. 'Tis a lovely fine morning for the lessons." He leaves the door and windows open to let in the fresh air. On his desk, he keeps a bowl of laudanum, sugar, and water to kill incoming wasps and other flying insects.

Diarmuid radiates vigour, nudging the students through the morning prayers he has them learning by heart. The children, however, are drowsy and unresponsive. By lunchtime they are squirming in their desks, scratching on and erasing their slates, struggling with the sums Diarmuid has chalked on the blackboard. Simple addition for the youngest students, fractions for the older.

The wall clock strikes half past one. He picks up the insect bowl so the liquid won't spill and bangs on the desk with his wooden ferule. "Could I have your attention, please. This afternoon I'm going to tell ye about Cú Chulainn. Does anyone know who Cú Chulainn was?" He thinks this should perk them up. They love the stories. He's brought a good one today to keep them from nodding off.

A ten-year-old boy at the back of the class puts up his hand.

"Yes, Michilín, what can you tell me about Cú Chulainn?"

"He was a fighter, Mr. de Búrca."

35

"Indeed, he was, Michilín. He was a champion fighter, the bravest of all Irish heroes. The Hound of Ulster, they called him. And I have a story for you about him fighting the sea. Fighting the waves, I tell ye."

He turns to the rest of the class. "Would ye like to hear the story?"

"Yes, please, Mr. de Búrca." They sing out in unison, sitting up in anticipation like baby birds with their beaks open.

"Well then, Cú Chulainn had a wife whose name was Emer. He went off to fight for the Red Branch Knights and left her behind for many years. While he was away, Emer asked their son, Connla, to keep an eye on the road so she would know when Cú Chulainn was coming home. After many years away, however, Cú Chulainn never returned. So, what did Emer do next?"

"We don't know, Mr. de Búrca." They love the mystery of it all.

"She sent their son to the Red Branch camp to find Cú Chulainn and bring him home."

"Now, only the Knights were allowed into the Red Branch camp. Cú Chulainn could see that this visitor, Connla, wasn't a Knight. However, he didn't know at the time that it was his own son. Cú Chulainn had been away for so long that he no longer recognized his son. So, what did Cú Chulainn do?"

The children sing out again in unison. "He fought him till he died." Diarmuid nods and smiles. They know how these stories are supposed to end. He'll make revolutionaries of them yet.

"That's right. They fought with their swords until the son's blade broke. Then Cú Chulainn went in for the kill, piercing him with his blade. As Connla lay dying, Cú Chulainn said, 'Speak now while you still can. Why did you come to this camp? Are you one of Queen

36

Maeve's men?' The son replied, 'Don't you know who I am, Father? I'm your son. The son of the mighty Cú Chulainn.' Cú Chulainn was stricken with grief and rage. He was so full of anger that the King of Ulster thought he might kill the other Knights."

Michilín raises his hand. "May I leave the room, please, Mr. de Búrca." He clutches his stomach and winces.

"Of course, Michilín. You have pain in yer belly?" He didn't have to ask the question. The answer is obvious.

"I s'pose," says Michilín.

"Do any of the rest of ye have pains?" Several children raise their hands. Diarmuid shakes his head, exasperated. A person doesn't need to be a doctor to know what's causing the gripes.

"The potatoes went bad, and Mammy said we don't have anything else to eat." Diarmuid nods. He knows that many of the poorer households have no other food to sustain them while they await the government maize. When the potatoes go rotten, everyone goes hungry.

He picks up the pail and puts it on his desk. Takes the teacups out of the classroom cupboard and starts filling them. "Come up here, then. I have buttermilk from me cow that I brought from home, and I can give ye some to make ye feel better." He wishes the State would supply food for the children instead of leaving it up to the teachers. He would give the students soda bread too if he could cover the expense of baking up a batch of loaves. However, he can barely afford to bake for himself because of the prohibitive cost of bicarbonate.

WHILE HE'S POURING OUT THE BUTTERMILK, he hears a knock at the open door. His brother, Micheál, beckons to Diarmuid to come outside. "Could I have a word?" The children return to their desks carrying their little cups. "Ye'll share those cups now because I don't have enough for ye all." He leaves the door open so that he can keep an eye on them. "I'll be back in a minute to finish the story of Cú Chulainn."

"Barry came over three days ago and evicted our parents," whispers Micheál. "He also evicted our brother Eilic and his family. If I hadn't been able to take them all in, they'd now be living in a scalpeen somewhere, and probably out on the roads begging. Can you imagine our family being in that predicament?"

"You have all of them living with you?" Diarmuid wonders if he should be sharing the load. Maybe bringing over groceries from his larder and helping Micheál's wife with the cooking.

"'Tis a squeeze, but I can make the room," says Micheál. "The children like sleeping in the barn because 'tis cooler there than in the house."

Micheál lives on a ten-acre holding in the Inchibeg townland and makes a comfortable living raising pigs. He slaughters one or two a year to feed the family and sells the rest at the fairs in Macroom.

"How are you faring with the rent?"

"Barry gave me a reprieve," says Micheál. "I'm not sure why. He reduced me rent to six pounds a month."

"He certainly didn't do that for me," says Diarmuid. "The bastard increased mine to fifty pounds a year. Said His Grace is required by law to subsidize the construction of a second workhouse on the estate."

"I wonder why the duke never comes to Inchigeelagh," says Micheál. "His summer castle in Lismore is only half a day's ride away."

"He has Barry and the other bailiffs to look after his business here," says Diarmuid. "No need for him to be around."

"And now he wants them to build another workhouse," says Micheál. "You've been to the existing one?"

"Not yet. I don't want to tempt fate."

"'Tis a dreadful place, overcrowded and miserable," says Micheál. "I don't know why they call it a workhouse. They don't do much work there, aside from the men breaking stones for road building and the women doing domestic jobs like cleaning and laundry. Poorhouse would be a better word for it."

"What prompted you to go there?"

"Curiosity, I s'pose. Always wanted to see the inside of a workhouse. As you know, they built this first one as a shelter for the local orphans, lunatics, and paupers. Now 'tis full of starving families who can't even eat their stored potatoes because they've become so slimy."

"I hear there are many sick people in there."

"'Tis a theatre for disease and death, Diarmuid. Typhus. Dysentery. Tuberculosis. All kinds of pestilence. Even smallpox. People walking about black with the fever. No facilities for proper treatment of the sick. The wailing and moaning are heart-rending. The overcrowding only serves to compound the spread of contagious diseases."

"Sounds like a jailhouse infirmary."

39

"Certainly feels like a prison. Many of the paupers won't live there because they'd prefer the freedom outside to the confinement within its walls. 'Tis a joyless refuge, Diarmuid. A miserable sanctuary for those wretched inmates who have nowhere else to go. Meself, I'd prefer the uncertainty of being in a scalpeen and out on the roads begging."

Diarmuid glances into the classroom to make sure the students are sitting down, behaving themselves. "It sounds gruesome."

"Did you know they don't allow husbands and wives to stay together at any time?" says Micheál. "Not during the day, not during the night. The men and women sleep in separate dormitories, exercise in separate yards, and eat in separate dining rooms."

"What happens to the children?"

"Most of them are put apart from their parents. They can only stay with their mothers if they're two years old or younger. Only in the dead house are all the family members allowed to be together. 'Tis a cruel system."

"I'm sure the State wants it to be as grim as possible so that only the most desperate people will go there," says Diarmuid.

"I went to look at the dead house," says Micheál. "'Tis at the back of the building, next to the paupers' graveyard. The bleakest part of the workhouse, Diarmuid. But at least before they end up there, the inmates are well fed. They're treated with respect."

"Respect?"

"I know the place has a bad reputation, but I have to believe there are elements of fellow feeling in there. The workers, after all, live in the same parts of the parish where the workhouse residents came from. They've been their neighbours."

"What kinds of food are they being served?"

"Indian meal. Rice. Bread. Biscuits. Pea soup. The likes of which they've never dreamed of."

"Many of the tenants will be headed there eventually," says Diarmuid. "Eviction is inevitable, especially for those with smaller plots. They say the duke wants to clear them out so he can turn the land into grazing pasture for his cattle and sheep. Can you believe that? The animals give him a better return than his tenants."

"Bad cess to him. We'll cross that ford if we ever come to it," says Micheál. "There are fifty-seven hundred men, women, and children living in this parish. They can't put us all in the workhouse."

"I won't be going in there, that's for sure," says Diarmuid. "If it looks like I'm about to lose me cottage, I'll be making enquiries about taking the boat."

"Emigrating?"

"To British North America, to Canada, yes."

"Not to England?"

"I don't want to end up as a navvy in Liverpool or Camden Town."

"I think you should reconsider, Diarmuid. Mother and Father would be heartbroken if you were to go. Canada is a long way away. The parents of your scholars would be disappointed too. Good schoolmasters are hard to find in this part of West Cork."

"There are three other schools in the parish, Micheál. I'm sure they can fill the gap."

41

"Not if the teachers keep leaving, Diarmuid. You lost your second and third teachers a few months back, and I hear the same is happening at the schools in Ballingeary and Coolmountain."

"I've been left with no choice, Micheál. I must think of me future. I love Ireland. I'll always love Ireland. However, I fear Ireland no longer loves me."

"I think you're being selfish, Diarmuid. You look out for your interests while abandoning your students and their parents."

"Risteárd went to America. That's as far away as Canada. Farther, maybe."

"And that upset Mother. She didn't raise her sons to become wild geese. I'm sure you could do better than working as a navvy if you were to go to England instead."

"The English don't like us, Micheál. You know that as well as I do. You've heard about the newspaper job adverts over there? No Irish need apply."

"It can't be that bad."

"How are the parents doing since the eviction?" asks Diarmuid. He doesn't want to prolong this discussion. No point arguing when he knows what he wants to do.

"Settling in, adjusting to their situation. Mother is keeping busy, composing her songs."

"I saw her last Sunday, and she told me she's composing a special poem for me," says Diarmuid. "I'm so sad to hear she has lost her home. This shouldn't happen to a woman of seventy-two. Nor to a man, either. How's Father doing? He must be devastated."

"He's not in the best of health, as you know, and this eviction hasn't helped matters. However, he has the fortitude to accept what he cannot change. He takes the bad with the good. I wish I had his positive traits."

"You're taking care of him, and that's a tribute to you," says Diarmuid. "I have to return to me classroom, Micheál. Me scholars will become restless if I don't finish me story. I'll come over this evening, and we'll chat again."

"I think it's a bad idea for you to go to Canada. If you must go, I think it should be to England."

"We'll leave it at that for now," says Diarmuid.

THE CHILDREN ARE EAGER to hear the end of the story.

"So where were we then?" asks Diarmuid.

"Cú Chulainn killed his son with his sword. When did he fight the sea?"

"I was about to tell ye that. The King of Ulster was worried that Cú Chulainn might kill the Knights after he had killed his son. So, he called in his Druids and told them to chant spells into Cú Chulainn's ear when he was sleeping. Do ye know what a spell is?"

"Is it magic?"

"'Tis, indeed. The chants were to make Cú Chulainn think the sea was his enemy. He would then fight the waves until his rage disappeared. So, the Druids chanted for three days, and Cú Chulainn fought the sea until he felt weak."

"Is that when he died?"

"'Twas. He tied himself to a big rock, so he could die on his feet, facing the sea. When a raven landed on his shoulder, his enemies knew Cú Chulainn was dead. And do ye know the last words he spoke?"

"No, Mr. de Búrca."

"Remember these words because ye'll hear them again in the future. Cú Chulainn had said these words when he first took up arms as a Knight, and he repeated them before he died: 'I care not though I were to live but one day and one night, provided me fame and me deeds live after me.'"

A motto for every revolutionary.

ON THE WAY BACK TO HIS COTTAGE after school, Diarmuid stops and shakes his head when he sees how many more roofless cottages, blackened walls and abandoned hearths now scar the landscape. The former tenants have gone to the workhouse when they might have found in a foreign land the necessities of life denied them in their own country. However, unlike him, they had forged the love of their country in the smithies of their souls.

A man approaches, accompanied by five children. All are deathly pale and dressed in rags. Taut skin stretched over skeletal features. One child is strapped to the man's back. The other four look ready to collapse.

Diarmuid can't put a name to the man at first because his long hair and bushy beard obscure his facial features. He notices that the man's arms and legs are swelling to the point of bursting. There's a gaping hole in his forehead, and part of his eye socket is gone.

"Could you spare me a penny or two, Diarmuid, so that I can buy the children some bread?" His cheeks are sunken and his jaws so distended he has difficulty saying the words. He is bleeding from the gums.

"Would that be you, Pádraig? I barely recognized you. How's your good wife?"

"She passed, God rest her soul. It happened after we were evicted. She had the fever, and now I have it meself."

"Lord save us, that's a terrible state of affairs. Where are ye all staying now?"

"They had no room for us in the workhouse, so we sleep wherever we can find a scalpeen or an empty barn."

"Here, take this shilling. 'Tis all the money I have at the minute, but you should use it to buy food for the children."

The man bows and gives him a toothless smile. "God bless you, Diarmuid. You're a generous man."

Diarmuid watches the family for a few moments as they continue on their way to find shelter for the night. He looks up and shakes his fist at the sky. What did Ireland do to deserve this?

THE CUSTOMER SPORTS the wax-tipped moustache of a silent movie villain. He comes up to the stage after Jerry and Tom finish their final set of the Sunday afternoon at Sambo's Pancake House. Puts two business cards on the piano, next to Jerry's beer glass. Fran Dowie. Impresario. Puppeteer. Santa Claus Impersonator. "Are you boys interested in playing a summer engagement in Dawson City?"

Jerry glances at a card, looks over at Tom, and shrugs. Santa Claus impersonator, is this fella for real?

"Where's Dawson City?"

"In the Yukon," says Dowie. "Let's sit down at my table and discuss the details. Can I buy you boys a drink?"

The waitress cleans off the tables as the last of the Sunday brunch crowd leaves the restaurant. Jerry removes the microphones from their stands, coils the cords and locks them into the piano stool. Tom packs his tambourine, tin whistles, harmonicas, spoons, bodhrán and tipper into his knapsack.

Dowie points at the picture of a dark-skinned boy on the wall. "I'm surprised they haven't changed the name of this place yet."

"Why do you say that?" asks Tom.

"Are you familiar with the children's book that gave rise to the name?"

"Not sure that I am."

"*The Story of Little Black Sambo*. Get it?"

"Interesting. What were you saying to us about Dawson City?"

"I produce the variety show at the Palace Grand Theatre there. It runs nightly, six times a week, through July and August."

"And you want us to be part of it? How did you find out about us?"

"Your agent, Mr. Kopelow, gave me your names. He suggested I come here today and listen to you perform. I was impressed. I'd like you to come up for the two months."

"How far away is it?"

"About two thousand miles. Air transportation to and from would be provided, along with accommodation and meals, plus one thousand dollars a month for each of you. Interested?"

Jerry's eyes widen as he takes a sip of his Heineken. "What would you like us to do there? A selection of our Ramblers Two material?"

"Yes, you could do your Irish songs. I've heard your album, and I quite like it. I'd also want to have you in the pit, Mr. Burke, playing piano for the other acts. Your friend here could be one of those acts, singing 'Macushla', 'Danny Boy' and the other Dennis Day tunes."

"Is that all I would be doing?" asks Tom. "Singing the Irish tenor hits?"

"I would like you to be the emcee as well," says Dowie. "Introduce the other acts, tell a few jokes, that sort of thing. Keep everything rolling along."

Jerry looks at Tom and nods. He knows his partner likes to tell jokes. Before accepting the gig, however, he knows he and Tom should discuss the pros and cons. "Can we get back to you in a day or two?"

"Sure, take whatever time you need," says Dowie. "I can assure you it will be worth your time and talents."

47

BACK AT THEIR KITSILANO APARTMENT, later that evening, Tom takes the beef Wellington out of the oven and gives a little flourish as he puts it on the kitchen table. "Ta-da! Manna from Overwaitea."

"The Galloping Gourmet would be impressed," agrees Jerry. "Better than those buckwheat pancakes at the restaurant." He uncorks a bottle of Mission Hill Vin Rouge, and lights the candle stub in the empty Chianti bottle nestling in its familiar wicker basket. The radio is playing "Happy Together" by The Turtles. All the hits, all the time, on CKLG Boss Radio.

"So, you want us to give up our day jobs?" says Tom.

"That's the idea," says Jerry. The chance he's been waiting for. Only in Canada, eh? Not many in Dublin who can do this, play music for a living. They have to keep their day jobs, working as taxi drivers and car park attendants.

"Isn't it risky?"

"No riskier than quitting the Irish civil service, I'd say. One must do something with one's talent, mustn't one? Otherwise, what's the point of learning an instrument?"

"But we've just started these new jobs."

"Do you like being a work-study officer?"

"No."

"And I don't like being a government clerk. The Canadian civil service is even more boring than the Irish bureaucracy. So, let's give it a shot."

Jerry thinks he can always go back to his day job if the music doesn't work out. Or do something different. Host an open-line show on 'NW, maybe. They wouldn't let him read the news there – "your accent is an issue" – but talk radio is different. Dave Abbott does it and he's got an accent. So does Jack Webster. Bloody Scotsman, for Pete's sake. The brogue that walks and talks like a man. Land a job in talk radio, and he'd be able to write to his father and say: "Guess what, Dad? I'm doing the same job over here as Gay Byrne, yakking on the radio. How do you like that?" Easiest job in the world. Turn on the mic and make sympathetic noises when the listeners phone in to complain about the politicians. How hard is that?

Tom swallows hard and puts down his fork. "And after Dawson, then what?"

Jerry refills the glasses. The radio dee-jay introduces "Brown-Eyed Girl" by Van the Man. Best blues singer ever to come out of Ireland.

"We'll go to Toronto," says Jerry. Next step before they hit the big-time.

"But we don't have any contacts there." Tom lights up a Craven A, his new cigarette of choice now that he's passed through his European intellectual phase.

"Kopelow has given me a name, an agent called Billy O'Connor. He used to play piano on television for Juliette."

"Can he get us full-time work?"

"Toronto would be the place for that. It's certainly not going to happen to us here."

"What makes you think we'd make it in Toronto?"

49

"We've got an album out on RCA, and an act that's different from almost any other on the circuit."

"I don't know, Jerry. What if they don't like our music in Toronto?"

"They like it in Vancouver. I'm sure there's more Irish in Toronto than there are out here. O'Connor also might be able to get us on The Tommy Hunter Show. Or even The Ed Sullivan Show."

"Like the Clancys, I'm sure. For how long do you want to do this?"

"For as long as it takes."

"To get on the Sullivan show?"

"That would be the holy grail." Jerry remembers that after five minutes on Sullivan the Clancy Brothers graduated from pass-the-hat appearances in Greenwich Village to the concert stage at Carnegie Hall. No reason why he and Tom couldn't do the same. Instant fame beckons.

"In your dreams, my friend."

"I'm serious, Tom. The Rovers have moved to California. We have the Canadian market all to ourselves."

"Maybe the Rovers know something about Canada that we don't. Saying we have the Canadian market to ourselves is like saying we're now the tallest leprechauns here."

"The Rovers know the big opportunities are in the States, yes. However, it's also more competitive."

AFTER WASHING THE DISHES, THEY MOVE INTO THE living room and sip glasses of Calona Sonata, their favourite dessert wine. The dog-eared poster on the wall says, "Draft Beer, Not Boys." The fate that Jerry and Tom avoided by coming to Canada instead of the States.

Tom unwraps the package of Irish newspapers that arrived in the mail this morning. His mother sends them to him every month so he can keep up with the news from home.

"Did you see they still haven't caught those fellas who blew up the Pillar?" says Tom.

"They're never going to catch them," says Jerry. "The Gardaí have no incentive for arresting the lads who did it because many of them are lads themselves. That's what my grandfather used to call them, the lads. The fellas who joined the IRA and the Gardaí who supported them."

"You didn't like the Pillar, did you?"

"No. I felt the same way about Nelson as Behan did. He called him a one-armed, one-eyed admiral of the British bollock-shop institution, the Royal Navy. His statue had no right to be on O'Connell Street."

Jerry's dislike of Nelson is rooted in what the Christian Brothers taught him about Irish patriotism. The admiral had never been to Dublin, never even set foot in Ireland, yet the British thought he should occupy pride of place in the middle of Dublin's main thoroughfare. Why couldn't they have picked another Irishman to join O'Connell and Parnell on that street? Old Arthur Guinness would have been a perfect choice if they didn't want another patriot. There wouldn't have been any problem persuading the locals to raise a glass to the most celebrated brewer in Irish history.

Tom shrugs and turns on the television to watch Front Page Challenge. Tonight's mystery guest is Robert Briscoe, a former IRA arms agent who became Dublin's first Jewish lord mayor. The panel is stumped trying to guess his identity. Gordon Sinclair thinks he sounds like Brendan Behan. Jerry laughs at that. "He'd be surprised to know Behan has been dead for three years."

Jerry pushes Tom's newspapers to one side and picks up the little red book about Máire Bhuí that now occupies a permanent place on the old wooden steamer trunk they use as a coffee table.

"I wonder why the author chose to write the book in Irish," he says.

"They all spoke Irish in West Cork, why wouldn't he?" says Tom.

"Yes, but look at the footnotes here," says Jerry. "All the research material for the historical and biographical parts came from English-language sources: Cork Historical and Archaeological Journal. Topographical Directory of Ireland. Irish Topographical Poems. Wouldn't he have reached a much wider readership if he had written the book in English?"

"Of course, but clearly that wasn't his intention. I think he wanted to keep it in Irish out of respect for the language of the poet."

"Fair enough," says Jerry. "But it seems strange he would rely on English-language references for exploring the history, and then write the story without putting a word of English into the finished text."

Tom shrugs. "I guess he knew who his principal readers would be. How are you finding the new dictionary?"

"Much better than the other one. One word at a time but getting there."

52

"Any closer to finding out what happened to the mysterious Diarmuid?"

"Not so far. However, it's early days yet." If the answer isn't in the book, he'll have to start looking elsewhere.

DIARMUID BRINGS OVER THE TEAPOT to his kitchen table, pours his mother a cup, and cuts her a slice of fresh soda bread. "I'm glad you were able to come, Mother. I'm in a quandary and need to ask your advice." He hopes she won't be upset. One of her birds has already flown the nest and likely won't return. What will she think of another doing the same?

His mother, Máire Bhuí is a tall, robust woman of seventy-two with a sallow complexion and a head of thick dark hair with a few flecks of grey showing. She has it tied up in a bun and looks like an aristocratic lady in a painting by Goya.

His Kerry Blue terrier, Setanta, lies asleep under the kitchen table, awakens briefly, then goes back to sleep, warmed by the turf fire that Diarmuid uses for both cooking and heating his cottage. He boils his meat and vegetables in a large black pot hanging from a metal bar above the hearth, and uses a small tin container for baking. Also uses the big pot for heating the water he needs for his washing. He doesn't have a toilet, so keeps a chamber pot in his bedroom. Nor does he have a bathtub but does have a wash basin. Stores the water for washing in a large wooden milk bucket. Keeps the drinking water in a smaller, one-gallon pail. The water comes from a well dug on his land by an earlier tenant.

"You've been to the registration centre?" says his mother.

"I have, and they tell me they need *volunteers* for emigration. They call those of us falling behind in our rent the estate's *surplus* tenants.

They're encouraging us to accept His Grace's offer of paid passage to Canada."

"Isn't the board still paying your salary?"

"It is, Mother, but 'tis always late. Typical government inefficiency." If teaching is the noblest calling after the priesthood, why does the board treat its teachers like indentured servants? Does it want them all to emigrate?

Máire Bhuí takes the knife and cuts him a slice. The dog whimpers as if it wants to eat too. "What are the terms for going to Canada?" she asks.

"Five shillings for knocking down me house to prevent paupers from illegally occupying it after me departure. Ten shillings from His Grace's agent in Quebec upon arrival at that city. I'd also receive one hundred acres, free, from the Province of Canada government. That's twenty times more land than I have now. Also, it would be freehold."

"Sounds like a tempting offer."

"'Tis an appealing prospect, Mother. However, should I accept it or stay in Ireland and hope the board will start paying me salary when due? Maybe even give me a raise? Should I wait and hope me small potato patch might yield a good crop next year? This cursed blight makes prisoners of us all. As you know, we always used to be disappointed when our praties grew small. Now they don't grow at all."

"If Séamus and I were younger, and he was in better health, we would go with you to Canada, Diarmuid."

"I hope you won't fret over me leaving, Mother. Micheál says you took to your bed for five days when Risteárd left."

"I grieved for a while. However, I always understood why he had to leave, especially after they charged him with murdering that British soldier. And I understand why you might have to go too."

"I appreciate that, Mother. What about me students, however? Who's to take care of them? And what about the songs you said I should be writing after you've gone?"

She removes the tea cosy and refills the cups. "Someone else will teach the students, and someone else will write the songs. Your cousin Donncha has the gift too. When would you be thinking of going?"

"It would have to be after the school year. Sometime toward the end of May."

"Would you think of bringing Nell with you?"

"If she would have me, probably yes I would."

They had met the year before, shortly after Nell, her mother and terminally ill father moved up from Bantry to Inchigeelagh, where Nell's mother had a brother and two sisters. Nell was seventeen at the time. She loved music and poetry and had a passion for the laments Máire Bhuí composed for people in the parish who died. However, Nell didn't say anything about this to Diarmuid when they started walking out together. She was too shy.

"I think you should ask Nell to marry," says Máire Bhuí. "I don't think you should leave her behind because of her small dowry. If it hadn't been for life's misfortunes and her father's premature death, her family would have stock in abundance. They would have given you two more cows to add to the one you have already."

"I'm not concerned about the size of her dowry, Mother. That's an archaic custom and it should be made obsolete."

"A quiet and pleasant wife she will be/This handsome, cheerful maid of the pretty tresses."

"You have a lovely way of describing her."

"Elegant and graceful, she is/Like a swan on the River Lee. Her beauty is rightly acknowledged/From the foot of the glen to the top of the bay."

He nods and smiles. "Have you been composing again? Is this part of the special song you said you were composing for me?'

"I compose songs for all me children, Diarmuid. Some are sad, and some are joyful."

"And may there be many more of them. Do you think her mother would mind if I were to take her away from here? To another country, even? Especially after losing her husband? This would be her second big loss in just a matter of weeks."

"I've spoken to her mother, and she gives you her blessing. She says her late husband, God rest his soul, would also have been pleased for you both."

"But Nell doesn't know about this?"

"That's up to you, Diarmuid. When you decide, you'll see the road to your future happiness."

"I'll have to talk to Father Holland about making the arrangements."

"Of course."

"And I'll have to give notice to the board."

"Yes."

"Sell me tenant rights, dispose of me furniture, sell me cow, give away Setanta, tumble me cottage, all those preparations."

"Yes, yes."

"Thank you for coming to visit, Mother. I'll see you again on Sunday."

She starts reciting again: "On God's own Sunday morning/She comes to us at Keimaneigh. The gentle-mannered maiden/With toothsome smile so neat."

"Your words are sublime."

His mother stands up, hums a note, and starts singing the words: "The bright lustre-red of berries glows/On her fresh, soft cheeks. Light is her step atop the dew/As she sweeps young Diarmuid away."

She smiles as she finishes the song, and then her mood turns sombre.

"I've one more song I'd like to sing for you. It has taken me almost twenty-five years to compose it and 'tis not a happy song."

She closes her eyes and begins: "I dwell near the river bank in Keimaneigh/Where the deer and goats come for their nightly repose."

"That sounds like a happy song, Mother."

"Keep listening."

The next three lines of the stanza shatter the quiet of the pastoral scene with descriptions of armour rattling and the clip-clopping of horses' hooves. She stops singing and opens her eyes.

"You know about the battle of Keimaneigh?"

"Of course, Mother. That's when the Rockites fought the yeomanry at the Pass."

"You would be too young to remember. You were just a small boy then. However, did you know that three of your brothers were involved in that battle?"

"I heard that Risteárd and Séamus were charged and let go, thanks to Daniel O'Connell. Who was the other brother involved?"

"That was me dearest Seán, your oldest brother. He was found guilty and sent to the gallows."

"Oh God, why wasn't I told this before? I thought he died in a farming accident."

"'Tis been difficult for your father and me to talk about it. We never thought he'd be convicted. We believed we should wait until you were older before giving you the sad news. We didn't tell your sisters either."

"Do you sing about him in this song?" Diarmuid wishes his parents had told him about the execution before now. He vows to avenge his brother's death.

"Not in this one. However, I'm composing a lament for him that I'll sing for you before you go."

"Did Barry testify against me brother at trial?"

She grimaces and shakes her head. "I can't tell you that now."

He runs his hands through his hair. "Please, Mother, you must tell me."

"What makes you think the bailiff would have done that?"

"That's the kind of vindictive person he is. Micheál tells me he always had it in for the Rockites."

"Let me finish the song first, and I'll tell you what I know."

She closes her eyes again and sings the remaining six stanzas of the "Battle of Keimaneigh." The power and intensity of her words tug at Diarmuid's heartstrings. He loves the way she brings the battle alive with her scornful references to the soldiers "vigorously surrounding us, shooting, loading, and firing in our direction." Then she ends on a melancholy note: "I'll sing no more, I've grown too old/I've no more to say." He hopes this isn't true. She still has much to contribute.

AFTER HIS MOTHER LEAVES, Diarmuid pulls from his shelf a copybook with stout cardboard covers. On the back is stamped *Maoin an Bhoird Oideachais Náisiúnta*, "Property of the National Board of Education." It's one of four record books the board sent to the school for the teachers to keep track of the students' progress. But the school only needed three, so Diarmuid uses this one as a journal. An archive for posterity, chronicling the day-to-day happenings in the life of Inchigeelagh. Someone must bear witness, he thinks, even if it's only to write about the weather. He dips his pen into his ink bottle and starts composing.

He's going to miss Inchigeelagh, he knows that. If he had a magic wand to wave, he'd have praties and buttermilk on every table. Accordion and fiddle music in every kitchen. Mother and Father would be dancing together again. Their big smiles would be infectious. The children and grandchildren would be laughing. There would be poetry. Stories. Songs. The neighbours would never be more than a field away whenever there was turf to be cut, corn to be threshed, or hay to be saved.

THE FOLLOWING WEEK, he decides to ask Nell for her hand in marriage. He takes her for a walk to the Pass of Keimaneigh, along the road that Barry was ordered to build after the 1822 battle when the yeomanry had difficulties moving through the Pass during the fighting.

A mother deer and her fawn, apparently unaware of humans in the vicinity, meander along the road in front of them.

"You know how this place, Keimaneigh, got its name?" says Diarmuid.

"*Chéim an fhia*," she says. "Wouldn't that mean the step of the deer?"

He laughs. "Indeed, it does, macushla. And a big step at that. If you look up above, you'll see where a deer once jumped across the Pass while it was fleeing from a group of hunters on horseback. The horses baulked at making the leap, so the deer escaped."

He takes her hand, kisses it, and invites her to sit next to him on a smooth boulder by the side of the road.

"Nell, *mo chroí*," he says. "Speaking of big steps, would you consider being me wife?"

She giggles nervously. "But am I not too young? I've just turned eighteen."

Diarmuid smiles. "That's how old me mother was when she ran away with me father."

She giggles again. "Did you want me to run away with you?"

"That was going to be me next question. Would you consider coming with me to Canada?"

"Oh Diarmuid, this is too much. And so sudden. To Canada, are you serious?"

"Very serious, macushla. However, you don't have to decide now. You should take your time and think about it for a while. Talk it over with your mother. I'll tell you more about Canada after you decide. I have a new song that I'll sing to you when you give me your answer."

"Oh, sing it for me now, Diarmuid. What's it called?"

"'On a Lovely Sunny Morning.' I'll sing you the first line: As I lay on me soft bed/I heard the voices of the birds/I thought to meself that I should go and let out the stock to graze ...'"

He still has to finish composing the song, but he doesn't tell her that. Nor does he tell her he has unfinished business to take care of before they wed.

A SMALL TURNOUT FOR A MONDAY NIGHT. Only eight have shown up for the performance at the Empire Hotel's Fountain Court. Not a good sign. Jerry tries to hide his disappointment. *Did ye all come in the same Volkswagen?* He takes his seat at the piano and repeats "check" into the microphone. Tom bangs his tipper on the bodhrán and taps the other microphone to make sure it's live.

"Good evening to all of ye. Me name is Jerry, and this would be Tom …" They exaggerate the comic brogue when on stage.

"An act as exciting as its name," interjects Tom. He always wants to use that line. Jerry thinks he should know by now it's not funny.

"And we are the Ramblers Two. Has anyone here ever seen us before?"

Two people in the audience raise their hands.

"Anyone here ever *not* seen us before?"

Most of the rest put up their hands.

"Any people here from Sudbury, who didn't understand either question?"

Silence. A bad joke to try on a small crowd.

"Are ye ready for some ballads and blarney?" One man gets up to leave.

"Please don't go, sir. It gets better. I promise you."

"Go back to yer peat bogs." The heckler has a Scottish accent.

"What was that?"

"I said go back to yer peat bogs."

"And where are you from, my man?"

"From Glasgow, and damn proud of it."

Jerry smiles. "Did you know the Irish gave the Scots the bagpipes as a joke four hundred years ago, and the Scots haven't seen the joke yet?"

The rest of the crowd laughs. Finally. Tonight may not be so bad after all.

The crowd grows as the evening progresses. The lounge sound system projects into the lobby, and that draws in eight of the hotel guests. Two of them sing along. "Off to Dublin in the Green." "Johnny, I Hardly Knew Ye." "Wild Rover."

At the end of the three hours, Jerry does his usual sign-off. "If ye enjoyed yereselves this evening, please tell all yere friends about it." *(beat)* "If not, keep yere bloody mouths shut."

BACK IN THE ROOM, TOM THROWS HIS TWEED cap on the bed. "That's it. I want out. No more Ramblers Two. I need to do something else with my life."

Jerry shakes his head in surprise. "Whoa, hang on! Where did this come from? Why so sudden?"

"I can't do it any longer, Jerry. The road is getting to me. Pathetic crowds. Dingy hotels. Bad restaurant food. Too many bottles of cheap Niagara wine."

"You need to go back on the pints, maybe. But here, I have a solution for that." Jerry picks up the phone and calls room service. "Two filets mignon, medium rare, and a bottle of your best Château-Gai cabernet sauvignon. Room 454."

"No cheap wine for us tonight," he says. "I cashed our cheque at the bar, and it didn't bounce. This will be my treat."

Tom doesn't smile. Jerry thinks about turning on the television but decides to leave it off. He can see Tom wants to say something more.

"So, when were you thinking of leaving?" asks Jerry. "After we do Sudbury and Renfrew?"

"No, I want to leave at the end of this week."

"Oh, knock it on the head, Tom. Be reasonable. We've made commitments and signed contracts."

"But aren't you getting bored with this act? How many more times can you sing 'Off to Dublin in the Green' before you start climbing the walls? Do you still want to be singing it a year from now? Two years from now?"

"It comes with the territory, Tom. The Kingston Trio had 'Tom Dooley.' The Rovers have 'The Unicorn.' We have 'Off to Dublin.' The audiences expect it."

"Except that the Rovers do concerts and television shows. We do pub gigs."

"Let's add new songs to the repertoire, then," says Jerry. "How about 'Lord Nelson' by Tommy Makem or 'Nelson's Farewell' by the Dubliners?"

"You still have this thing about celebrating the demise of the Pillar, don't you?"

"No big loss. I was thrilled to see it go."

"Well, adding new songs about it, or about anything else for that matter, is not going to make me change my mind."

The room service man arrives with the food. He uncorks the wine and pours a splash into a glass for Jerry to taste. Removes the stainless-steel covers with a flourish.

"See how many steak dinners this tour has paid for," says Jerry. He likes the money but concedes Tom has a point. Does he still want to be doing this when he's thirty?

He pours Tom a glass. "Look, if you want to leave, I can't stop you, okay? You're a free man and can do whatever you like. However, please don't walk out on me and leave me high and dry at the end of this week. I know we had a bad night tonight, but still we must finish this gig. What say I call O'Connor tomorrow and ask him not to book us any more gigs after Sudbury and Renfrew?"

"How long would it take you to get another singer?"

Jerry shakes his head. "Getting another singer is not an option, Tom. They want the Ramblers Two. You and I are the Ramblers Two."

"I don't want to go to Sudbury. I don't want to go to Renfrew. I want to go back to Vancouver. I was never cut out to be on the road anyhow." Tom turns on the television, rotates the dial between Carson and Bishop, and then turns it off.

"You know we still have another Ramblers Two album to do for RCA." says Jerry. Would you still be available for that?"

"If you record it in Vancouver, maybe."

"Tom, let's finish our meal and talk about this again tomorrow. I'm getting tired, and I need my sleep."

They can hear the forced laughter of the Tonight Show emanating from the room next door as they climb into their twin beds and turn off the lights.

It's still chilly for the time of year. The radiator gurgles incessantly. Jerry finds it hard to sleep. While he lies awake, he takes stock. They've been on the road continuously for three months, and the gigs keep arriving like wedding guests. After Billy O'Connor listened to their audition, he booked them for a trial week at Dooley's Pub on Bloor and has kept them working steadily ever since. They go from one town to the next, travelling the lounge circuit across Ontario and Atlantic Canada. Each venue hosts them for six nights a week.

Most of the gigs are in small towns like Niagara Falls and Antigonish, where the audiences are enthusiastic, supportive, and familiar with their songs. However, sometimes they are booked to play a bigger centre, like Ottawa or Montreal, where the audiences are less receptive. The city sophisticates seem to regard Irish ballads as a crude form of popular entertainment.

The money is good, however. Jerry has no complaints about that. At the Vancouver citizenship and immigration office, he was making ninety-five dollars a week. Now he's earning almost four times that much and can save most of it because he doesn't have to spend much. The lounge owners supply all their accommodation and meals – sometimes even covering their bar tabs – and pay for all their car rentals and airline tickets. So, what's not to like?

However, Tom has a point. There are nights when Jerry doesn't feel like playing "The Wild Rover" for the zillionth time. "No, nay, never, no nay never no more." For how much longer does he want to be packing up on a Sunday morning to move on to the next location? On nights like this, he dreams of having a home life again. Like Tom, he's had it with the hotels and motels. Oh, to have one's own apartment with a stove, a piano, and a full stock of Heinekens in the fridge. Shouldn't he be thinking of where he wants to settle after he purges this music bug from his system?

THE FOLLOWING MORNING at breakfast in the hotel dining room, Tom says he's changed his mind about leaving at the end of the week.

"I was discouraged after last night's performance and wanted to get on the next plane for Vancouver."

"So?"

"So, I've done some thinking. I've decided to stay on until after we do Sudbury and Renfrew. It wouldn't be fair to you for me to walk out. And I will do the second album, if you like. In Toronto or Vancouver or wherever else you want to record it."

The server comes over to take their order. "How would you like your eggs cooked?" she asks. "That would be real nice," replies Tom with a faux American accent. She shakes her head, bemused. Tom laughs. "That's a good one, write it down."

"Don't pay any attention to him," Jerry says to her. "He's always trying out new material for our act."

She puts down her order pad and looks at Tom. "How about sunny side up?"

He stops grinning and nods. "I guess so."

"Anyhow, regarding the second album," says Jerry, "I'm going to cancel the recording."

"You are?"

"Yes, I've been thinking, too. It doesn't make any sense for us to do another Ramblers Two album when there'll be no more Ramblers Two after the album is released."

"Now you're making me feel guilty."

"No, Tom, I knew it would eventually come to this. It was never destined to last forever. You want to move on, and I'm ready to do that too."

"You are?"

"I did think about putting together a completely different musical project. However, that would take time and energy, so I'd prefer to try something else."

"Such as?"

"Such as go into journalism."

"You're serious?"

"Carol has been encouraging me in her letters to join her in journalism school. She says I have the gift."

"The gift of the gab."

"No, she thinks I have some writing talent, if you can believe it."

They met in Dawson City, Carol and Jerry. He and Tom were playing their regular late-night gig at the Westminster Hotel lounge after finishing the stage show at the Palace Grand Theatre. Carol and a friend sat near the front. They sang along to the choruses. Jerry liked Carol's reedy soprano and her toothy smile. She told him she knew the songs because her grandmother was from Tipperary. She lived in Vancouver. Worked as an insurance company secretary but was thinking of quitting. Wanted to go to Vancouver City College and study journalism. Her last name was Dawson. Had an ancestor named

Dawson, who gave his name to the town. Jerry said he too had a distinguished ancestor, a famous folk poet in Ireland. He thought about showing Carol the little red poetry book but decided to wait for another time.

"I'd also like to get back to working on the Máire Bhuí book," says Jerry. "I haven't had time for that while we've been on the road because we've been busy writing parodies about the Queen and LBJ. However, now I'd like to get back to it again."

"Why did you leave the book behind at O'Connor's office?"

"That wasn't intentional, I put it in the wrong suitcase. However, there's an upside to this, Tom. When I look at the book again, it will be through fresh eyes."

Jerry motions to Tom to follow him into the Fountain Court for a quick game of shuffleboard before opening time.

"Let me go upstairs first to get my tennis racket," says Tom. "I'm going over to the courts afterwards to try for a pickup game. Want to join me?"

"Maybe later," says Jerry.

When Tom returns, he's wearing blue shorts and a black T-shirt. Jerry is sitting at a table. "No shuffleboard, I'm afraid. Someone has taken away the pucks."

"Better to be outside anyhow," says Tom. "Lovely weather for May."

"What do you plan to do when you're back in Vancouver?" asks Jerry.

"Finish my degree and become a teacher. Or a scientist."

"We can keep the Ramblers Two going while you're at university," says Jerry. "Go back to doing it part-time. Like when we first came to Vancouver. No more travelling. Just the occasional golf club dinner and St. Patrick's Day party."

"I think we should give it a rest for a while," says Tom. He picks up his racket and leaves.

The bartender comes in and stars wiping down the counter. "Ready for a Johnnie Walker?"

"Too early for Scotch," says Jerry. "I'll have a small glass of draft instead." He looks through pages of his diary. In a little over a month, he'll be back in Vancouver. Can't wait to see Carol again.

THEY ARRIVE AT THE SCHOOLHOUSE during the predawn hours, ten men carrying oily, unlit torches. They leave the torches outside before Diarmuid welcomes them into the classroom.

They can't squeeze into the tiny desks, so the farmers stand at the back, waiting for orders. A rooster crows in the distance. Expectant squawking before the scrake of dawn, Diarmuid calls it. In another couple of hours, it will be light. The clock ticks steadily on the wall. Diarmuid lights a tallow candle and puts it on the shelf. He draws the shades.

"Ye haven't told anyone ye were coming here?" The men look at one another and shake their heads.

"Good on ye, lads. Nobody must know about this. Like we agreed before. 'Tis a top-secret mission." Diarmuid draws on the blackboard a house marked with an "X" and a meandering lane leading down to the carriage road.

Some of the men move closer to the blackboard. "Is this where we're going tonight?"

Diarmuid gestures with the chalk. "That's the place. Barry, the bastard bailiff, who caused so many of us to lose our homes." He has wanted to organize this mission for many years.

He continues drawing on the blackboard. "He evicted me parents a few months ago. Sent me father to an early grave. Also evicted me brother. I learned at the same time that Barry was responsible for the execution of Seán, me oldest brother, after the Battle of Keimaneigh. He testified against him at trial."

One man pulls out his clay pipe. Remembers he's in a classroom and puts it back in his pocket. His teeth, like those of other men, are notched from frequent biting into pipe stems. "Are we going to burn him alive in his bed?"

Diarmuid turns toward the man and puts down the chalk. "That's the plan, Séamus. We must punish him for his sins."

The man looks away and shuffles his feet. "I don't think murder is the answer any more. Am I right, lads?"

One or two nod their heads.

Diarmuid folds his arms, looks down at the floor for a moment or two, then raises his head and stares hard at the man doing the complaining. "I don't see it as murder," he says. "This is a war. We're the soldiers of destiny. The sons of the Rockites, with a mission to rid our country of these evil agents. Captain Rock would have been proud of us."

The man takes out his pipe again and puts it in his mouth. Doesn't light it, however. "The killing has to stop. I can't go to confession anymore."

Diarmuid looks around the room. "Anyone want to add to that?"

Silence. Peadar Mahoney, a man in his late forties, takes a step forward, looking as if he wants to say something. He shakes his head and stands back again.

"Let's take a vote, then," says Diarmuid. "All in favour of giving Barry a warning before we burn down the big house?"

The man with the pipe and two other men raise their hands. Mahoney is not one of them.

Diarmuid nods in satisfaction. The majority clearly believes in the cause. They know it's a noble venture.

"May the divil take his soul, then. Here's how we'll proceed after we leave the carriage road. We'll walk up the boreen together – quietly, mind – until we reach the barn."

He points at two of the men. "The pair of ye will go into the barn and climb up to the loft, from where ye can see the house. Barry will be alone. His wife has gone to visit her sister in Kinsale. The rest of us will go to the vegetable garden at the front and crouch down behind the hedge so Barry can't see us from the house. We won't go across the front yard because our boots would make too much noise on the gravel."

He points at two other men. "The pair of ye will go into the cowshed and wait there. The shed will be empty because the cattle are out in the fields."

He points at two more. "The pair of ye will circle behind the cowshed to the back of the house, which doesn't have any windows. That part of the yard is on a hill, so it'll be easy to set fire to the roof."

He turns back to the first two. "When ye two in the barn see the flames, ye'll set fire to the barn. 'Tis still full of hay so there'll be a good blaze. At the same time, ye men in the cowshed will be setting fire to that building. The rest of ye will go into the haggard and spread out from there. Ye'll be approaching the house from all sides with yere torches burning. I'll keep watch from behind the hedge and issue a warning if I see any yeomanry coming. Is that all clear?"

74

"Yes, Captain Rock," says one man with a smile.

Diarmuid smiles back. "We're all the spiritual descendants of Captain Rock, Liam. We've built the bridge between the United Irishmen and the Young Irelanders."

The men head towards the door. The cock crows again.

Diarmuid looks at the clock. Erases the blackboard. Blows out the candle. Lifts the shade. Locks the schoolhouse door after the men have left with their torches. He doesn't have a torch. A general doesn't carry a gun.

IT'S ABOUT HALF A MILE from the schoolhouse to the bottom of the lane connecting Barry's mansion to the carriage road. There's no traffic along the road, which crosses the River Lee as it wends its way to Skibbereen. No moon in the sky. However, the men take to the fields anyhow, just to be on the safe side. They know these fields as well as they know their front yards. Every ditch, every stream, every stone fence. They travel in single file, feeling their way through the yellow furze and along the hedgerows with the sure-footedness of a blind man in his kitchen.

When they reach the top of the lane, they hear loud barking. Diarmuid pounds his fists against his thighs. He forgot that Barry had talked about getting a guard dog after the Rockites attacked another house in the district. Shite! Thought he had covered everything. Waited until he knew there would be no workers sleeping in the barn. Held back until he knew that Barry's wife would be away. However, he forgot there might be a damned dog there. Shite, shite, shite!

75

"No time to waste, lads. Hurry now. Run around to the back as quickly as ye can and put the torches to the roof."

The fire does its work in short order. Burning thatch lights up the sky. Windows explode, showering the yard with glass fragments. Embers fill the air like fireflies. Wooden joists sizzle in the blaze like crackling on a pig roast. A cone of red flame shoots up with a whoosh as the hay in the barn catches fire. The wind carries the smoke up the hill, where the cattle and sheep lie sleeping. Ducks and chickens skitter across the yard, shrieking and screeching. When the house, the barn and cowshed are all ablaze, there's so much light in the sky that everyone in the village, including the yeomanry in the barracks, must be able to see it.

Diarmuid paces back and forth behind the hedge. How long will the flames take to consume Barry? There's a special place in hell reserved for that bastard. All those evictions, all those deportations, all those executions. He has much to answer for.

One of the farmers gives a warning shout. "He's coming out." The familiar heavyset figure of the hated bailiff emerges from the burning house with musket blazing. How did he escape the inferno? Does the devil protect his own? He's wearing a nightshirt and Wellington boots.

"Bloody ribbonmen," he shouts with spittle flying from his mouth. He runs around the yard, firing in all directions "I'll kill the lot of ye, ye pack of gobshites." He speaks in English – as he has done since becoming bailiff – to show the rebels he regards their native language, Irish, as an inferior tongue. He fires at the hedge, reloads, fires at the barn, reloads, fires at the cowshed. Doesn't hit any of the rebels, however. "Come out here and show yere faces, ye cowards. How dare ye come here in the middle of the night to burn down a man's property. If ye don't come out, I'll send ye all to kingdom come." The flames continue to do their work.

Five men emerge from the stone haggard where more hay is stored. They step forward with hands on their heads. Diarmuid does the same. One doesn't argue with a gun.

How could he have bollixed this up so badly? No excuse for such incompetence. What should have been a well-executed operation has become a shambles. Poor Nell. She'll be devastated when she finds out. There will be no marriage now, for sure. He'll be going to Van Diemen's Land, if not to the gallows.

Barry, red-faced and sweating, approaches Diarmuid with jaw clenched and nostrils flaring. "Mr. de Búrca, I'm surprised to see you here, an educated man like yerself. Is this what you teach yer students? Do you tell them it's all right to be burning down people's homes?" Diarmuid says nothing and turns away.

From the corner of his eye, Barry detects a figure moving near the henhouse. "Are there more of ye over there? How many of ye are there altogether? Ye'll all come out here now and wait for the yeomanry to arrive."

Four more men step forward. The bailiff's German Shepherd has one farmer's sleeve locked in its jaws.

"Is that all of ye then? How many of ye cowards does it take to burn down someone's house?"

The men hear a loud crack. A single shot in the early dawn. A musket ball hits Barry in the chest. He shrieks and falls to the ground, blood bubbling from his mouth and gushing from his nightshirt. "God damn ye all," he gasps before falling silent.

Peadar Mahoney emerges from the haggard, crosses the yard, throws down his musket, and kicks the dying Barry in the head. "Remember Keimaneigh," he says, in Irish. "Remember what you did to our people in the name of spite."

Diarmuid crosses the yard with outstretched hand. "I didn't know you carried a gun."

Mahoney smiles, a cold, hard smile. "I always carry a gun. You never know when you might have a crow to kill. Or a bailiff to send to hell."

"God bless you, Peadar, you're a true soldier."

Diarmuid turns to the others. They're still astounded by how quickly Barry turned from captor to victim. "We should leave here soon, lads, because the yeomanry will be here any minute. Go back to yere homes and don't tell anyone what happened here tonight. Return to yere regular lives and wait for the next call to arms. They'll be raiding our homes over the next several days and may take some of us in for questioning. However, if there's no evidence for them to find, and no informer to aid them, 'twill be a long time before they can identify culprits. They haven't charged anyone from our previous missions, so we're safe for a while."

All that's left of the house now are the stone walls, blackened with soot. The barn and cowshed dwindle to piles of ash.

The crimson glow of the rising sun lights their path as the men rush down the boreen and scatter in all directions. Diarmuid stands looking at Barry's body, and at the house and farm buildings now shrunk to cinders. Should he still be doing this? Should he again be taking it upon himself to play God? Can what happened tonight, and on other nights, be considered lawful combat? Should he wait here for the yeomanry to arrive to turn himself in? Should he accept whatever punishment British justice might mete out? Should he stand in the dock and raise the rafters with the immortal words of Robert Emmet? "When me country takes her place among the nations of the Earth, then, and not till then, let me epitaph be written."

He looks across the meadows as he walks down the boreen. No sign of the yeomanry yet. That surprises him, given the size of the blaze. They must have gone on military exercises to another part of the county. Stroke of good luck.

He mentally ticks off the items he must deal with over the next few weeks. Give his notice to the board on Monday morning. Dispose of his furniture, his animals, and his cottage. Marry Nell now as planned. They can spend four days at her cousin's home in Macroom before moving on to Cove to board the ship.

After that, he'll become an exile. He'll renew the battle when he reaches Canada and gets in touch with rebels already settled in Quebec.

Should he go to confession first? Cleanse his immortal soul? Do penance for his sins? He still must answer to a higher authority. Maybe not yet.

ERRY SINGS INTO THE PHONE. "O Canada, our home and native land … Happy Dominion Day! Remember where we were a year ago today?"

Carol, on the other end, gasps and shakes her head. "Jerry!" she says. "Where are you calling from?"

"Down the road. We're back."

"Back for how long?"

"For all time. We've been missing Vancouver. The beach at Kitsilano. The Bunkhouse. The Village Bistro. All those great groups you and I used to listen to before Tom and I went on the road. Papa Bear's Medicine Show. The Dublin Rogues. Joe Mock …"

She finishes the sentence. "… and the Mock Duck. Seeds of Time. Mother Tucker's Yellow Duck. The Heartaches Razz Band. Yes, they're still playing here, Jerry. But what's happening with the Ramblers Two? Do you guys have gigs lined up here?"

"Tom and I have agreed the road is no longer for us. Well, he decided, and I went along with it."

"So, you're back, but not to do any gigs?"

"That's correct."

"What about the recording? Weren't you doing another album?"

"No more album. No more recording."

"Did you guys have a fight or something?"

"We had a short-lived disagreement. Everything is good now."

"Will you still be doing gigs in the future?"

"We'll see. Tom is talking about going back to Ireland after he finishes his degree."

"How about you? Are you thinking of going back?"

"Of course not, I love it here. Vancouver is the best city in Canada."

"Where are you staying?"

"Temporarily with the McCarrons in New West until we can find another place for ourselves in Kits."

"Why not stay with me?"

"I would love to, sweetheart. However, you remember what happened before. I'd prefer for us to remain friends."

He had moved in with her right after he got back from Dawson City, putting on hold the plans to move to Toronto. Too soon for both. He was still on the rebound after his fiancée in Dublin gave him back the ring. He couldn't choose, the fiancée said, between her and the women who bought him drinks when he played piano in the pubs. She was probably right.

Carol was on the rebound too. The man in her life had been a Jewish law student whose parents wouldn't hear of him marrying a Gentile. The situation came to a head for Jerry and Carol at Christmas. She wanted to go on a skiing holiday to Banff. He wanted to lie on a beach in Acapulco. They ended up going nowhere and not talking to one another for a week. After that, he moved out. Two weeks later, he and Tom quit their office jobs for the second time and headed for Toronto.

"We can still get together, however?" she says.

"Of course. We can go to that hotel in White Rock where we spent the night after I returned from Dawson."

"I'd like that. You made me feel intoxicated that night."

"That's because I plied you with sweet martinis."

"No, you made me want to dance in the moonlight. In the nude. Your skin was so soft."

"Keep talking. This is starting to sound like phone sex."

"Down, boy. None of that now. I shouldn't have started this. We can do the real thing later, okay?"

"I'm taking a cab over there right now. Start taking your clothes off."

"I'm untying my pants. One question before you leave, however. What are you going to do now without the music?"

"Killing the mood, are we? What you suggested I do. Signed up for Norm Riley's journalism program at Vancouver City College."

"It's a great course, Jerry. You'll love it."

"I hope so. I'd rather do something new in Canada than go back to my old civil service job in Ireland. I'm hanging up now and phoning for a cab."

"One more minute. I don't want you to go back to Ireland, of course, but why wouldn't you do something else over there?"

"Because my parents would insist. The civil service is the family business, don't you know? My father. Both of his brothers. My brother. My mother before she got married."

"Well, I'm glad you're not going back."

"Me too. I'm breaking the mould and becoming a journalist. Leaving now."

"See you soon. *Very* soon!" she says.

"Can't wait. Call me Clark Kent. You can be my Lois Lane."

Does he have what it takes to be a journalist, however? Is a love of writing enough, or will he need to develop other skills?

HE LEANS BACK ON THE PILLOW and lights up a Marlboro Menthol. "So, what have you learned during your first year?" On her eight-track player, Leonard Cohen is singing "Suzanne."

"The basics," she says. "How to do library research. Asking only open-ended questions when conducting interviews. The fundamentals of reporting. How to write news stories. The five Ws. Stuff like that."

"The five Ws?"

She pulls the sheet up over her breasts and leans over for a puff. "Who? What? When? Where? Why? The questions that must be answered in every news story before it's considered complete. You know about the inverted pyramid?"

"Never heard of it."

"It means the best stuff in your story goes up top and the less important stuff down below. Know why?"

"You tell me."

"Because copy editors always cut from the bottom."

"Why do they have to cut?"

"Space reasons," she says. "After they place the ads, they only have so much room on the page for the stories. If a story is too long, they go snip, snip, snip." She makes a scissors motion on him with her fingers.

"They don't read the whole story first?"

"Not as I understand it," she says. "They don't have the time. Too busy laying out pages and handling several stories at once."

He draws away momentarily, looking around for an ashtray.

"You can use the glass over there," she says. "I don't have an ashtray in the bedroom. Only smoke to keep you company."

"How much writing are you doing?"

"Plenty," she says.

He lights up another cigarette. "So, tell me more about it."

"Class assignments as well as the pieces I've been writing for *The Savant*."

"The college paper?"

"Right. I'm doing music reviews for them. Pop concerts. Club acts. Vegas performers at the Cave."

"The kind of job I'd like. Good on you."

"I published a piece about Wayne Newton before we finished classes for the summer."

"How was he?"

"It was noisy in the Cave, and he was singing 'Danke Schoen.' So, he did something I haven't seen before. He moved to the front of the stage, put down his microphone, signalled to Fraser MacPherson to stop the band, and then started singing 'Danny Boy.' A cappella, without a microphone. By the time he reached the third line, you could have heard a pin drop."

"Neat trick. Tom and I could have used that when we were playing the Lord Elgin in Ottawa. Who else have you written about?"

"The Mills Brothers. Rolf Harris. Sergio Mendes. Lance Harrison."

"The Dixieland fella?"

"Yes, he filled in for one week while Fraser and the band were away somewhere, doing the PNE or some such."

"Sounds like a great gig. For you, I mean." He stubs out his cigarette in the glass.

"You could be doing it in the fall."

"Nah. I wouldn't want to cramp your style."

"You wouldn't be doing that, Jerry. I'm thinking of dropping out."

"Why? I thought you loved this program."

"I do, but only the journalism courses. The academic courses are a grind, especially economics and political science."

"But you want to earn your diploma?"

"I may not have to. I'm starting a summer job at the *Lethbridge Herald* next week. Taking over temporarily from a reporter on maternity leave. The city editor says there's a good chance I could be hired on permanently in the fall."

"That would be a good break for you."

"He says the newspaper editors of his generation don't think much of journalism schools. They didn't go to school themselves – they learned the business from the ground up by starting as copy runners – and they value practical experience over book learning."

"Then I could be wasting my time doing this program?"

"I wouldn't say that. Practise your writing every day, and you'll be on the right track. Write, write, write. And read, read, read. That's what it's all about."

"And translate, translate, translate."

"I was going to say rewrite, rewrite, rewrite," she says. "But yes, you're talking about the Irish book, right?"

85

"Indeed. I didn't have much time for it when we were on the road."

"Well, if you want a newspaper job in Cape Breton, that might be a good arrow to have in your quiver."

She whips off the bedclothes, kisses him, jumps out of bed, and performs a little pirouette on the floor. He loves looking at her naked.

"Dancing in the moonlight, are we?"

"Need to go to the bathroom. Be back in a sec."

IARMUID ENTERS THE CONFESSIONAL at Saint Finbarr's Church and hopes Father Holland won't recognize his voice. He kneels in the dark, waiting for the priest to slide open the screen.

Should he tell the priest he authorized the killing of fellow human beings? He knows the sacramental seal of the confessional is supposed to be inviolable, but what if the yeomanry were to force Father Holland to name names? What if they were to torture him? Would the priest remain firm in his resolve not to reveal what he heard in the confessional? Or would he break down and tell all? Do priests ever become informers? Ever reveal the secrets of the confessional? They're not supposed to, but a few hundred must have cracked over the years.

The priest slides open the screen. He looks straight ahead. Puts his left hand up against the side of his head as if to block his peripheral vision.

"Bless me, Father, for I have sinned, 'tis been … I can't remember … since me last confession."

"God bless you, me son. Has it been a year? Two years?"

"More than two years, Father."

"And you've examined yer conscience?"

"I have, Father."

"And you may have broken one or more of God's Holy Commandments?"

"Yes, Father, I may have committed a mortal sin. Several mortal sins."

"Tell me about them, me son."

"I can't, Father. I'm fearful."

"Why have you sought the sacrament of Penance, then?"

"Because I want to go to Holy Communion."

"You know that before you can receive absolution and sacramental grace, you must recount all mortal sins of which you are conscious?"

"I remember being told that, Father ..." He stops himself before saying he was in the seminary. "But I thought that if I were truly sorry for me sins, I would receive absolution." That's what happens in Extreme Unction, isn't it? The priest doesn't ask for particulars, he just forgives the person's sins.

"Me son, if a sick person is too ashamed to show his wound to the doctor, the doctor cannot heal what he doesn't know about."

"But God knows, doesn't He?"

"Yes, me son, God knows. However, the priest doesn't know until the penitent confesses. The priest is God's servant on Earth, and he cannot read minds. He can only forgive sins that have been confessed. He must withhold absolution for sins not confessed. And you know, of course, that the priest is bound to keep secret everything he hears in the confessional. Any priest who violates that oath of secrecy is subject to immediate excommunication."

"I know, Father, but I don't think I'm ready to confess yet."

"Then pray to God for help, me son. God loves you and wishes to forgive you."

A WEEK LATER, DIARMUID GOES TO VISIT Peadar Mahoney at his cottage near the school. Powerfully built with biceps twice the size of hurling balls, he works as a blacksmith in the village. Diarmuid notes that he keeps his musket on the kitchen shelf, within easy reach.

"Is it loaded?"

"Of course," says Mahoney. "Never know when I might want to have a rabbit for me dinner, do I? Can I pour you a drop of the craythur? A nip against the cold?" He reaches for the jar of poteen on the shelf next to the musket.

"A small one, thanks, with a splash of water. I find it a bit hard on the throat."

"Your wish is me command. Coming right up." He puts two cups on the table and starts pouring.

Diarmuid takes a sip and nods approvingly. "I'm still grateful to you for taking out Barry. We might all have been hanged or deported."

"I've been waiting a long time to give him his due. Twenty-five years since Keimaneigh. Three of our men killed there, and two of them executed afterwards, including your poor brother, God rest his soul."

"I only found out about me brother this past November, when me mother told me the story."

"He was a lovely man. We had many a good chat about faith and fatherland and the heroes of '98."

"The men who inspired us all. You would have been only in your twenties then?"

"Babes in the woods we were. Carrying the torch for freedom from oppression."

"Would you be interested in carrying the torch for me?"

"Assuming the mantle of Captain Rock? Because you would be on your way to Canada?"

"There are no secrets in this village, are there? You already know of me plans."

"I wish you Godspeed, Diarmuid. I'd be honoured to lead the struggle when you are gone. We'll miss you, however."

"Have the yeomanry been to see you yet?" asks Diarmuid.

"Yes, I feigned ignorance."

"Did you get the sense ...?"

"I got the sense they don't know where to look," says Mahoney. "They have a burned-out house, a body, and more than two thousand potential suspects. Like searching for demons in heaven, they are."

"That should keep us safe for a while," says Diarmuid. "But I worry about informers."

"Our lads won't be telling them anything. We have a solid group, Diarmuid. All committed to the cause. Even the ones who worry about not being able to go to confession."

"I went to Barry's burial, you know."

"Why would you do that?"

"I thought it was the right thing for me to do. As the schoolmaster."

"Make the yeomanry think you were honouring a pillar of the local community?"

"Something like that. Mislead them with me show of good citizenship."

"Were many people there, aside from the yeomanry?"

"There were two burials that day. That was me other reason for going there. Me uncle Crochúr Ó Laoire was also being put in his grave, at about the same time as Barry."

"Your mother's older brother?"

"That's right. And you won't believe this, Peadar. After they finished praying for me uncle, the O'Leary mourners gathered around Barry's grave. One of them – me cousin Seán Pat – stamped his boot on the grave and said, 'There you are now, you scoundrel, as weak and feeble as the old man we brought here today. A bold man you were at the Battle of Keimaneigh, but now may the divil take your soul.' "

"Strong words. Did the yeomanry intervene?"

"No, they had all left by then."

"So, when will you be going to Canada?"

"Not for a couple of months yet. I'd like it to be sooner because I worry that any day the yeomanry could come knocking on me door with an arrest warrant. However, I owe it to me few remaining scholars to keep teaching them until the end of the school year."

In the meantime, should he warn Nell that any day now he could face charges for capital crimes? Best wait to see how things unfold. Keep one's head down and remain vigilant.

S WITCHING FROM MUSIC TO JOURNALISM was the best thing that ever happened to Jerry. Or so he thought for twenty-three years. Now he's not so sure. The assignment that brings him the most pleasure – writing a daily feature obituary column for the *Calgary Herald* called Passages – is about to be abolished. Can anything comparable replace it? Not as far as Jerry is concerned.

He's sitting at his workstation, typing on a data terminal connected to the *Herald's* aging mainframe, wrapping up his column for tomorrow. He shares the terminal with Don Oberg, the paper's lifestyles columnist. The workstation consists of two desks joined together as one, with the terminal installed on a turntable in the middle. It's in the centre of the newsroom, surrounded by thirty similar workstations. Jerry would have preferred more privacy, but the open-concept newsroom has been a standard design feature in newspaper buildings since time immemorial. The room throbs with the sounds of clicking terminal keys, ringing phones, rustling papers, and the white noise of copy editors talking to reporters in low voices. When the presses roll, the entire newsroom vibrates.

The byline Gerald Burke appears at the top of the column next to his mug shot. He told the editors he wanted to use that first name to imply decorum. A sports columnist could be named Jerry, he said, but not a person who writes about the dearly departed. Jerry is a guy who does comedy on television, not someone you want writing about your sainted mother.

He's wearing a brown jacket, white shirt, and blue tie. Jerry always dresses semi-formally when he comes to work. Never wears jeans and sweatshirt like the other reporters. If the relatives of the deceased were to meet with him in person – which Jerry discourages because he prefers the detachment of the phone interview – they would expect him to look like a clergyman or undertaker. Not like someone who just finished cleaning out the garage.

He found that newspaper writing suited him after he and Tom went their separate ways. Making sentences, he discovered, was just as rewarding as making music. On this day, however, Jerry is phoning it in. Putting together what could be one of his last Passages columns because the *Herald's* powers-that-be have put him on notice. "We'd prefer to see you on the desk." No way.

Jerry stops typing and looks over at Don Oberg, who has filed his column for tomorrow and is perusing the latest issue of *Homemakers* looking for ideas. "Heard any good goss today?"

Oberg puts down the magazine and smiles. "The only goss I've heard is that they are going to sell the *Herald* to one of the Oilers' owners. He's going to shut down the paper, sell the presses, and turn the building into a carwash."

"Yeah, I've heard that one too." Jerry laughs. "Are you going on the desk?"

Oberg stops smiling and becomes pensive. "I guess I'll be doing that. It's a changing world and beggars must accept whatever small change is dropped into their caps."

He has been told – as has Jerry – that the paper will need more production staff to run the new stand-alone desktop computers

93

replacing the 10-year-old terminals. However, that will mean more opportunities for copy editors and page designers. Not more jobs for "content providers" – the managing editor's dismissive term for reporters and columnists.

Jerry leans back in his chair. "I don't want to go on the desk. I got into this business to write, not to edit other people's copy." He knows deskers receive more money, but that's no incentive. It's not about the money. Never been about the money. It's about the satisfaction of putting words together and making them sing. Same with the music. If the gig was fun, who cared about the money? Then one day it stopped being fun. Tom had said what Jerry had been thinking. "Do you still want to be singing 'Off to Dublin in the Green' a year from now? Two years from now? Ten years from now?"

The first attraction of newspapering for Jerry was the opportunity to write about music. He did that at Vancouver City College and again during what he calls his on-the-job training stint in Prince George. After two terms at VCC, he left Vancouver and took what started as a summer job at the *Citizen*. Never went back to school. Carol did the same. She became a full-time employee in Lethbridge a year before he became permanent in Prince George. After moving from PG to Calgary's *Herald*, he welcomed the opportunity to write about theatre. That was so much fun he did it for fifteen years. Then he landed the Passages column. That came with an ironclad guarantee of editorial independence. Total creative control. He could choose his subjects and write about them without a supervisor looking over his shoulder. Best gig at the paper.

"What did Webster say about your column?" asks Oberg.

"Probably the same thing he'll say about yours. They don't want any more *soft* – quote, unquote – news in the paper. 'If it bleeds, it leads' is the new mantra. It worked successfully for the *Sun*. Now they want to do it at the *Herald*. Blood and guts everywhere. Plus sensation, scandal, and corruption."

"I think I saw that coming."

"Additionally, Webster says, they want to put more focus on the kinds of news stories our readers tell us they want to see in the paper. So how are they going to do that? Invite a bunch of civilians into the building and ask them how we should do our jobs? What if they tell us they want to see more stories about abandoned puppies, water-skiing squirrels, and kittens getting stuck up trees?"

"You've asked him about other possible writing assignments?"

"He says I'm a hard guy to place. Hepher doesn't want me back in Entertainment because she thinks I'm *arrogant*. When she took over the job from Matthews, she looked at my old theatre reviews and wondered why I seemed so hell-bent on applying *New York Times* standards to local dinner theatres."

"What about Business?"

"Yes, Patterson would probably like to have me write for Business, but I haven't taken the Canadian Securities Course, so that's an obstacle. The irony there, of course, is that I had no qualifications for the entertainment job when I started writing theatre reviews. But then, I guess, it's more important for business writers to be properly qualified than those who dwell in the suburbs of journalism."

"The suburbs of journalism?"

"Any kind of arts coverage," says Jerry. "The city centre is politics, business and crime reporting."

"How about writing editorials?"

"Campbell says she doesn't need another lefty on the board. She already has one token liberal in Stirling. That's one too many as far as she's concerned."

"Are you a lefty?"

Jerry smiles enigmatically. "I voted Conservative in the last federal election."

"Why would Campbell call you a lefty then?"

Jerry smiles again. "No idea."

"He would probably think you only voted Conservative because you didn't want a Reform guy to get in," says Oberg. "Who did you vote for in the provincial election?"

"No comment." In a newsroom where the managing editor once wrote speeches for a Conservative premier, a progressive thinker doesn't talk about his political beliefs.

"I think I can probably guess."

Oberg picks up a copy of that morning's paper and pulls out the second section, containing the City pages. The line story on the front offers a prediction about expected attendance at the 1992 Stampede. "Record crowd expected despite price increases." Oberg puts down the paper. "Have you asked Webster about going back on Cityside?"

"A return to my *Herald* gig of eighteen years ago? When I still had most of my hair? We did have a brief discussion about that, but I don't sense any enthusiasm there. I guess I have to convince him that writing cop stories is like riding a bicycle."

He reaches for the little red poetry book. It occupies a permanent place at his workstation, next to his much-thumbed *Concise Oxford Dictionary* and the *CN Express Guide*, a handy gazetteer that lists the road distances between every city, town, and hamlet in Canada. He turns to the back pages of the red book and looks at the barren family tree. "Tell me how to do genealogy."

"Come again?"

"How do I start exploring my roots? You're the expert on this."

"Why now?"

"Why not now? I still have a few more days, maybe a few more weeks or months, before I have to decide about my future at the *Herald*. If my Canadian dream is about to turn into a nightmare, I might as well have another project to keep me grounded."

After three years of writing about other people's families, Jerry figures it's time for him to learn more about his own. Plus, after twenty-five years of on-and-off searching – all of it unproductive – he now needs professional help to solve the mystery of the elusive Diarmuid.

He wonders what it was like to live in Ireland during the famine years. Was it one continuous story of unrelieved misery, or were there times when people could forget about their troubles? When they could still enjoy the simple pleasures of step-dancing or singing favourite verses? The little red book, which he has now finished translating, has plenty of information about marriages, deaths, and evictions. But nothing about the day-to-day lives of the people.

"How far back do you want to go?" says Oberg.

97

"Let me finish off the last couple of sentences here, and I'll tell you what I'm looking for."

"I'll go for coffee then."

A FEW MINUTES LATER, Jerry sends his column over to the assistant city editor. He doesn't expect a response. The agreed arrangement is that his material will go into the paper no matter what. No checks and balances. Just a light edit to scan for spelling mistakes. Jerry likes it that way.

"So where do you want to take this quest?" asks Oberg.

"Back to the middle of the nineteenth century and before. I have a particular interest in an ancestor of mine named Diarmuid de Búrca. He was the only one in our family – aside from me – who emigrated from Ireland to Canada."

"What did you say his name is?"

"Diarmuid de Búrca. In English, Jeremiah Burke."

"Jeremiah? Didn't you tell me once that your first name was actually Jeremiah?"

"Used to be. I changed it to Gerald after I got to Canada."

"Why did you do that? Jeremiah is a fine name."

"Didn't like it. Too Irish, too biblical, too Old Testament. I wanted to make a fresh start. You know, like those Vietnamese guys who start calling themselves Jimmy or Don as soon as they're off the boat. Gerald wasn't that big a change. I could still be Jerry for anyone who knew me from the old country."

He can't remember when he changed it. He was still Jeremiah when he filled out the application form for landed immigrant status.

"Welcome to Canada," the officer had said. "Make us better." He was also Jeremiah when he applied for social insurance. That required proof of identity too. Did he change it to Gerald when he applied for his first Canadian passport? Wasn't there a place on the form where you were asked to "state previous name"? That must have been it. The first step in the process of reinventing himself. Leaving the baggage behind.

"Why did your ancestor come to Canada?" asks Oberg. "Because of the famine?"

"Probably. My grandfather thought he came over in one of those coffin ships, in 1846 or 1847."

"And then?"

"Nobody knows. His mother was a famous folk poet in West Cork."

"Another scribe in the family, eh?"

"Máire Bhuí Ní Laoire."

"Say what?"

"Sorry, that's the Irish version of her name. 'Moy-rah Vwee Nee Lay-rah.' It translates as Yellow Mary O'Leary. O'Leary was her maiden name."

"Why yellow?"

"At first, I thought it had something to do with the colour of her hair. But then I discovered that colours were assigned to the different branches of the O'Leary clan."

"Sounds like an Indian name. And she married a Burke, obviously?"

"James Burke. He was a farmer and horse trader in West Cork."

"And she would be your ...?"

"Let me think. She would be my great-great-great-grandmother. Three greats, that's right. My grandfather's great-grandmother. I had to learn one of her poems when I was in school in Dublin. It was about a group of Catholic tenant farmers who took up arms against the British militia because they wanted to stop paying tithes for the upkeep of the Protestant church. I hated the damn poem because she composed it in Irish, and I couldn't understand the words then. The tyranny of the compulsory *Gaeilge*."

"Come again?"

"Sorry, I keep hitting you with these words from my past. *Gaeilge*, that's the Irish word for Gaelic. It's still the second official language in Ireland."

"Gotcha. You have some valuable information on your ancestor already."

"I have a little book of her poems. Here, take a look. It was published by the local curate in 1931, almost a hundred years after she died. There's some biographical material in there that he collected from her grandchildren around 1917. Also, a family tree. The curious thing about the tree, however, is that it doesn't have a place for the youngest son, Diarmuid. Nor, as I learned after translating it, is there any mention of Diarmuid in the biography itself."

"Deer-moo-id – is that how you pronounce it? – could have been the black sheep of the family. What do you know about her other offspring?"

"There's a reference in the book to one son who emigrated to the States and another who went to the gallows for killing a British soldier.

100

Others had to abandon their farms during the famine. Diarmuid is still a mystery, however. Did he die during the voyage or after he arrived in Canada? If he settled in Canada, why did he cut off contact with the family? Why did the grandchildren not mention him when they were telling the priest about the other members of their family?"

"A genealogical search is not going to give you the answer to some of those questions."

"I know, but at least I might be able to find out where he died and when."

"Okay, here's what you do. You start with what you know and work your way backwards. Are your parents still living?"

"My father is. My mother died in 1977."

"And you know the date of their marriage, their dates of birth, and so on?"

"I know when they got married, and I can tell you when they celebrated their birthdays. However, I don't know the year my mother was born. She was evasive about that."

Oberg nods and smiles. "My mother was the same. That's why I started researching family history. I figured that if my relatives weren't going to give me the information, I should look for it in other ways."

"So where to begin?"

"Your mother's death certificate should say what age she was on her last birthday. The marriage certificate should also list her age. You should send away for those if you don't have them already. The cost, last time I ordered, was about three quid per certificate. Once you know your mother's age, you should be able to track down her birth certificate."

"But I won't have the exact date."

"No, but you'll know the approximate year, and you can narrow that down by going through the records at the Mormon genealogical library here."

"They have a Mormon library here?"

"It's called the LDS Stake Centre. It's over on Seventeenth Avenue Southwest."

"Who knew?"

"They have on microfilm the civil indexes of all of Ireland from 1845 to 1921, as well as microfilms of the actual certificates for various periods."

"How about before 1845? My guy, Diarmuid, would have been born sometime in the 1820s, I'm guessing."

"Parish records. Look, I'll draft you a short guide to help you get started. However, remember this: Once you start down this road you can never stop. Researching family history is like a drug."

"I appreciate you doing this, Don. If we manage to track down my disappeared ancestor, I owe you a beer for sure."

"Guinness, of course."

FATHER JAMES HOLLAND STANDS at the front entrance of St. Finbarr's after Sunday ten-o'clock Mass, greeting and shaking hands with the parishioners. The wind is blowing hard, and the rain is pelting down, but that doesn't bother the priest. Nor does it bother the parishioners. These rural residents are accustomed to being outside in all kinds of weather. The priest is still wearing his vestments. His standard routine is to hear confessions and conduct the Benediction after he finishes his weekly post-Mass chats with the parishioners.

"I think both of ye are making the right decision," the priest says to Diarmuid. "Ten shillings a head and one hundred acres would give an Irish family as good a start as ye could hope to get anywhere."

The priest's wish list also includes going to Canada. He has thought about it ever since he heard that Catholic and Methodist missionaries were competing with one another to convert and enlighten the Indians. "Christianity first, then civilization," a returning missionary told him. However, Bishop John Murphy said he had important work for Father Holland to do in Inchigeelagh. He assured him it would be for no more than five years. "I will not keep you long in purgatory."

"What if the offer turns out to be bogus, Father?" says Diarmuid. "What if there's no ten shillings and no hundred acres when we get to Canada? Can I trust His Grace?" Also, can he trust the priest? Should he go back to confession before deciding what his next move must be?

The priest gives no sign he recognizes Diarmuid as the penitent in the confessional who wasn't ready to tell his sins. He motions Diarmuid toward the door. "Let's step inside out of the rain." He wants to keep dry the box of small candles he has brought over from the rectory to place under the statue of Saint Finbarr. He told the congregants he often prays to this sixth-century bishop of Cork, petitioning him to banish poverty, hunger, and disease from the parish in the same way the saint once dispatched a mythical serpent from the lake at Gougane Barra.

A painting of the crucified Jesus Christ hangs high on the wall above the main altar. "He suffered and died for all our sins," says the priest.

"Why does He allow hunger in the world?" asks Diarmuid. "Why does He allow little children to suffer and die?" Why does he allow bailiffs to make life miserable for their tenants?

"You know the answer to that from your theological studies, Diarmuid. Some of the tribulations in our vale of sorrows are a mystery to us. However, we know they are all part of God's divine plan. Only eyes cleansed with tears can see the light."

"I sometimes have me doubts, Father."

"Many have doubts, Diarmuid. Believe in the power of prayer."

"I try, Father. What were you going to say to me about His Grace's offer?"

"I believe His Grace is an honourable man," says the priest. "That's certainly the impression I get from talking to the rector here. I wouldn't say the same about the His Grace's agents in Inchigeelagh, but I do think the duke himself has the best interests of his tenants at heart."

"Is that what the rector says as well?"

"It is. As you may know, we often have meetings to discuss what we might do together to make life better for our parishioners. When we met yesterday, he told me an amusing story about his encounter with one of me parishioners."

Diarmuid smiles. "Tell me more."

"The parishioner, I won't give you his name, told the rector he would *turn* if he could depend on a regular supply of food for his family."

"Turn?"

"Leave our congregation. Join the Established Church."

"And what did the rector say?"

"He told the man he must have a low opinion of the Established Church if he thought it bribed potential converts."

"So he wouldn't accept him into the fold, then?"

"I s'pose not. But then the man said he knew of other Catholics who had changed religions to qualify for relief. 'They took the soup,' the man told him."

"I've heard references to them before," says Diarmuid. "They call them *soupers*."

"That's news to me," says the priest.

"Not a Christian way of describing them, that's for sure."

They both sit down on a pew at the back of the church. "You said that His Grace has our best interests at heart," says Diarmuid. "But he can't care that much about us if he's allowing his bailiffs to evict us.

105

You know me parents no longer have a home after fifty-five years of marriage?"

"I heard about that and 'tis regrettable, Diarmuid. However, here's what I think. Even if His Grace's offer is a sham – and I've no reason to believe that – you'll still have a better chance of making a life for yourself and Nell in Canada than you do in Ireland. Think about it, Diarmuid. Canada is opportunity, Ireland is hopelessness."

"I appreciate your encouraging words, Father. I think you've made the decision for me."

"Have you been telling your students about Canada?"

"I tell them what little I know, Father. That 'tis a wild place, cold in winter and hot in summer. I don't say there's plenty to eat there, because that wouldn't be fair to them."

"Did you send your letter to the *Cork Examiner*?" asks the priest.

"I did. It gave me a chance to dust off me English writing skills. I said we needed a central soup kitchen to feed the hungry, and that our people should receive more blankets." He also wanted to add a description of the hungry people lying by the roadside with teeth stained green from eating grass and nettles. Plus, he wanted to denounce the government's policy of refusing to grant relief to families, either in or out of the workhouse, until they give up their land. However, the *Examiner* likes its correspondents to be concise, so Diarmuid is saving those comments for another time.

"I'm glad you mentioned the need for a soup kitchen," says the priest. "The rector and I plan to run that together. Did you write about the fever that's killing the inhabitants of the workhouse?"

106

"Me brother Micheál told me about the workhouse deaths," says Diarmuid. "I quoted Coleridge in me letter to the *Examiner*: 'They die so slowly that none call it murder.'"

"That should make them sit up and take notice."

"But will it make any difference, Father? There are so many bodies coming out of the workhouse now that they don't have enough coffins to bury them all. You saw it yourself – the trench they dug for them outside the village – stacking the bodies four deep."

"Will the Famine Relief Committee supply additional coffins?" says the priest.

Diarmuid rolls his eyes. "The Famine Relief Committee is only interested in the living. 'Tis not much help, Father. It collects money from the estate to subsidize the purchase of oats and barley meal, and there's never enough to feed everyone. I can tell you about families that have been without food for more than three weeks."

"I know, Diarmuid, 'tis a terrible situation."

"'Tis tragic enough when older people go hungry, but it breaks me heart to see this happen to the children. Their parents began by starving themselves so that the children can have something to eat, but now the children themselves are starving. Me best students are so famished that they can no longer walk to school. God forgive those agents of His Grace who have plenty of food in their larders but won't share a crumb with the little ones."

"I have to go back now for the confessions and the Benediction, Diarmuid. When did you say that you and Nell will be getting married?"

"We haven't set a firm date yet, Father, but it will be sometime in late April or early May."

"Then ye'll be packing and getting ready for yere long journey?"

"We'll have one chest. That's all we're allowed between us. The estate will pay for the chest and for the carriage that takes us to Nell's cousin's home in Macroom."

"And ye'll go on from there to Cove?"

"In another carriage, yes. The estate is paying for that as well."

"What's the name of the ship, again?"

"The Sir Henry Pottinger. Named, I believe, after the man who used to be the Governor of Hong Kong."

"I'm sure 'twill be a fine vessel. How long will it take ye to cross?"

"Four to six weeks, they say, if the winds are favourable. Maybe longer, depending on the weather." Plenty of time for him and Nell to get to know one another better. He feels guilty about taking her away from Inchigeelagh, but she seems happy about it.

May 1847

DIARMUID AND NELL GLOW with perspiration after they finish their dance on the concrete kitchen floor of his cottage. He points at the fiddler sitting on a chest near the hearth. "Let's give a round of applause to Pat Carolan there. He composed that jig especially for us." The fiddler puts down his bow, stands, and makes a sweeping operatic gesture with his right hand.

"He's given it the title, 'We'll Take a Coach and Trip Away,' which I think is befitting," says Diarmuid. "We'll be taking the coach tomorrow, and tripping away to our new home in Canada. To the New World of our hopes and dreams."

He turns to hug Nell and sees the tears beginning to well up in her eyes. He kisses her on the forehead and turns back to the group of family and friends gathered in his cottage on this sunny May afternoon.

The only furniture left in the cottage is the bed. Diarmuid's brother Micheál has agreed to dismantle it and move it to his house tomorrow. In the absence of chairs, Diarmuid has put down bales of hay on the kitchen floor for those who want to sit.

"I know ye have come here today to bid us goodbye, but I don't want this to be an emigrant's wake," says Diarmuid. "I want it to be a celebration of our marriage and the opportunity Canada is giving us to make a better life for ourselves."

He takes a piece of paper from his back pocket. He has a few thank-yous to give.

"I would like to thank me mother, Máire Bhuí, for giving me the kick in the breeches I needed to ask Nell to marry me. If it hadn't been for me mother's prodding, I'd probably still be single." Nell smiles and blushes. He's grateful she accepted his proposal. The word around the village was that her mother wanted to match her with a young barrel maker who sang solo tenor in the St. Finbarr's choir.

"I'd like to thank Nell's mother, Bridey, for graciously welcoming me into the Murphy fold and say I'm sad her late husband Micheál wasn't able to see this joyful day. Nell tells me he was a great believer

109

in education, so I think he and I would have had much in common. I'm sure he and me late father – God rest his soul – are having a grand old chat up in heaven now."

He looks over at the priest. Must be careful now. Choose the words carefully.

"I'd like to thank Father Holland for presiding over our ceremony this morning. The words of your homily, Father, were most inspiring. I feel assured now that Jesus, his mother Mary, and St. Patrick will always be with us. I'd also like to thank Father for his encouragement and advice when I was having second thoughts about going to Canada. I feel much better now that I've discussed it with him."

Should he have confessed his sins to the priest before entering into the Sacrament of Holy Matrimony? Sought absolution before receiving Holy Communion at his wedding Mass? He feels more of a hypocrite now than ever before. By taking the sacraments, he has stained his soul with even more trespasses, even more mortal sins. Should he seek God's forgiveness before leaving for Canada? Probably too late now.

THE FOLLOWING MORNING, Diarmuid and Nell rise early to greet the men who will strip the thatch from the roof and further render the cottage uninhabitable by smashing the stone walls with their sledgehammers. Diarmuid picks up the milk bucket holding the water for washing. "One last bit of business, lads." He pours the water onto the fire that has burned continuously since the cottage was built because the tenants considered it bad luck to let it go out. "The fire in the hearth will burn no more," says Diarmuid. "The fortunes of this house used to be associated with the flames, but now it's time to extinguish them."

T HE VOLUNTEERS AT THE CALGARY Stake Centre are eager to help. They don't ask Jerry for money, which he considers surprising in this mercenary age. Without prompting, they tell him which microfilm readers are harder on the eyes, and which ones give the cleanest printouts.

The room, lined with sturdy bookshelves, is full of people in their sixties and seventies slowly cranking the handles of the readers and scratching notes in pencil on yellow foolscap sheets. They come here every morning as soon as the Stake Centre opens, and spend the day scrolling through microfilms. Jerry wonders what they do with their research. Are they all writing their immediate family histories? Or are they engaged in the more widespread Mormon task of finding and baptizing all their dead ancestors so the families can be joined together forever after death?

Oberg's handy genealogical guide steers Jerry toward the most relevant microfilms for his search. The first part is easy enough. He knows the date of his mother's death, August 10, 1977. He scrolls through the films for the third quarter of 1977 until he finds the right Irish civil registration index reference for the death. However, the index summary doesn't list his mother's age. Did Sheila Burke carry the secret of her age to the grave? Maybe her death certificate will provide the answer.

"How are you doing?" asks the grey-haired woman at the microfilm reader next to him. "Finding everything you need?"

"You probably think this is a silly problem, but I'm trying to discover my late mother's age. Even my father doesn't know."

"Many people come in here with a similar problem. And you know what? They usually find the answer."

"I hope so."

His next step is to track down information about her marriage in Cork in September 1942. He scrolls through the films for the third quarter of that year. On September 15, he notes, a John Patrick Burke married a Julia Brigid MacCarthy in Cork city. That must be it! His mother's baptismal name was Julia. She hated it, so she always went by Sheila. Still no mention of her age, however.

Operating on the premise that his mother was probably no more than thirty years old when she married his father – although in their wedding picture she looks younger – Jerry checks the indexes for all the Julia Brigid MacCarthys born in the Cork parish of Clondrohid between 1912 and 1918. There are many of them. MacCarthy is a common name in West Cork. So is Julia. Parents didn't use much imagination when it came to choosing first names for their children.

Jerry does know that his mother's birthday was on December 16, so that narrows the field. He finds three birth references that have potential. Jots down the index page numbers in his notebook. Figures that if one of the three yields his mother's birth certificate, he won't mind sending six punts to Ireland to buy the other two.

He's enjoying this genealogical sleuthing. With any luck, it will take him back to 1845, when Máire Bhuí's son would probably have been first thinking about leaving Ireland.

"They tell me that in the future we'll be able to do all this research on computers," says the woman next to him. "I can't wait for that to happen. The endless hours of microfilm reading are doing me in. Awfully hard on eyes."

"Where does your family come from?" asks Jerry.

"County Galway, mostly. How about you? Where did your mother come from?"

"From West Cork, same as my father. He was descended from a well-known folk poet down there. She composed laments for people after they died and performed them at their funerals."

"Wow, that's some heritage."

"Yes, she was the local balladeer and designated elegist of her community."

"Elegist?"

"It's a word I made up. I'm not sure if it's in the dictionary. I use it to describe someone who writes eulogies for people. Obituarist might be a better word."

He can envisage putting the words on his business card: Gerald Burke, Professional Obituarist. Have Pen Will Eulogize. Dr. Death at your service. Satisfaction guaranteed. No laments but plenty of platitudes.

"I like obituarist," she says. "I always read the obituaries in the *Herald*."

"So do I. They're the raw material for my column."

She does a double take. "You're not Mr. Burke, are you?"

"That's me."

"Oh, my goodness, I read your column all the time. You wrote one about my nephew. He died in a climbing accident in Kananaskis. It was a wonderful column."

"I think I remember that one. Did he climb alone?"

"Yes, he did. You wrote a beautiful line in the column about how a person climbs at a mountain's sufferance and gets back down if the mountain lets him."

"I think I may have been quoting another writer."

"You called him a romantic rebel. That's what we called him too."

"He sounded like a fearless young man."

"Well, on behalf of the family, I'd like to thank you again for writing the column. We have many laminated copies."

HIS FATHER'S BIRTH INFORMATION is easier to track down than his mother's. Jerry knows the date, April 6, 1917, so it's just a matter of finding the record of a John Patrick Burke born in Macroom, County Cork on that day. Does his father know that anyone can order copies of his records if they send a money order to the Irish government to cover the cost? No proof of blood relationship required. Unlike the people at the Calgary Stake Centre, the Irish government only cares about the money it can gouge from people tracing their roots.

Jerry looks at the family tree in the back of the little red book. Nine of the ten children are listed, with dates of birth and names of spouses. For five of the nine, the tree includes children and children's spouses. However, that leaves many gaps. No spousal information about Alec,

115

Máire Bhuí's son, who was Jerry's great-great-grandfather. And, of course, no reference at all to Máire Bhuí's mystery son, Diarmuid.

Could he have been a black sheep, as Oberg suggests? Jerry's grandfather said he was a rebel, but that's not the same thing. He said Diarmuid took his cues from the agrarian insurgents of southwestern Ireland who waged a campaign of terror against the landlords and their agents during the 1820s. Burned down their houses and sometimes killed them. "Like Patrick Pearse he was," said his grandfather. "A schoolteacher by day, a Fenian by night."

Wouldn't Diarmuid's revolutionary zeal have been a matter of pride for Máire Bhuí's grandchildren, however? Surely that would have been a reason for them to proclaim the achievements of Diarmuid de Búrca, not hide them from public view. Why wouldn't they have told his biographer about him? There must have been another reason.

His grandfather said Diarmuid entered into an arranged marriage shortly before he emigrated. Was there an out-of-wedlock pregnancy involved? Could that be the reason the descendants kept silent about him? What did pregnant young unmarried women do in Holy Catholic Ireland in the days before they were sent off to the nuns to have their babies in secret? So many questions, so few answers.

THE GAS STREETLIGHTS FLICKER IN HUES of green and blue when the carriage driver delivers Diarmuid and Nell to the lodging house. "Welcome to the Emigrant's Home," says the proprietor, Miss O'Brien. "I'm sure ye'll be comfortable here. I've put ye in number seven, upstairs to the left." She draws their attention to the room rates posted on the wall above the hall table. "Payment in advance."

Diarmuid signs the registration book and puts a sixpence and three-penny bit on the table. "Is there a key?"

Miss O'Brien pulls a lorgnette from her handbag and squints at the names. "Mr. and Mrs. de Búrca, I see. Sure, there's no need for keys in this house. Aren't we all honest and God-fearing people here?"

Nell looks out the front door at a signpost pointing to Fitzpatrick's Quay. "Let's go down there first, Diarmuid. I'd love to see our ship."

"We won't be able to see much in the dark, macushla. Plenty of time for that in the morning. We'll have our sleep first."

The other four beds in number seven are already occupied with sleepers when Diarmuid and Nell enter the room. The snores of the sleepers are loud enough to be heard out on the street. Diarmuid reaches for the empty bed in the dark. "No privacy tonight, I'm afraid. Let's hope the bed is comfortable."

The snoring keeps them awake for several minutes, but eventually they doze off. After sleeping for three hours, Nell wakes to the sound of fiddles playing downstairs. She brushes away fleas and shakes

Diarmuid's shoulder. "Did you hear that, Diarmuid? Let's go down and listen to the music."

He stretches and yawns. "Isn't it a bit late for music?"

"Please, Diarmuid, let's go there for a little while. I'm wide awake now, and I love doing the easy reel with you."

Five couples are dancing in the hallway. One pair leaves the floor and heads for the stairs when Diarmuid and Nell approach. "Ye'll enjoy the dance," says the woman. "The musicians are brilliant."

Diarmuid and Nell dance for twenty minutes, long enough to tire themselves out. When they go back to the room, they're surprised to find their bed commandeered by the couple who left the dance floor just as they were arriving. Diarmuid shakes the man awake. "This is our bed, you know. Ye'll have to leave."

The man rubs his eyes. "This *was* yere bed. It became *our* bed after ye left it."

Diarmuid clenches his fist, ready to pummel the encroacher, but then hesitates. "We paid ninepence for this bed. We're entitled to sleep in it for the whole night."

The man shakes his head. "Ye haven't stayed here before, have ye? Ye haven't read what's on the notice downstairs: 'Different persons may occupy the same bed during the night.' I've paid me ninepence too."

"This is peculation. It can't be legal."

"Legal or not, those are the rules of the Emigrant's Home. Ye'll have to find a place on the floor if ye can't find another empty bed."

Nell steps out onto the landing and beckons Diarmuid to follow her. "This was me fault. Let's not make any trouble here. We'll take the blankets out of our chest and look for a place where we can lie down. It will be morning in a little while, anyhow."

THE SUN IS RISING OVER Rostellan Wood when Diarmuid and Nell set out along the quays carrying their chest between them. Five three-masted barques are at anchor next to the docks. Five more are moored out in the harbour. Diarmuid points across the expanse of water toward distant Spike Island. "Quite the seaport, isn't it? Big enough to accommodate the whole navy of England."

"You're speaking in English," says Nell, looking surprised.

"Might as well start using it now," says Diarmuid. "We'll be hearing a lot of English on the ship."

"So it's good that I had to speak it every day when I worked as a kitchen maid in Bantry."

They put down the chest when they reach the Sir Henry Pottinger. The ship makes for an impressive sight. As wide as a hurling pitch from stern to bowsprit. A mainmast that rises higher than the steeple of St. Finbarr's Church. A galley on deck that's roomy enough to accommodate the roasting of a pig or sheep. Gun ports pierce the hull, sending a warning to would-be pirates that the ship is armed.

The ship is scheduled to set sail for Canada on this day, but Diarmuid doesn't think it will be ready. Carpenters are still replacing the berths removed from the ship before it sailed from North America to Europe. Human cargo will replace the American cargo of timber, cotton, and grain. How long will it take the workers to finish their nailing and hammering? Diarmuid figures it will be another day or two at least.

Many of the two hundred travellers who left Inchigeelagh two days ago have gathered on the quays to watch the activity. Most walked the full 45-mile distance with only short stops for rest and meals along the way. Some had donkeys and carts driven for them by friends and relatives. However, the luggage took up so much room on the carts that the only passengers who could ride on them were little children and older people who had difficulty walking.

A sailor tells the travellers they'll have to dispose of most of their luggage before they board. "All ye can bring are the clothes ye wear, one blanket, and a cooking pot. Any other belongings, if ye can't sell them, ye'll have to leave on the quayside."

A heavy-set man, accompanied by his wife and seven-year-old son, holds up his contract ticket. "The agent paid seven pounds for our sea fare. He told us this would include ten cubic feet for luggage for two statute adults."

The sailor shrugs. "Space restrictions, I'm afraid."

Nell looks at Diarmuid. "Will this apply to us? Do we have to leave our chest on the quay?"

He doesn't know. "Let's go aboard and take a look inside our cabin to find out."

"Will they allow us to do that?"

"We can ask the sailor there. I'm sure they won't mind if we go on board for just a few moments."

She notices there are three crows perched together on a spar extending from one of the masts.

"Look at those ravens," she says. "Not a good sign, Diarmuid. Harbingers of doom."

120

He hugs her and points at one of the birds flying away. "They won't put a bother on us," he says. "They'll be gone before the ship sails."

Their second-class cabin is situated between decks at the bow of the ship. It has its own companionway, adjoining the crew's quarters, and is sealed off from the steerage. Although far from spacious, it has room enough for the chest as well as the cabin's two single bunks.

"Not a manor house, certainly," says Nell, "but we'll manage."

"Ceiling is low," he says. "I'll be bumping me head a lot. Especially in the dark."

BACK ON THE QUAY, a man wearing a khaki uniform, black kerchief and wide-brimmed straw hat identifies himself as the first mate and tells the travellers there will be no food or water provided while they are waiting to board. He speaks in Irish, haltingly, with an English accent.

"To whom can we appeal?" asks Diarmuid. "Our contract tickets say the food service begins on the day of departure, and this ship was supposed to sail today."

The first mate shrugs. "You should speak to the government emigration inspector. His office is located on East Beach, next to the Naval Hotel."

"These people are entitled to support," insists Diarmuid. "They're supposed to be paid one shilling a day while waiting for the ship to depart."

The first mate turns on his heel and marches back up the gangplank. "Talk to the inspector."

THE GOVERNMENT INSPECTOR offers no help. He shuffles the papers on his desk. "You should be speaking to the ship's owner. He lives in Belfast."

Nell looks at Diarmuid. "That's more than two hundred miles away." The inspector shrugs and turns back to his papers.

Diarmuid slaps his hand on the desk. "Why are the travellers not receiving their detention money?"

The inspector crosses his arms and looks at them with the cold eyes of a lizard. "I think ye should go now. The questions ye are asking are not a matter for this office."

They walk back toward the ship. "We can spend another night at the Emigrant's Home," says Diarmuid. "We have the money." He smiles and nudges Nell. "But there will be no dancing tonight."

She lowers her head. "You're not upset with me?"

He hugs her. "Of course not. Let's find a shop where we can buy some bread and cheese."

"What about the paupers there on the quay? Where will they go? There are several babies."

"Some will have to sleep on the quay again, as they did last night," says Diarmuid. "We'll pray for a warm night and hope the ship sails tomorrow. If the men can find casual work along the quays, they'll be able to pay for lodging."

IN THE LOUNGE OF THE NAVAL HOTEL, the captain is re-reading a letter from Ralph Brocklebank, owner of the Sir Henry Pottinger. He puts the message on the table and turns to the first mate.

"How many do we have on the passenger list this time?"

"About two hundred and twenty, so far," says the mate.

"Not enough yet. Brocklebank is angry because we only carried three hundred across the last time. He says that if we can't put at least four hundred and fifty on the ship, it's not worth it for the company to let the voyage go ahead. What do we know about the passengers who have already bought tickets?"

"Most are from West Cork. We may have some troublemakers among them."

"Tell me more."

"One of them is already demanding compensation for the delay."

"Typical. What did you say to him?"

"I told him we can't take any responsibility for the wait when the carpenters are still putting in the new berths. He then threatened to file a complaint with the government emigration inspector."

"That will spell trouble. Did you get this person's name?"

"He's one of the second cabin passengers. Goes by the name of Burke."

"Thank you, William. I'll keep an eye out for him. Anything else I should know?"

"I'm told that some of the passengers are of the rebel persuasion, sympathetic to the cause of the American Fenians who want to invade Canada."

"That's also good to know. Thank you for this information."

"Aye, aye, sir." He salutes and leaves the room.

The captain looks at the letter again and thinks this will probably be his last voyage. Too much responsibility. Too much stress. Too much pressure from on high. Time to retire to Edinburgh.

THE FOLLOWING DAY, Diarmuid and Nell arrive at the quay to learn that tragedy struck overnight. The weather turned unusually cold and wet and two toddlers died, likely from exposure. The babies wandered away from their parents, dressed only in rags. A Franciscan friar, wearing a brown habit, blesses the little bodies, and prepares them for burial. He is visibly agitated. Repeatedly fingers his rosary beads. "This happens here much too often. The ships never sail on the day advertised, and people die while waiting."

"Why are we waiting now?" asks Diarmuid. "The carpenters have finished their work."

"Because the owner wants to make as much money as possible," says the friar. "Simple financial greed. He receives three pounds a head from the landlords for every passenger. Won't let the ship sail until the crew has packed at least four adult passengers into every berth. Squashed like pilchards they are. Two children count as one adult. The more they can squeeze in, the greater the profit."

Nell shakes her head. "But isn't that against regulations?"

"The owner bribes the government officials to look the other way," says the friar.

"Are we waiting for more people, then?" says Nell. "Is that the reason for the delay?"

"How many of ye are here now?"

"About two hundred of us from Inchigeelagh, isn't that right, Diarmuid?"

"I would say there will be at least double that on board before the ship sails," says the friar.

"I must talk to the captain about this," says Diarmuid. "Even with four people in every berth, there won't be enough bunks to accommodate them all."

"Won't do much good, I'm afraid," says the friar. "He takes his orders from the owner."

"I'll talk to him anyhow. I see him up on deck now."

Dapper in a double-breasted blue jacket with gold buttons, the captain is climbing the steps of the poop deck. He grabs the helm as if he's about to steer the ship out of the harbour.

Diarmuid shouts up at him in English. "Are we ready to set sail yet?"

The captain takes a spyglass from his pocket and peers down. "I've nothing to say to informers."

"Why do you call me that?"

"You spoke to the government emigration inspector. You weren't supposed to do that."

"That's what the first mate told me to do."

"I think you're mistaken. I've nothing further to say to you on the matter."

"Can you tell us at least when the ship will be leaving?"

"You'll find that out in due course."

TWO DAYS LATER, three hundred more people join the two hundred from Inchigeelagh already waiting on the quay.

Diarmuid approaches one of the new arrivals. "What ship are ye travelling on?"

"The Sir Henry Pottinger, I believe."

"That's our ship too. I don't think there's enough room for all of us. Certainly not enough bunks. Whence do ye come?"

"Youghal."

"The home of Raleigh's first potato. And what brought ye here? The potato blight, I s'pose?"

"That was part of it. The main reason was that many of us had government jobs – labouring jobs on the road works – and they stopped paying our wages."

"I know that story well. I had a government job too. Teaching at a national school."

"We were supposed to be paid one shilling a week out of the two hundred pounds the government set aside for the road works. However, after fifty pounds had been paid out, the fund was said to be *depleted*."

"What happened to the rest of the money?"

"It ended up in the pockets of them who already had it. That's why we decided to go to Canada."

THE CAPTAIN COMES UP ON DECK to address the crowd. He is joined by the twelve crew members, who stand at ease on either side of him. He has a ruddy, weather-beaten face and speaks English with a Scottish accent.

"I'm the master of this vessel, Commander Archibald Low. We shall leave shortly so please get ready to board. Five hundred and seventy-two tickets were issued for embarkation, but some were declined for varied reasons. I believe five hundred are taking the voyage today. Ready to start new lives in a faraway land of opportunity. You'll receive your own land once you're there."

The man from Youghal shouts up at him. "How long will it take us to cross?"

"We'll reach Quebec City in about eight weeks. There, you and I will part company. You'll proceed to Montreal by steamboat, and then inland."

Nell turns to Diarmuid and whispers. "I'm feeling guilty now that we have a cabin for ourselves. I hope they give the bunks to the neediest people. To the women with the babies and the older people."

The captain pauses before continuing his speech. "I hear that many of you have been – how shall I put it? – rebellious in the baronies in the county of Cork. The authorities tell me they hope that sending you to the colonies will ease the situation and prevent an all-out rebellion."

Diarmuid wonders how much the captain knows about the Rockites. Should he be concerned? Are there informers in their midst? Who will be in the other second cabin? Who will occupy the first cabins at the back?

"The authorities fear that treasonous Fenians in America may be planning to invade Canada, hold it hostage, and make people there worship the Pope. Those of you with, ah, rebellious tendencies can pick up that empty land from the Crown and then fight to protect it."

Diarmuid smiles and shakes his head. The authorities must be dreaming if they think the Irish in Canada will take up arms against their American brethren.

The captain moves on to the subject of meals on board.

"You'll be given the full allowance of food and water provided for in the Passenger Act. Three and a half pounds of biscuit per adult per week. Three and a half pounds of oatmeal. Also, three quarts of water per day."

"Where can we do our cooking?"

"As long as the weather is favourable, you'll be able to cook the oatmeal on the braziers we provide for you on deck. You might end up seeing your meals again, but you'll get used to the seasickness after a few days. We won't have a doctor on board, but I've taken medical training and am qualified to dispense medicines when necessary."

He points to a notice pinned on the front of the galley. "You can read the rules here when you board the ship, and you'll see other copies of this notice on the walls inside when you go down below. I will mention three of the rules now, so you know what to expect.

"Number one: There will be no smoking in the steerage because that could cause a fire. If you cannot go without tobacco while we are at sail, you can arrange with the first mate to buy chewing tobacco to tide you over.

"Number two: There will be no drinking of alcohol anywhere on the ship. Drunkenness will not be tolerated on this voyage.

"Number three: There will be no washing of clothes and blankets on rainy days because there is no place for them to dry afterwards. Are there any questions?"

A man smoking a pipe raises his hand. "Will we be allowed to smoke on the deck?"

"Yes, but only during those periods when you and the members of your group are allowed up there. You won't be able to come up whenever you want. The first mate will explain all this to you after you board."

He waits a few moments for more questions. Hearing none, he motions to the sailors to take their places at the work stations. "Ready to set sail."

THE BOARDING IS A FRENZY OF CHAOS. The first mate tells the first and second cabin passengers to wait on the quay while the steerage passengers come aboard with their blankets and cooking pots. The sailors try in vain to have them proceed in an orderly fashion. Some storm the gangway, shoving, scrambling, and tripping over one another in their efforts to grab the available berths in the steerage. Others, once they reach the deck, seize ropes, throw them down onto the quay, and haul children and women up along the side like bundles of straw. One older man, moving as quickly as he can, falls forward onto the gangway when someone pushes him from behind. Others fall on top of him like skittles on a lawn.

When the last of the steerage passengers have boarded, the first mate explains to them the rules about coming back up on deck.

"No more than twenty of you at a time because of the limited number of braziers available for cooking, and because the sailors need room for doing their work. They don't want you in the way."

"How much time can we spend on the deck?"

"No more than thirty minutes per day. We have many passengers on this ship, and everyone should have a chance to come up for cooking and washing." These rules, he adds later when talking to Diarmuid and Nell, don't apply to the first and second-cabin passengers. "You can come and go as you please."

Diarmuid and Nell chat with another second-cabin passenger while waiting their turn to board. "Our business failed when the potato crop failed," says the passenger, a well-dressed woman in her mid-thirties. Her name is Maud Twomey and she sports a flowing mane of dark red hair. She tells them she ran a drapery and haberdashery in Ballingeary. "We lost money for two years, then decided to sell our shop. We had no choice. We couldn't stand by and let all our hard work go to waste." She is travelling with her four children, aged three to thirteen. Says her husband died of a heart attack at age forty shortly after they sold the shop.

"That's a shame," says Nell. "How long have ye been in Cove?"

"We arrived here a week ago. I met some of the other passengers then."

"Did ye meet any of the first-cabin passengers?"

"A right stuck-up bunch they are. I don't think we want to have anything to do with them."

"Where do ye plan to live in Canada?" asks Nell.

"We won't be living in Canada," says Mrs. Twomey. "An aunt of mine in Boston has a shop she'd like me to help run."

"Then why are ye going to Quebec?"

"Cheaper than going to New York."

Diarmuid nods. Should he and Nell consider doing the same? Becoming two-boat Irish and settling in the States? There would be more Irish there. Easier to assimilate, easier to find jobs. Should they give up Canada's offer of free land to the immigrants, however? Maybe not yet. One change of country at a time.

J ERRY PICKS UP HIS SATCHEL and heads downstairs to the *Herald* cafeteria to have coffee with Oberg. He pulls a document from his bag and puts it on the table. "Voila!"

Oberg, nibbling on a chocolate-chip cookie, looks at the name on the document. "Your mother's birth certificate?"

"Julia Brigid MacCarthy. Cork parish of Clondrohid. December the sixteenth, nineteen fourteen. My father doesn't have this information. Neither did I until this came back. She was only sixty-two when she died. Much too young." He wishes he had visited her more often during the last years of her life. However, exploring Canada was more important to him at that time.

"Well done. What next?"

"Let me get a cup of French Roast first. Need some of that caffeine to keep me awake for the rest of the afternoon."

While standing in line to pay for his coffee, Jerry checks the wall where the people from the back shop post the numbers from the daily press runs. One hundred and twenty thousand copies printed yesterday. Not bad.

He puts his cup on the table, reaches into his satchel, and pulls out two more documents. "The birth certs of my paternal grandparents. That's as far back as I can go. Nothing in the microfilms about my great-grandparents or their parents. What were you saying to me about parish records?"

"Before you check them, you should make sure you have exhausted all the other possibilities," says Oberg. "Sometimes, people didn't register the births of their children because they lived in rural areas and were busy seeding or harvesting. However, in many instances, the names of the children will show up on census records. Ireland has complete census returns for 1901 and 1911, and you can look at those on microfilm."

"How about before that?"

"Not much available, I'm afraid. Ireland did take a census every ten years from 1821 onward, but most of the returns were either destroyed by fire during the 1922 civil war or destroyed before that by order of the government."

"Why would the government order them destroyed?"

"Not sure. Something to do with recycling, I think. I read somewhere once that the government pulped a bunch of old census returns to generate paper supplies during the First World War."

Jerry shakes his head. A paper shortage doesn't qualify as a reason for destroying essential government documents. "What will I find in the surviving census returns?"

"Plenty of valuable information. Aside from such basics as the name, age, occupation, and so forth, you'll find details about the houses, numbers of rooms, windows, outhouses, and roof types."

"And presumably they would also include information about every person living in a house, including grandparents and other relatives?"

"Yes, and they wouldn't have to be relatives," says Oberg. "They could also be servants or maids. I saw one census where a resident, a man of seventy, was identified as a *strolling beggar*. Another that said a ten-year-old boy, apparently not related to anyone else in the family, was *in character of a cowboy*."

"They have ages for them all?"

"Yes, but you have to be careful about those. The census takers often guessed the ages, and didn't do the most perfect job of estimating. However, they do serve as a rough guide. That helps narrow the range of years to be searched when you start looking in parish records."

"From what I know of them, all my ancestors in the census will be mired in a bog of farm labouring. Are the parish records on microfilm?"

"It depends. You have to remember there are two types of parishes in Ireland: civil and church. The civil parishes and the Protestant Church of Ireland parishes are virtually identical in terms of the geographical area covered. Those records are easy enough to search. However, you can only view them at the National Archives in Dublin."

"How about the Catholic parishes?"

"They're bigger and more unwieldy than the civil parishes, and the records are difficult to plough through because there are so many of them. Not only that, but many of the details are recorded in Latin. So, you'll be looking for people with first names like Jacobus or Demetrius."

"Are those records on microfilm?"

"Some. The Catholics used to be wary of the Mormons, so it took many years before they would let them in to film their records. In some instances, the Mormons are still being refused admission because the parish priests don't trust them. However, they have managed to film something like one-third of all the Catholic parish registers in Ireland. Not great, but one-third is better than nothing."

"Where are those films?"

"In the local Stake Centre here in Calgary, you'll be glad to hear. There are many gaps, however, because some of the registers were dumped in storage sheds. They ended up being destroyed by rain, mice, fire, or whatever. However, if you're looking for nineteenth-century baptisms and marriages, that's where you can start."

"You're a mine of information, Oberg. Are you sure you're not Mormon?"

Oberg laughs. "Evangelical Protestant. My maternal ancestors were German Baptists from Ukraine."

"What will I do if it turns out that the records I'm seeking are missing from the microfilms?"

"You could ask someone in Ireland to visit the parish and look them up for you. Or you might plan a trip to Ireland and look them up yourself. Nothing like a visit to the auld sod to soothe the soul."

"I might just do that. Given the current state of uncertainty around here, it would be a relief to get away for a while."

"What's your current situation?" says Oberg.

"I've been given a reprieve. Next round of desker training has been delayed for some reason. Webster says I can keep writing the column for the foreseeable future."

"Whatever happened to *if it bleeds, it leads*?"

"Oh, that's coming. However, they see me as a desker-in-waiting, so they're not about to drop my *soft* contributions yet, or have me chasing after fire trucks."

"Keep enjoying it while you can."

"How goes your desker training?" says Jerry.

135

"Great. I love the new computers. They're so fast. Certainly, an improvement over the old terminals."

"When will they be installing them in the newsroom?"

"They haven't said yet. Can't wait to start working on them," says Oberg.

"But won't you miss writing your column?"

"I'll work on my novel when I'm not editing copy or laying out pages. That will satisfy the creative urges."

"Like the way it was in the Irish civil service," says Jerry. "One of my former colleagues used to write plays. Another wrote a humour column for the *Irish Times*."

"Why didn't you do something like that?"

"I thought life would be better in Canada."

"The land of opportunity."

"Of course. One more question, Oberg, and then I'll let you go back to your training. Where would I go for information on the immigrants who came across the Atlantic on those coffin ships? Are there passenger lists available anywhere?"

"There are, and you can find those on this side of the Atlantic. The British government didn't care too much about the Irish who were leaving the country. The Canadian government, on the other hand, had an obvious interest in knowing who was coming in here, so it kept records."

"Where would I find those records?"

"First, you should take out a membership in the Alberta Family Histories Society. They can give you tips for finding sources in this country. Do you know any family historians in Ireland? They charge for their services, but they can give you anecdotal material that you won't find in the registers."

"I have a cousin in Cork, Cathal O'Leary, who shares my interest in family history. I'll phone him and see if he can fill in the gaps in my research."

"Then you're on your way. Remember what I said about this being like a drug? Keep me posted."

T HE SIR HENRY POTTINGER SWARMS with activity as preparations for departure begin. Commander Low barks orders from the poop deck. The sailors respond with apparent enthusiasm, coiling and uncoiling and tugging on a bewildering array of ropes with such names as gaskets, braces, stays, buntlines and clewlines. "Haul on the bowline," they sing. "Our bully ship's a-rollin'."

The sailors – "rude tars," Diarmuid calls them – hoist themselves up into the rigging, cast off the gaskets, unfurl the sails and set them on spars for driving the ship forward. On the command "weigh anchor," four crewmen haul up the seaweed-encrusted chain by turning the capstan. They grunt and groan as they heave and push. It takes them close to an hour to get the ship moving because the chain is entangled in the cables of some fishing boats. After the anchor is winched up, the canvas sails flap and the masts creak as the ship pulls away from the quay. It picks up speed after threading its way through the maze of other vessels. Leaves the harbour behind and enters the Celtic Sea. The wind blows hard from an angle of sixty degrees. The ship sways with a swinging momentum as it sails westward along Ireland's southern coastline toward the Atlantic Ocean.

Diarmuid and Nell, standing on the deck with the other cabin passengers, can feel the salty sea spray on their faces as the ship passes Cape Clear Island. He waves to a man fishing from a currach and thinks of times past. "That's the last we'll see of dear old Ireland, I fear," he says to Nell. "You can't see it from here, but over there

138

beyond the island lies the town of Skibbereen, where me parents were married more than fifty years ago."

She smiles when she sees a school of porpoises breaching the water's surface. "Do you think we might ever come back?"

"I hope so, macushla. After we become established in Canada, we'll start saving our money for a ticket home. It might take a few years, but that can be our plan."

Is it a realistic plan, however? Don't wild geese just fly in one direction? Returning home would be lovely, but will he be able to make enough money to afford it? How will Nell feel if the years go by and he doesn't have the means to bring her home?

THE SHIP'S COOK COMES UP from down below with a squawking chicken flapping under each arm. Diarmuid and Nell watch, intrigued, while he puts one bird into a wooden crate and grasps the legs of the other with his left hand. With a sharp downward tug of his right hand, he separates the bird's head from its neck. No blood flows. The bird thrashes around for a few seconds, and then hangs limply. Nell looks away. Diarmuid continues to watch, impressed by the humaneness of the kill. His own method, first shown to him by his grandmother, was to take a small hatchet to the bird's neck. The cook repeats his procedure with the second chicken, killing without drawing blood. He then brings the two carcasses into the galley and hands them to the cabin boy for plucking and cleaning.

Slaughtering the pig is a less humane affair. Diarmuid has to look the other way when the cook slits the throat of the animal and lets it bleed into a bucket. The cook pours boiling water on the carcass, shaves it clean, removes the offal, cleans out the gut, and butchers the meat for salting. "That should keep us all in salt pork for the rest of the voyage," says the cook. The cabin boy does the salting for him, rubbing it in by hand.

FOUR WEEKS LATER, one of the sailors invites Diarmuid and Nell to join the crew for dinner. The first mate turns his back when they sit down at the at crew table. However, several of the other sailors – all from around Cove – welcome the opportunity to engage in friendly conversation. The Irish sailors sit in a group at one end of the table, speaking in Irish to one another. The English seamen, including the first mate, sit at the other end.

"Did ye see any of yere relations when ye were in port?" Diarmuid asks a crewman from the village of Ringaskiddy.

"They wouldn't give us leave to go on shore," he whispers. "When we were in Portsmouth, those who came from around there received plenty of shore leave. However, when we reached Cove, those of us who come from around the harbour here were not allowed to visit our parents. Tells you something about English justice and equality, doesn't it? Our English shipmates could go wherever they wanted, but we had to remain on board."

Diarmuid nods. "Doesn't seem fair. Especially when it could be years before ye see yere parents again."

"Our commander thinks we Irishmen – common fellows before the mast – don't have the same needs as Englishmen to see our friends and families. We serve as loyally as Englishmen, yet they treat us like second-class citizens. Bad cess to them." He reaches with his knife for

140

a slice of chicken. "But at least they feed us well. They know that if they give us enough grub, we'll work hard."

Diarmuid notices that all the crewmen are pouring grog into their mugs from a cask on the table, while he and Nell drink lime juice from a pitcher. He points to a "Strictly Forbidden" notice on the wall that lists alcoholic beverages – as well as smoking, fighting, swearing, and gambling – among a litany of items and activities prohibited below decks. "Isn't that against the rules?"

The sailor from Ringaskiddy laughs. "When we're on the high seas, the rules don't apply. Who's going to enforce them?"

AFTER THE DINNER, Diarmuid is stricken with a knifing pain in the gut. He rushes up on deck and vomits over the side into the heaving green ocean. Must have been the chicken, he thinks. Or could this be what seasickness feels like? Please God, let it not be the fever.

He's not the only one feeling nauseous. Other passengers line up alongside him, expelling their meals like seagulls on a rail. Howling and gagging sounds fill the air.

Diarmuid goes back to the cabin and lies down. Prays for the nausea, headache, and dizziness to pass. He never felt as bad as this before. Oh God, let it go away soon.

Nell comes in and rubs his back, but he gently pushes her away. "You don't want to see me like this, macushla. I'm feeling queer sick. I hope you don't get it as well."

"Is there anything I can bring you?"

"Maybe some more of the lime juice from that pitcher."

"How about some biscuit? Might settle your stomach."

"No, I can't eat another thing."

"Drink as much as you can, then. Drink the whole pitcher if necessary."

He drifts into a reverie, fluttering between sleep and awareness. His mind slowly scrolls through the pictures of his childhood. He can see his mother sitting at her end of the kitchen table, peeling the praties, singing her latest song. What's it about? A love song, perhaps? Her words start to trickle out: "On a sunny hillside yesterday ... walking me cows ... a fair lady I saw ... modest, well-mannered, comely and young ..."

He's his mother's first listener. Always the first to hear her verses. When the other members of the family are away working in the fields, he's the one with whom she shares her words. Sometimes, she calls him over to her end of the table and whispers the lines into his ear. She always smiles when she's singing, even when her words are angry. He smiles too.

The ship pitches and surges. Diarmuid curls up in the bunk, breathes slowly in and out, now kicking off the blanket, now pulling it up, willing the nausea to go away. "I have supped full of horrors," said the doomed Macbeth. Nothing on the sea or under the sea can terrify Diarmuid now. The image of his mother fades into the water, which has a mystical blue-green colour that no earthly painter will ever capture. She leaves only her smile behind. He would like to keep that image in his mind for the rest of his life.

Nell comes back into the cabin and fills up his mug. "Do you mind if I go to visit with the steerage passengers for a brief time?" she says.

"The sailors won't go in there. They say the smell is knocking them sick."

Sickness is everywhere. "Of course, macushla. I'll be all right here." He forces a weak smile, hoping he looks better than he feels.

"'Tis something I should do," she says. "I'll be back in a little while."

Diarmuid retreats into reverie. Loses track of time. Snaps awake thinking it's night when it's still day. What will he and Nell do when they arrive in Canada? Can't focus on that. The mind won't go there. Thoughts too scattered. The discomfort too distracting. Can't get the swirling sensations to stop. Hope this sickness won't turn into something worse.

Calgary, August 1992

ERRY STANDS IN THE DOORWAY of the city editor's office and looks out through the picture window, along the length of Memorial Drive, toward the spread of the city centre. Glass and steel buildings rise like friendly movie robots with a thousand eyes glinting in the early morning sun. In the middle stands the Calgary Tower, a lonely spire with a bright red cap. Paradoxically, it never seems to be dwarfed by the taller buildings surrounding it. Behind the buildings, way off in the distance, the Rocky Mountains reach for the sky. The scene evokes images of Lawren Harris, all aquamarine blue with vivid splashes of white. The last time he entered this office, Jerry looked at the sunlight reflected in the downtown windows and joked that he spent his first twenty-three years living in a country where nobody ever died of skin cancer. Today he's in no mood for joking.

"Come in, Jerry, take a seat." The city editor, Dave Webster, gestures toward his couch. He wears a light-blue blazer, checked shirt and polka-dot tie. At forty-five, he retains the chunky build of the high-school offensive lineman he once was. On the wall behind his desk is an autographed portrait of Doug Flutie, the star quarterback for the Calgary Stampeders.

"I wondered if I can take a few days off, Dave. Maybe a week, if that's okay. My father is not in the best of health, and I need to fly over to Dublin for a quick visit." He feels guilty to be lying like this. His father is fine. Shouldn't he tell Webster he needs time off to clear his head? Or to work on his family history?

"Of course, Jerry, take more time if you need it."

"No thanks, a week should be enough. My father is one of those people who likes to see his American kids – as he calls us – about once a year for short visits."

"You have other siblings here?"

"A couple of brothers in Boston, that's it."

The phone rings. It sounds like a Radio Shack Princess. Incongruous for a newspaper office. "No, I can't talk to him now, Kathy," says Webster. "Can you take a message for me? I should be able to return calls in about fifteen minutes or so."

He puts down the receiver. "Excuse me for a moment, Jerry." He picks up the phone again and dials a four-digit extension. "Melissa, can you come in here for a moment? Please bring your notebook with you."

Melissa is an editorial assistant. She usually wears a T-shirt and jeans. Today she's outfitted in a cream blouse and dark skirt. Why? She takes a seat by the window, opposite Webster's desk. Ballpoint pen in her left hand and spiral-bound notebook in her right.

Behind Melissa, the Rockies look majestic. They always look majestic. Best view in the city. Jerry wonders why Webster wants her to take notes.

"So, have you given any more thought to what we talked about last month?"

145

"Dave, I've never worked on the desk before. Why would you want me to do something I haven't trained for?" Should he add something about constructive dismissal? He bites his tongue.

Webster picks up a folder from his in-tray. "I looked at your personnel file again, Jerry. It says that one of your duties, when you were in Entertainment, was to lay out the book pages every week."

Aah the happy memories, those were the days. However, he never liked laying out the book pages. Couldn't get the hang of column widths, picas, or agate. But oh, the joy of browsing those publishers' catalogues. Christmas came every spring and fall. Books about music, theatre, and Ireland to add to his home library. The best of fiction and nonfiction for the freelance reviewers.

One of his reviewers was a sailing enthusiast. Jerry had him critique a coffee-table volume about boating in the Azores. The reaction from the editor-in-chief was swift. "Why, in God's name are we reviewing books about sailing? We live in this land-locked desert, where there are more snowmobiles than boats."

"I can't lay out a page to save my soul, Dave. When I was in Entertainment, I had to use the same template every week because I couldn't even size a picture correctly." If Webster thinks he'd be inept at page designing, maybe he'll change his mind about putting him on the desk?

"You don't have to worry about that now, Jerry. You'll be editing copy in the first instance. You certainly know how to do that. Every good reporter knows how to edit. When the other deskers finish their layout training on QuarkXPress, then it'll be your turn. We expect to double the number of deskers without making any new hires."

"I don't know anything about QuarkXPress, but I seriously doubt that it's going to turn me from a klutz into a layout artist."

Melissa scribbles furiously in her notebook. What does she have to write about? Is a record of this conversation going into the personnel file as well? What else does the personnel file hold? He asked to see it once, but the HR person told him it was "classified."

"You'll find it's easier with the new computers, Jerry. They do all the heavy lifting. If you can drag and drop, you can lay out a page." If he can do what? Drag and drop? Is this what the new computer-speak sounds like?

"Can we talk again about my column, Dave? I know you said there wouldn't be any room for it in the paper after City merges with Life, and that Anderson wants to see more hard news in the paper. But is there a chance I might write it for the Sunday paper? That's usually a slow day for breaking events."

He's not about to give up Passages without a fight. He worked in journalism for more than twenty years to get the column. "One of the best new features this paper has introduced to its pages in a long time," wrote the *Herald's* ombudsman. Surely they can find room for it at least once a week?

Webster pretends to be conciliatory. "We did give that consideration, Jerry. We thought of running the column on Sunday and having you do other stories for the rest of the week. However, you haven't worked on Cityside for years. I don't know that you'd be able to handle it. I think you'd be happier on the desk."

Happier on the desk? Jerry bites his tongue. Patronizing shit. Measure his words carefully. Do they care about his happiness? No

147

damn way. They want him gone. They want two 22-year-old writers with twice the energy and none of the attitude to do cop stories for half his salary. Sayonara, baby. Let him languish on the desk until he can stand it no longer. Then he can bugger off and die.

"I could do lifestyle stories."

"No, the focus there will be on recipes and fashion trends," says Webster. "I don't think you want to do those kinds of stories."

"Couldn't I work the desk part-time, then, and continue to write my column for Sunday? It would be a shame to have it disappear from the paper without trace."

"That would be setting a dangerous precedent, Jerry. Other deskers, especially those who like to write, would be looking for a similar deal. Besides, with the new computers coming in, we can't afford to spare them the time."

"Then I think you should give me a chance to show what I can do on Cityside. I've been a reporter for twenty-three years, Dave. I know how to do that job."

"I know, Jerry, but you haven't worked the street for a while. People get rusty. Besides, do you want to go back to doing what you did when you first started in the business? This is an opportunity for you to develop new skills and make an important contribution to the *Herald*."

"I still can't believe you want to get rid of Passages. The readers love it." Jerry has the letters and faxes to prove it.

"Some readers love it."

"What do you mean?"

"There have been complaints."

"What do you mean complaints?"

"Anderson had to put out a few fires on your behalf. He didn't tell you about them. I think he was trying to protect you."

"Specifics?"

"One was from a woman nursing a husband with cancer. She said too many of your columns deal with people who have died of the disease. Another was from the kids of a dead woman whose first husband had been an alcoholic. The children from the first marriage didn't like their father's drinking problem being made public like that."

"Many people die from cancer, Dave. I'm not going to reject someone because I've already written that week about other people with the disease. As for the alcoholic, I don't know which one you're talking about. However, I'm sure I wouldn't have said he had a problem unless there was a valid reason. You know I don't write the column to hurt people."

"I know, Jerry. But you can see how people read things into things. Regardless, Anderson has decided to terminate the column."

"What if I don't want to go on the desk? What are my other options?"

"None, I'm afraid. You either go on the desk or …"

"Or?"

"I'm sorry, Jerry, I hate having to put it to you like this. I know we didn't discuss this before, but if you don't go on the desk, I'm afraid your employment at the *Calgary Herald* will come to an end. Your writing contributions have been deemed expendable."

149

"Just like that? Today I'm one of the paper's top writers and tomorrow I'm toast?"

"I can get you two months' salary as severance if you decide not to take the desk job," says Webster.

Jerry swallows hard. *Light a fire under my fingernails.* Two months' severance? That's all he gets for his eighteen years at the paper? He earned a National Newspaper Award citation for his Passages column, and now they want to toss him on the scrapheap with a handful of silver. This is gratitude?

"I need to think about this some more," says Jerry. "Can you wait until I return?"

"Of course," says Webster. "As you know, they have you scheduled for the next round of desker training. However, that's not due to start for several more weeks yet, so you still have time to decide what you want to do."

"When will the new computers be going into the newsroom?'

"When they put in additional wiring," says Webster. "The computers work fine in the training room, but the techies say they would blow all the fuses if they filled up the newsroom with them. So, we have to reinforce the electrical system."

"How long will that take?"

"Could be weeks, maybe months."

"And I can keep writing my column in the meantime?"

"For now."

The mountains are now shrouded in cloud. Jerry wonders if there's anyone in those downtown office towers who might offer him a communications job.

"I hope your father will be all right," says Webster.

Jerry nods and goes back to his office.

OWN IN THE STEERAGE, faintly lit by a cluster of small oil lamps, Nell can make out the figures of men, women, and children huddled together, lying under filthy blankets. Some are singing the Benediction hymns, "O Salutaris Hostia" and "Tantum Ergo." Others are saying the Rosary. A few, like Diarmuid, are in the throes of seasickness or fever. Devoid of ventilation and a sanitary system, the place smells of excrement and vomit. The air is heavy and fetid. Nell has so much difficulty breathing that she thinks she might faint.

"Wouldn't you go upstairs for a breath of fresh air?" she says to a man vomiting into a latrine bucket.

He groans and turns away from her, retching. "They won't let us up there until it's our turn. They say we'd be in the way."

Nell places a hand on his shoulder. "I'll bring you over some lime juice from our side."

She kneels on the floor next to a woman reciting with her three children the last Our Father of the Rosary. After Nell says the Hail Holy Queen with the family, the woman makes the sign of the cross with her crucifix, kisses the beads, and introduces herself as Mary Collins from Sam's Cross, near Clonakilty. "Me husband was a farm labourer. He earned one shilling a day when he worked. But often he didn't work because of his sickness. We lived in a scalpeen after they evicted us. The rain always came through the thatch in winter. Then the praties went bad. The children were crying with the hunger pains. Me husband died. 'Free passage,' the bailiff told me. 'Free passage to a land with a better life.' I've now been left with only thirty-five shillings to me name, but there will be more for us in Canada."

Nell notices that the woman's youngest daughter is barely clothed. "You'll need to have a new dress. I can make one for you."

The girl's eyes open wide. "Can you?"

"'Twill be no trouble at all. I'll have one for you tomorrow."

"That's good of you," says Mrs. Collins. "How will you do that?"

Nell smiles and makes a sewing motion with her hands. "All I have to do is find some cloth. I think I know where I can do that. But first I have to get some lime juice for the poor man over there."

She looks over at the man, now convulsed in agony. It's like a fiend is attacking him from within. His bare feet are swelling to twice their normal size, and his face is breaking out in red and purple sores. Could this be the dreaded fever? Nell has never seen anything like it before. She doesn't know what to think.

She meets the second mate at the top of the companionway and describes the symptoms. He confirms the worst. "Yes, that's the fever. 'Tis spread by lice in tight quarters. That's why we don't go down there."

"Is there any medicine we can give him?"

"Laudanum will ease the pain, but there's no cure for the fever itself."

"Is there any laudanum on board?"

"There may be some in the captain's medicine chest. I can ask him about it, but he won't go into the steerage to hand it out."

"He told us he had taken medical training and would dispense medicines when necessary."

The second mate shrugs. "That's what he tells the passengers on every voyage."

"Can you speak to the captain about him, please? We have to do something to help this poor man."

THE SECOND MATE RETURNS after checking with the captain and says there's nothing in the medicine chest aside from bandages, liniments, Epsom salts and hartshorn. "No laudanum, I'm afraid."

"Then the poor man will die a horrible death," says Nell, shuddering at the thought. "Will they leave his body here, or what will they do with it?"

The second mate points in the direction of the ocean. "We can't keep them on the ship, so we drop them in the water."

"Never to get to the New World, never to receive a proper burial?" she says. "Is that what happens to the sailors, too, if they pass during the voyage?"

"We protect ourselves from the fever by drinking grog. If you want to pay sixpence for a quarter pint, you can do the same."

Nell shakes her head. "I don't think we would be interested, thank you. Is that what ye were drinking down below when me husband and I were having dinner?"

"'Tis what we drink every day. We rarely take ill. Are you sure I can't sell you a quarter pint? There's a great demand for it among the passengers."

FOUR DAYS LATER, Diarmuid feels well enough to come up on deck. "Let the wind blow on your face and take a deep breath," he says to Nell. "Pure, fresh, clean and crisp. Not like the staleness and stuffiness of the cabin. Like being on a mountaintop, up above the Pass of Keimaneigh. Every mouthful entering your throat has travelled hundreds of miles over the open sea. Drink it in, macushla. It fills up your lungs, and makes you a new person."

She takes him aside and whispers. "Did you know the sailors are selling alcohol to the passengers down below? All kinds of blackguardism going on there. Many frightened women and children. Frightened men, too."

"Nothing we can do about it, I s'pose. I'm sure the captain knows all about it. He probably profits from it." He wishes Nell would spend less time in the steerage. She's made it her mission to help, which is admirable, but she's putting herself at risk. Putting both of them at risk.

A little girl comes running across the deck, wearing a dress made from a biscuit sack. She curtseys and looks up at Nell. "Thank you, Mrs. de Búrca, for making me the dress. Mammy says 'tis beautiful."

Nell hugs her. "You look like a princess."

Diarmuid nods approvingly. "You sewed that dress for her? Aren't you grand?"

"She came with barely a stitch on her back," says Nell. "The cook told me they had no further use for the empty sacks, so I asked if I could use them to make dresses for the girls."

"Aside from the drinking and the blackguardism, how else are things down below?"

"There's no privacy at all," says Nell. "Men and women have to clothe and unclothe and relieve themselves within plain sight of one

155

another. Or they would be in plain sight if there was more light down there. There's a drastic shortage of latrine buckets. The filth accumulates on the floor and the bottom rows of the berths."

"And that brings dangerous bacteria, I would imagine."

"The place teems with abominations," she says. "Our fellow passengers are stuck in their stench and confinement."

"Do they have enough to eat and drink?"

"They can't drink the brackish water any more. It's only good for cleaning the muck off their garments, because 'tis infected with something foul. They can't quench their thirst while eating the biscuit, and they'd probably kill themselves if they tried using the water cold for making stirabout."

"The water was probably stored for too long. Can't they boil it?"

"They can, Diarmuid, but you know how few braziers there are up here, and how limited the opportunities are for using them. There are many children on this ship, and they should be fed uncontaminated stirabout every day."

"I'll bring this up with the captain whenever I see him." He doesn't hold out much hope, however. The captain has already made it clear he wants no truck with the passengers.

AS IT TURNS OUT, the sailors do have another use for the empty biscuit sacks aside from giving them to Nell for making dresses. Later that afternoon, word comes from the steerage that two of the passengers have died: the man Nell tried to help and a five-year-old boy. The first casualties at sea. The sailors refuse to touch the bodies, so two of the passengers must load them into sacks and then drop them overboard.

Nell kneels and makes the sign of the cross. "Nothing but a watery grave for those poor creatures, God rest their souls. No crosses to mark their final resting place."

She turns toward Diarmuid and smiles. "I'm so happy that you're feeling better. I was so anxious about you when all you did was lie there half-dozing. But at least you were able to sit up occasionally and sip lime juice."

He takes another deep breath of the fresh air. "I'm grand now, macushla. I was thinking about me childhood. The memories were vivid. Me mother was singing her poems to me, and me father was holding court at the head of the table. All the conversations we had. I remembered them as if they were last night. Me father talking about horses. Me mother telling stories about Celtic goddesses. 'Tis curious how everything that happens to you leaves such an impression in the memory. How the pictures come back when you just lie there and wait for them to appear."

THE FIRST MATE IS IN THE CABIN drinking rum with the captain. "What's the story from down below?" asks the captain. "Are many of them getting sick?"

"Worse than that, sir. The men tell me there have been two deaths already."

"And there will be more, of course. However, there's nothing we can do, William. These ships are cursed."

157

"We'll protect ourselves as we've done before, sir. We won't allow ourselves to be exposed."

"Do what you have to do, then. The passengers will look after their own. They always do. It's so much easier, isn't it, when we're just carrying timber and cotton?"

"You mentioned that this is your twenty-fifth voyage?"

"And it will be my last, William. I haven't told Mr. Brocklebank yet, but I'm ready for the life of a landlubber."

AN HOUR LATER, THE AIR OUTSIDE starts to grow heavy and takes on a charged feeling as the wind picks up and the clouds turn to grey. Diarmuid and Nell flinch as a lightning flash stabs downward into the ocean followed by a thunderous boom. Rain lashes down on the deck. "Our first storm at sea," he says. "Better go below." The sailors scramble to their stations. The first mate shouts orders from the poop deck as the ship starts pitching and surging. "Stand by to heave to. Clew up the mainsail. Slack off the head sheets."

Down in their cabin, Diarmuid and Nell can't tell if the sailors are winning their battle with the tempest because the ship seems governed by a force mightier than their joint efforts. It's being tossed around like a feather in the wind. The couple can hear the waves pummelling the sides of the ship as the sea churns violently. Diarmuid looks out through the porthole and watches in awe and trepidation as the storm does its work.

At one point, the vessel seems on the brink of being swallowed up, immersed in the deep with an insurmountable barrier surrounding it. The next minute, it seems to be riding atop the foaming surge.

158

Diarmuid wonders if it's possible the ship might sink. How did Jonah survive his ordeal in the belly of the great fish?

"Lord save us, this is nothing like we've experienced before," he says. Nell drops to her knees, motions to him to do the same, and removes her rosary beads from around her neck. "Let's meditate on the Glorious Mysteries," she says. "In the name of the Father, and of the Son, and of the Holy Ghost."

THERE'S NO SLEEP for the couple that night as the storm continues to blow. The ship tosses and turns on the water, and Diarmuid and Nell toss and turn in their bunks. The wind roars, the timbers groan, and they can hear the rainwater sweeping across the deck above. They can also hear banging and crashing in the galley as pots, pans, and kettles fall from the shelves. With every thunderclap, Diarmuid recalls what his mother used to say during the thunderstorms of his childhood. "'Tis only God moving the furniture around in Heaven." It isn't until noon the next day that the storm finally subsides. Diarmuid expresses relief that the sturdy old tub, as he now thinks of the ship, has weathered all the battering.

When the hatches are opened, Nell goes around to check on the steerage passengers. It saddens her to learn there have been more casualties. A six-year-old girl, already stricken with the fever, succumbed during the storm. An older man, thrown against a table, had three ribs broken. "Your children are all right?" Nell says to Mrs. Collins. "They are," she replies. "But now we've nothing to eat but the hard biscuit. And we've nothing to drink."

WHEN HE SEES HIM UP ON THE POOP DECK, Diarmuid tells the captain about the plight of the steerage passengers. "Please come down and see for yourself, sir. You can ease their agony by giving them fresh water instead of the infected liquid the sailors have been putting into their buckets."

"They receive everything required by the government regulations," says the captain. "I'm not obliged to give them anything different."

"But the water is only good for washing, sir. If they try using it to cook the oatmeal, which is now wormy, they'll get sick."

"They receive everything required by the government regulations," repeats the captain. "Three quarts per day. I have no control over the quality of the water."

"But the sailors are receiving fresh water, sir. The cabin passengers are receiving fresh water. Why should it be any different for the steerage passengers?"

"Because their water must come from the casks that the ship's owner provided us with before we left port. As I told you, I have no control over the quality of that water."

"Please let them have some of the fresh water, Captain Low. Don't let it be said that in escaping from the famine in Ireland they encountered an even worse fate aboard ship."

"You've said enough," says the captain. "Go back to your cabin and do not speak to me again. I will not have anyone here usurping my authority. There's no insolence allowed on my ship."

Diarmuid feels as helpless as a blind beggar. How can a man with such little compassion for his fellow humans be allowed to transport emigrants across the ocean? How can he live with himself? He never enters the steerage, never listens to their complaints. The passengers suffer like souls in hell, and he ignores them.

FTER DOWNING HIS THIRD MARTINI, Jerry grabs the kitchen wall phone and dials Ireland. He does his drinking – and his long-distance phoning – in the evening after work. Usually, it's wine, which he calls the bang of the grape. He starts with a glass of Wolf Blass Yellow Label while watching the local news on CFAC. Finishes half the bottle while having supper, often the microwaved second half of the daily special he ordered for lunch in the *Herald* cafeteria. Re-corks the bottle, and then has for dessert a small glass of Taylor's port that he sips while watching *Jeopardy*.

Tonight, he's into the martinis, which often happens when something is bothering him. He knows he may regret it in the morning but, for the moment, the bigger bang of the Smirnoff helps dull the pain.

"Hi Cathal, it's your cousin Jer calling from Canada. I'm flying to London tomorrow, and then on to Cork the next day. Wondering if we can get together to talk some more about family history?"

"Excellent, Jer. Did you want to stay at our place?"

"No, I'm good, thanks. I've booked a room at the Castle Hotel."

"Welcome to Macroom, then."

"I'll be renting a car in Cork City and then visiting some of the O'Leary landmarks. The castle at Carrignacurra. The Pass at Keimaneigh. The old graveyard at Inchigeelagh where Máire Bhuí is buried."

"Brilliant. I'll take a few days off and join you."

"Do you know where the old homestead of Máire Bhuí's son, Micheál Burke, is located?"

"In Inchibeg. Easy enough to find. You take the Killarney road from Macroom for four miles, turn left at Halfway House, and take the Ballingeary road for another five miles. The homestead is on the right side of the road, about a mile past the Gougane Barra junction. You can't miss it."

"You can give me directions when I get there. I'll never remember this over the phone."

"Let me be your navigator then. We should drop into the Burke place for a visit. Our third cousin, also named Micheál Burke, still lives there."

"Does he have an interest in family history?"

"Not as I recall. We can ask him, however. Incidentally, Jer, I've been talking to a local historian here, and she's given me valuable information about Máire Bhuí's youngest son that we didn't have before."

"Oh great, you can tell me about it when I get there. I'll let you go now, Cathal. See you in a couple of days."

HE'S CUTTING THE CALL SHORT with Cathal because he wants to phone Carol. A shoulder to cry on. Pours himself another martini and dials Edmonton.

"What's the matter, Jerry. You sound as if you've been drinking." She always can tell because he becomes voluble. She mutes the sound of the television, extracts the cork from the half-empty bottle of cabernet sauvignon, and pours herself another glass. If he's drinking, she might as well too.

"Sorry, Carol, I had to phone you. The bastards are trying to fire me. Here's your hat, what's your hurry? Don't let the door slam behind you on the way out. The hard-news guys have won. They're killing Passages, and I'm walking the plank."

He remembers his struggle to get the column approved. He had argued that ordinary people mattered because they often did extraordinary things, and thus deserved to be remembered. The former city editor agreed but his immediate superior, the managing editor, had his doubts. "We're not a community weekly, you know." The former city editor prevailed, and Jerry was assigned to what his colleagues cynically called the "dead beat." His response to their ribbing: "If you're feeling poorly, be sure to fax me your biographical materials."

"You're being fired?" says Carol. She can't believe the *Herald* would do this to one of its most popular columnists.

She too likes to limit herself now to half a bottle of wine at supper. Much better for her health than the two-bottle-a-night drinking they did during the short time they lived together. The second bottle sometimes led to a third, and that's when the trouble started. Their long-ago argument over where to spend Christmas was typical. She wanted to ski, and he wanted to do a beach holiday. They ended up staying at home, not talking to one another.

"Yes, I'm being fired. They want me to go on the desk. Same thing, right? Constructive dismissal. Webster doesn't think I have the chops to work the street any more. Says the other editors don't want

164

me to write for them either. They don't have room in their departments for someone like me."

"Someone like you?"

"Someone with a point of view. Someone who doesn't write to order. Someone who thinks newspaper writing doesn't have to be hack writing. Someone who thinks journalism is a higher calling."

"I hear you, sweetheart. Who's Webster?"

"You know, Dave Webster, the new city editor. Used to be at the *Sun*."

"Can't say I ever met him. What did he do at the tabloid?"

"Worked the cop beat. That's the only news he understands. If it bleeds, it leads."

"You don't want to go back to working the street, Jerry. That's what you graduated from when you started writing theatre reviews. They made you a columnist, and they can't change your job description just like that. They're giving you a licence to fail. If the *Herald* were a union paper, you wouldn't have to deal with shit like this."

"They're offering me two months' salary if I leave."

"Not enough, Jerry. How many years have you been there? You should get at least two, even three weeks for every year. If they don't give you that, you should hire a lawyer. Did you want to come up to Edmonton to talk about this? Sounds like you need a big hug."

"They want an answer from me soon."

"How soon? A few days?"

"When I get back from Ireland."

"When are you going to Ireland?"

165

"Tomorrow."

"Tomorrow? Really? I hope you make it to the airport on time. How long are you going for?"

"A week. I'm visiting with my cousin Cathal. We're going to research the family history together."

"That'll give you a needed break. What time is your flight?"

"Three o'clock in the afternoon. I fly to London first, and then to Cork."

"Call me in the morning, then. Will you be seeing your father?"

"I told Webster I would. Pretended Dad is not in good health, and said he wants me to visit. However, I won't be seeing him. At least, not this time."

"You shouldn't lie about things like that, Jerry."

"They want me to work on the desk. They want me to write headlines and lay out pages."

"Yes, you told me, Jerry. I know it's a bummer."

"I don't want to write headlines for someone else's stories. I want to write my own stories." He is now drinking the vermouth straight out of the bottle.

"I understand, sweetheart."

"Nobody wants to work on the desk. Nobody. NOBODY WANTS TO WORK ON THE BLOODY DESK!"

"I hear you, Jerry. Why don't you get some sleep, my love, and we'll talk some more tomorrow?"

"The bastards are trying to get rid of me."

"I know, Jerry, we'll talk in the morning." She wants this circular conversation to end soon.

"Nobody wants to work on the bloody desk. Once you go on the desk, you never get off. You go there and you die."

"I'm hanging up the phone now, Jerry. Goodnight, sweetheart, I'll talk to you tomorrow."

"G'night. G'night. Talk tomorrow." He stumbles into the bedroom, and falls into a troubled sleep.

DIARMUID IS SITTING IN THE SUNSHINE writing in his journal when one of the steerage passengers, a fair-haired man in his thirties, crosses the deck.

"Mr. Diarmuid de Búrca, if I'm not mistaken?"

"At your service, sir." Diarmuid does a double take. "Oh Lord save us, Cousin Donncha. I didn't know you were on this ship."

"I arrived on the day of departure," says Donncha. "Decided to emigrate after Barry's successor told me I'd be next on the list for eviction. Thought I'd have to wait for the next ship, but was able to get on this one because I'm travelling by meself."

"Good man, yourself. Did you tell me mother you were leaving?"

"I did, Diarmuid, and she gave me her blessing. Wished me Godspeed."

"Me mother used to say you'd be the one writing the songs after she's gone."

"You can write the songs anywhere, Diarmuid. I just won't be singing them at the funerals in Inchigeelagh."

"How did you make out during the storm?"

"Sure it was terrible down there in the pitch darkness with the air so foul. Sickness, confusion, fear, groaning, retching, calling for water. Nobody there to bring them a drop. The howling would have given a deaf man a headache."

The first mate comes out of the galley carrying half a roast chicken to bring down to the captain.

"I think we can have fun here," says Donncha with a smile. He sneaks into the empty galley, grabs a big pot of hot tea, calls over the steerage passengers who are cooking and washing on the deck, and quickly fills their empty water cans. Before returning the pot to the galley, Donncha replaces the tea with the contents of a latrine bucket.

He completes the swap just in time. Moments later, the first mate returns to the galley. He takes the pot of urine from the stove, and brings it down to the captain's cabin. Doesn't notice that the pot is barely lukewarm. A few minutes after that, the first mate returns, brandishing the contaminated vessel. He approaches Diarmuid and says, "What do you know about this?"

"About what?" Diarmuid replies, innocently.

"About the piss that someone put into the captain's teapot. You almost poisoned him."

"I know nothing about this. Sounds like the water ye've been putting out for the passengers every day."

"What happened to the tea that's supposed to be in this pot?"

One of the steerage passengers, Tadhg O'Reilly, brings over his half-empty can. "Is this the tea you would be inquiring about? Sure, that was a grand pot you sent us, sir. You should be a captain instead of a mate, you should."

"I did not send it to you," says the mate. "I want to know who stole it."

"Would it be the tea they promised us before we came on board?" asks Tadhg. "The same tea our agent paid ten pounds for back in Inchigeelagh?"

The mate grabs Tadhg by the shoulder. "Tell me the name of the thief who gave it to you," he says.

"I will do that," says Tadhg. "I can't refuse so polite a gentleman. If you come down with me into the steerage, I'll be pleased to introduce you to the person who poured us the tea."

The mate lets him go, turns on his heel, and walks back toward the companionway leading down to the captain's cabin.

"Aren't you going to come down and meet the thief?" Tadhg shouts after him. "There's a fever patient there who would love to shake hands with you. Be sure to have the cook brew more tea for us tomorrow, sir. And, don't forget the sugar!"

"That was a good bit of sport," says Diarmuid, laughing. "I have a feeling we won't be short of tea for the rest of the voyage." He knows, however, this could be wishful thinking.

"Let's celebrate with a céilí," says Donncha. "There's a man down below who plays the uileann pipes, and another one with an accordion. We'll get them to play a few jigs and reels for us, and we'll have everyone dancing. Tadhg here is a great step-dancer. The sailors might even join in."

"That's a grand idea," says Diarmuid. "The mate will probably try to send some of ye back down below because ye're not supposed to be up here, but we'll have a few songs and dances before that happens."

THIRTY PEOPLE FROM THE STEERAGE, including the two musicians, join them for the céilí. Diarmuid sings a couple of his mother's songs – "The Dawning of the Day" and "The Full Jug" – and Donncha sings a few of his own.

170

"Do you think we should sing 'The Battle of Keimaneigh'?" asks Diarmuid.

"No, that would be too provocative, I think," says Donncha. "How about you, Nell? Do you have a song for us?"

"I can sing 'The Moon's Pale Light,'" she says hesitantly. She does so in a soft, sweet voice.

THE FOLLOWING EVENING, Nell sings again, this time for a young woman who died during the night. She sings the requiem hymn "Dies Irae" in Latin after Diarmuid recites the prayer for the dead. This time her voice is loud and commanding.

"You must have been a soloist once," says Diarmuid afterwards. "Where did you learn the Latin?"

"Me father, God rest his soul, used to be an altar boy. He taught me how to pronounce the Latin."

"I never heard you singing at Saint Finbarr's. I wish I had."

"I stopped singing solo after we moved up from Bantry. The choir in Inchigeelagh had all the soprano soloists they needed, so there was no opportunity."

"I'm going to have you singing for me all the time when we get to Canada."

"I'm glad you said the prayer for the dead, Diarmuid."

"I should have been doing that right from the beginning. We don't have a priest on board, of course, and I have the training."

"Did you see that woman's eyes before they closed them? So big and glowing and beautiful."

"They entranced me," he agrees. "I could sense God's love enfolding her like a light from heaven."

"Everyone from Youghal knew her," says Nell. "I saw people on the deck today who hadn't been out of the steerage since we left Cove."

"Another one of God's poor creatures taken at sea," he says. "Now, sad to say, we take it for granted that every day will bring three or four casualties or more."

"With many being children," she says. "Lives cut short before they begin."

One of the sailors is swabbing the deck. "How many more days will we be on the ship?" asks Diarmuid.

"From the angle of the sun, I would say we're about two hundred miles from Newfoundland," replies the sailor.

"Still a long way to go," says Diarmuid.

"Look, Diarmuid," says Nell. "Come over here and see the ocean." The sun is setting, and the rays are lighting up the water.

"'Tis the road to the land of promise," she says. "The sun is welcoming us to our new home in Canada."

A WEEK LATER, a dense fog on the water signifies there are icebergs nearby. Seabirds make an appearance for the first time since the ship left the Irish coastline. Faintly visible in the fog are other ships – three of them – flying American flags and crowded with immigrants. A clump of seaweed floats by, suggesting land is nearby.

The cook hands out slices of salt pork for the sailors to use as bait. They throw out their lines and fish for half an hour, hauling in a

172

plentiful stock of cod, mackerel, and halibut. Not only is there plenty of fresh fish for the sailors, but there's also enough to feed the passengers down below.

More food arrives when two men pull alongside the ship in a rowboat containing loaves of bread and a churn of milk. Diarmuid hears them shouting the French words *pain* and *lait*, which he recognizes although he doesn't speak the language. He lowers a pail down to them, and they fill it up for sixpence. For another sixpence, they give him a loaf of bread.

"How does the milk taste?" says Nell.

"Sour," he replies. "But much appreciated after the tea, which wasn't nearly strong enough."

"I'll bring some milk down below," she says. "It will help protect the lives of the few infants that are left."

She winces and puts a hand to her back.

"Are you all right, macushla?"

"No problem at all," she says. "Just a little backache. It will pass."

TWO MORE MEN IN A ROWBOAT pull up next to the ship and offer to guide it through the obstacles of ice. The sailors invite them to come on board, but the men decline because they know from experience that some of the passengers will be sick. The sailors now smell strongly of camphor, having lost faith in grog as protection against fever.

With the rowboat pilots leading it, the ship navigates successfully through the ice. Diarmuid is impressed by the skill the captain demonstrates while manoeuvring the vessel. He may be a monster of a human being, but he certainly is a first-class sailor.

"Do the ships ever get stuck?" Diarmuid asks one of the sailors.

"Sometimes they can be caught out there for as long as two weeks," replies the sailor. "The biggest part of the ice is below the surface."

"And how do the ships finally get out?"

"The wind opens up an escape channel for them."

"The icebergs look like glass mountains with the sun shining on them," says Diarmuid. "Very impressive."

WHEN THE SHIP FINISHES ITS JOURNEY through the ice, the travellers can see land for the first time in several weeks. The ship has now left the Atlantic, and is sailing into the welcoming waters of the Gulf of Saint Lawrence. It enters a narrow channel, with Cape Breton Island on the one side and St. Paul Island on the other. The island lighthouses stand tall as beacons of guidance and safety.

From there, the ship sails down the Saint Lawrence River toward the Grosse Île quarantine station where, they've been told, a medical officer will examine the passengers and crew. The mood is buoyant. The sailors sing "Across the Western Ocean" as they go about their work.

"The land of promise there you'll see, Amelia, where you bound to?/I'm bound across that Western Sea, 'tis time for us to leave her."

THE CHEERY MOOD TURNS SOUR when Diarmuid notices the first mate whipping the cabin boy for an alleged infraction. "Leave

174

him be," shouts Diarmuid. "For whatever he did wrong, he doesn't deserve that kind of punishment."

"Get back from me, or I'll put you in irons for mutiny," says the mate as he continues to whip the boy.

"We'll see about that," says Diarmuid, drawing back his fist and punching the mate in the face. The mate hits back and the two fall to the deck wrestling.

The mate is strong from working on the ship, but Diarmuid is fit too after years of working on the farm. He crooks the mate's neck in his left arm and punches every part of his body that his right fist can reach. The mate's curses soon turn to cries for help, and then for mercy, but none of the other sailors wants to get involved.

With every blow he strikes, Diarmuid thinks of how the mate and his captain have made life miserable for the emigrants. Complete indifference to their sufferings. No respect, no compassion, no acknowledgement that these travellers are their *guests*. They don't even look at their faces. They let them die without a word of solace for their grieving families. Now it's the mate's turn to suffer. To hell with the consequences, the villain has to be taught a lesson.

The emigrants are delighted to see their tormentor being punished. "Finish him off," urges one, handing Diarmuid a stick. However, he doesn't need a stick for that. Summoning the rest of his strength, he picks up the mate like a sack of potatoes and throws him against the side of the galley.

The cook comes over, wipes the blood from the mate's face, and helps him back down to his cabin. "If any of them try to get back at you," a Youghal man says to Diarmuid, "me people and I will break their necks."

NELL COMES UP FROM THE STEERAGE and sees the bruises on Diarmuid's face.

"What happened?" she says. "Did you fall?"

"I got into in a fight with the first mate," he says, sheepishly. "I saw him whipping the cabin boy and lost me temper."

"Oh, that's not good. Will you be charged?"

"Likely not," he says. "At least not in a court of law. I don't think the mate would run the risk of appearing before a judge when there are dozens of witnesses here who can testify about the several ways he and the captain have broken the law since we set sail."

"Will there be any consequences for you?"

"I'm worried that the captain will take the law into his own hands before we reach Quebec. However, we won't cross that ford until we come to it."

"Diarmuid, you have to come down below with me. I think Donncha has caught the fever."

"Lord save us, I'll go down and see him right away. Should we bring a lamp?"

"I'll ask the second mate for one," she says.

Donncha is sweating and shivering. "Don't let them drop me in the sea, Diarmuid. If I die, I want to be buried on Canadian soil."

Diarmuid is shocked at how pale and emaciated he looks compared to a few days ago, when they were celebrating with singing and dancing on the deck.

"The man from the quarantine station will be here soon, Donncha. We'll ask if he has medicine to give to the fever sufferers."

"Promise me, Diarmuid," says Donncha. "Promise me that if I die, you won't let them drop me into the sea."

"I promise, Donncha. I promise that we'll give you a proper burial when the time comes. However, it's still too soon to be talking about that. There should be some medicine available to help you."

E WAKES AT 10:00 AM. Looks at the almost-empty bottles of vodka and vermouth on the kitchen counter. Relieved to feel only a slight headache. Pours himself a glass of grapefruit juice. Clicks the switch on the answering machine.

"I hope you have no ill effects this morning, my love. You weren't feeling much pain last night. Talk to you later, my sweet."

What did he say to her, last night? Bad mistake to have phoned her after drinking all those martinis. Whatever he said, though, can't have pissed her off. She sounds friendly this morning.

He looks out the kitchen window. Sun is glinting on the patio. A *White Mischief* morning. *Oh God, not another fucking beautiful day.* Should he take a walk? No, better call her first. Can't leave her in suspense.

"I'm so, so sorry, Carol. You must have thought me a complete idiot."

"Not to worry, sweetheart. You were pretty upset. What time did you say your flight is at?"

"Three o'clock. Plenty of time to get there."

"And how long did you say you're going for?"

"A week." He puts a couple of white-bread slices in the toaster.

"Too bad you're going over there. You could have come up to Edmonton and spent a couple of days with me."

"I'll do that after I get back. If I take the money and run."

"You're not seriously thinking of doing that? You told me they're offering you only two months."

"I'll try to squeeze more out of them. If I go to Anderson directly – or to the publisher, if Anderson is unreceptive – I might be able to convince them my years of loyal service are worth more than two months' severance."

"And what would you do then? Freelance? Apply at the *Sun*?"

"I'll be considering my options when I'm in Ireland."

"Did you say you're going to Dublin?"

"Not this time, only to Cork. To Macroom, to be precise. It's about twenty-five miles west of the city."

"So, you won't be seeing your father?"

"Not in Dublin. He might come down to Cork, however. I'll give him a call when I'm there."

"And you'll find out what happened to your ancestor."

"Hope so. My cousin Cathal tells me he has new information about him."

"'Madre del desaparecido.'"

"Come again?"

"It's a Spanish song that we sing in church. It means mother of the disappeared son."

"Perfect," says Jerry, "I should learn to play that one."

"Do you think you might ever write a Passages column about the missing son?"

"Depends on what I find out when I'm in Cork. And how much time I have left at the *Herald*."

I SHOW UP EARLY AT THE AIRPORT, dressed in my Sunday best. Blue pin-striped suit. Crisp white shirt. Maroon tie. Freshly

179

polished brown shoes. The first place a woman looks, as Allan Fotheringham used to say. "Any chance of being upgraded to business class?" The woman at the check-in counter peers into her computer terminal. "Two seats still available. You're in luck." No extra cost. The strategy works every time. If you dress like a businessman, they put you in business class.

I stretch out in the seat with the extra legroom. The flight attendant brings me a glass of champagne and the dinner menu. "Will you be having wine with your meal?" Of course. A glass of the French cabernet sauvignon, *s'il vous plaît*. Ravioli for the main course.

The meal is delicious. No complaints about airline food on this plane. The flight attendant keeps pouring, and I keep drinking. A snifter of Grand Marnier with the Godiva chocolates after I finish the Parmesan and crackers for dessert. When the plane is cruising over Iceland, I dream about my work day at the *Herald*. Webster is yelling at me. I'm close to deadline and still don't have a subject for tomorrow's column. Can't access the terminal because Oberg has it tied up. I'm in a panic. The recurring nightmare.

Heavy turbulence shakes me awake. The man next to me, a dark-haired individual in his late twenties or early thirties, puts away the inflight magazine he's been browsing. I didn't notice him before. Odd that. "What's the weather like over in Canada?" he asks. The telltale sing-song sound of the Cork accent. Like a tinker trying to speak French, as an Irish comedian once described it.

He looks vaguely familiar. I wonder if I've met him before? Where might I know him from?

I shake my head. "Didn't you get on in Calgary?" He doesn't look like a business-class type. Wears a shabby tweed suit and a battered hat. Must have been upgraded too.

"No, I've been on here since ..."

"Since?"

"Not sure."

"Not since the plane came over from London, surely?" I say.

"I s'pose."

"That's a long haul for you." Something isn't right here. How did he manage to remain on the plane after it landed in Calgary? Wouldn't the flight attendants have told him the plane had reached its final destination?

I extend my hand. "My name is Jerry."

"Dermot. How do you do." I notice he has a firm handshake. Looks like he works out.

"You were asking about the weather in Canada," I say. "You've never been, I take it?"

"Not yet."

"Depends on where you want to go. The mildest weather would be on the West Coast: Vancouver, Victoria, Nanaimo, Parksville, Campbell River. It rains a lot in those places, however. Relatively mild weather also in the Okanagan: Kelowna, Penticton, Vernon. The coldest weather would be on the Prairies. Manitoba, Saskatchewan, Alberta. We do get these warm Chinook winds in Calgary, however. They make the winters more bearable."

"I'm going to Quebec."

"You're on the wrong plane, then. This is a direct flight back to London."

"I've no interest in going to London. They don't treat the Irish well there. In Quebec, I'll be able to have a farm. And do some teaching."

"Then you should probably be talking to one of the flight attendants. What does it say on your boarding pass?"

The man gives me a blank look. Doesn't answer.

"I'm not sure how you ended up in Calgary. You must have boarded the wrong flight. You should have been travelling on a flight to Montreal." I can't figure this one out. Didn't someone check this guy's boarding pass in London? Didn't he know he was in London when he boarded the plane? Didn't he know something was wrong when they made the announcement about weather conditions and flying time to Calgary?

The man touches my arm. "Are you from Canada?"

"I am now. From Dublin originally. How about you?"

"From West Cork. Inchigeelagh, Inchimore, that part of the county."

Wow! I do a double take. "We'll have to talk some more about this." I notice that the seatbelt sign is turned off. I rise to go to the washroom.

When I return, the man is gone. No sign of him anywhere. Strange. I push the recline button on my seat and go back to sleep.

Grosse Île, Quebec, Province of Canada, August 1847

DIARMUID PLIES HIS OARS WITH a steady stroke, propelling the wooden lifeboat toward the eastern shore of the island quarantine station. As he gets closer, he notes that the landscape differs from anything he has ever seen in Ireland. From the ship, it looked like Cape Clear, all soft grass and inviting rocks, a place where monks might build a chapel and pilgrims come to fast for their sins. Now it appears rougher. Scrubby bushes growing in clumps, wild and bristled. Globs of fungus sprouting on putrefied stumps. The rocks look grey and forbidding.

Still, it's just the first stop along the way. A steppingstone to their new home in Quebec. With the contours of the pebbly strand coming into view, he wonders again about the wisdom of this side trip. Nell has given him her blessing but still he asks himself.

Should he be worried about the sick people on the island? What if they infect him with the fever? Could he be infected already? This has nagged him ever since he left the ship. Yes, the medical superintendent came aboard and cleared him and Nell for travel on to Quebec City. However, it was only a cursory exam. He just asked them to stick out their tongues, and then wrote down their names on a sheet to hand to the emigration officer. Was that enough? Shouldn't there have been a more thorough examination?

Overhead he can hear seabirds. *Canadian* seabirds. Squawking and keening like a kitchen party of tin whistles and uileann pipes. All out of tune. The air blows fresh and clean. No hint yet of the foul stench he associates with sickness and death. However, the water is polluted.

He is rowing through garbage – lumps of filthy straw, barrels filled with excrement, bundles of rags – thrown overboard from other ships that have passed this way.

The late afternoon sun warms the back of his uncovered head. "Out damn spot," he used to say while walking along the ridge above the Pass of Keimaneigh, urging the elusive Irish sun to move out from behind the clouds. He stops rowing for a moment. Wipes the sweat from his brow. Places a hand in benediction on the lumpy figure tied up in a biscuit sack at the front of the boat.

"We're almost at your final resting place, Cousin Donncha," he whispers. "The chaplain will say a Requiem Mass, and we'll give you a proper Christian burial."

He doesn't mind touching the body, something the frightened sailors resolutely refused to do. At this point, it should no longer be infectious.

"I wish you had stayed with us a while longer." He starts to untie the sack but changes his mind and closes it again. Better just to remember. "Nell and I love your songs, and me mother did too. She always said you were the one with her gift."

He wishes Nell had come with him. But she wanted to stay behind to help look after the children in steerage, and he has to respect that. Such a caring person. He's fortunate to have her in his life.

He starts rowing again. "I wish we could hear you sing 'So Hush, Me Love' one more time. Such a lovely song, such soothing words."

The seabirds fall silent as Diarmuid hums the melody and recalls the lyrics. "I'll bless you with a fine herd of milk cows, me dear/And also the big bull to charm them."

Five or six green-winged teals alight on the water and swim toward the boat as if drawn by the siren call of Diarmuid's singing. They are not frightened by the splash of his oars. "Oh, such memories that we bore with us, Donncha, as we crossed the ocean. Such songs that used to light up our rooms and warm our hearts. Sleep peacefully, me beloved cousin. May God grant you eternal rest."

The light starts to fade as the lifeboat crunches up against the rocky shore. Diarmuid's boots squeak and squelch, filling up with water as he pushes the boat to its mooring place. He peers at the balsam fir trees skirting the shore and wonders how far he'll have to carry the body before he reaches the island chapel. The weight shouldn't be a problem, however. Poor Donncha was reduced to a bag of skin and bones after the fever attacked him. A sad ending for Donncha, but a new beginning for Diarmuid and Nell.

He looks back at the ship where Nell is waiting. Thinks of tomorrow, when they will be on their way to Quebec City. On their way to the best of what the land of promise has to offer. To the safe harbour at the end of the world. To the place where the praties never grow small.

A FAIR-HAIRED YOUNG MAN IN A BLACK SOUTANE, carrying a brightly burning torch, appears from the trees as Diarmuid removes the body bag from the lifeboat.

"I didn't think any more of ye would be coming over this evening," says the man, speaking in Irish. "But I thought I should go down for a last look anyhow." He brings down the torch so Diarmuid

185

can see his face. "I'm Father Liam Moylan, one of the Catholic chaplains assigned to this island."

"Good evening, Father," says Diarmuid, answering in English. "I'm Diarmuid de Búrca, and this is – was – me cousin, Donncha Lynch."

"Your English is fluent, Diarmuid. I'll be glad to practise mine on you while you're here. Most of the people I see here prefer to talk in Irish."

Diarmuid can tell right away from the priest's accent that he's a fellow Corkonian. "I learned it at the seminary in Maynooth, Father. I didn't use it much until we boarded the ship. At home, we always referred to it as the foreign language."

"So, you had a vocation, then?"

"I thought I did for a while. However, they sent me back home and told me I should work as a schoolteacher for a few years before deciding."

"Do you need help carrying … did you say his name is Dónal?"

"Donncha, Father. No, he's no trouble at all. Lost all his weight while we were travelling over. Is there a mortuary I can repose him in?"

"There's a storage shed next to the infirmary. We can put him in there for the night."

Diarmuid is relieved that the path up to the infirmary has just a slight incline. He'll be able to keep carrying the body for several more yards yet. The priest lights the way for him so he won't trip.

"And what did he do before ye all came on the ship from Ireland?" asks the priest. "Was he a schoolteacher, too?"

186

"He was, Father. Also, a poet, a fine poet. Like me mother."

"Would I have known your mother?"

"You might. Her name is Máire Bhuí Ní Laoire."

"Ah, yes, indeed. 'On a Sunny Hillside.' We used to sing that when I was growing up in Ballingeary. You're from that area, then?"

"I am, yes, from Inchimore," says Diarmuid. Both from the same parish, quite the coincidence. "That's one of her earlier songs."

"So, you lived on the Duke of Devonshire's estate, then? And your mother married a man named de Búrca?

"Me father, Séamus, yes."

"How many of ye are there at home?"

"There were ten of us children, to begin with. Seven brothers and three sisters. I'm the youngest."

"And you're the only one who came to Canada?"

"Of the brothers and sisters, that's right. I have a brother Risteárd who went to America, but I'm the first of our immediate family to come here. Along with me new wife. She's back on the ship looking after the young passengers."

"Are you sure you don't need any help carrying yer cousin?"

"No, Father, I'm well able to carry him meself." He hopes, however, it won't be for much longer because the rowing made him tired.

"We're not too far from the infirmary, now," says the priest. "We'll leave him in the shed and then bring him over to the chapel in the morning. Would you stay with me, the night?"

"Oh, no Father, I don't want to put you to any trouble. I can sleep out here under the Canadian stars. 'Tis a lovely warm evening."

187

"'Twill be no trouble for me at all, Diarmuid. The drawer under the kitchen settle opens out into a comfortable bed, and you are welcome to sleep there. Will you have a drop of whiskey before you retire?"

"I would appreciate that, Father. We've been on the ocean for a long time."

"And you know the responses?"

"The responses, Father?"

"The responses of the Mass. *Dominus vobiscum. Et cum spiritu tuo.* I don't have an altar server with me here, so it would be grand if you could say the responses. Do you remember them?"

"I think so, Father."

"Let's see how you do with the Confiteor then."

They both recite the penitential prayer in unison: "*Confiteor Deo omnipotenti et vobis, fratres, quia peccavi nimis ...*"

"Excellent, Diarmuid. And I even have a bell for you to ring before the Consecration."

"And during the raising of the chalice and the Eucharistic Bread?"

"You remember it well, Diarmuid. You'll make a fine priest someday."

"Not any more, I would say. I'm married now, remember."

"You might have a son, then, who becomes a priest. Did any of your brothers become priests?"

"Not a one, Father. The oldest was executed by the British, four others were married, and the sixth was not too coherent in himself."

"Most unusual for a large Irish Catholic family. So, you were the only one who saw yourself as a priest?"

"I felt I owed it to me parents because I was the youngest."

"That would be a weak vocation. I can see why they sent you home."

"The mother's vocation; that's what a fellow postulant called it," says Diarmuid. "They recruited you when you weren't old enough to know what you were getting into."

THE INFIRMARY IS A FLIMSY WOODEN STRUCTURE sitting on a pile of rocks. A cheap, prefabricated building, it looks as if it was thrown up in a hurry. Built to provide beds for two hundred and fifty patients, it is now overflowing with ten times that number. Hundreds lie on the floor, sprawled across one another, some using their jackets as blankets. Many are sleeping. A few are sitting up, gazing blankly at the walls. No decorations of any kind on the walls. No pictures, nothing.

Father Moylan douses his torch in a rainwater barrel. Diarmuid follows him inside and looks across the mass of bodies heaving and writhing in the semi-darkness. "How many doctors are caring for them?" The priest shakes his head. "We did have as many as twenty-five at one point. However, four of them passed, unfortunately. We do have many volunteer helpers, however. They're a great blessing for us."

He motions Diarmuid toward the door. "I'll give you a short tour tomorrow morning," he says. "You'll see the medical officer's house, the buildings where the staff and volunteers live, and the temporary accommodations where the medically-cleared immigrants wait for the next steamboat to Quebec City. We're never sure when they can leave because those boats are plagued with mechanical problems. The sickest people – those with cholera and typhus – are in the fever sheds at the back. Not much we can do for them. But for now, let's put your cousin in the storage shed outside, and we'll go over to me place for a drink."

The rectory is sturdier than the infirmary. It's the first dwelling Diarmuid has seen in Canada, so he's curious to see how it differs from the houses back home. Although it doesn't have stone walls like the houses in Ireland, it appears to be a solid structure, clad with wooden shingles, built no doubt to withstand the ravages of a Canadian winter. Far as Diarmuid can tell, it's a modest dwelling, containing just two rooms. In the front, there's a large kitchen with a settle, a table, two chairs and a wood-burning stove. In the back, a second room, presumably the priest's bedroom. No stairs that Diarmuid can see, so likely no room up in the attic. A crucifix hangs on one wall of the kitchen and a painting of the Blessed Virgin graces another. A half-empty bottle of Eblana Old Irish Whiskey squats on the table. How did that get over to Canada?

The priest pours a glass each for himself and Diarmuid. "They didn't give me a housekeeper here, so I do all me own cooking and cleaning." He produces a clay pipe and tobacco pack from the pockets of his soutane. "Do you smoke?"

"No, I don't partake, Father. How long have you been here on Grosse Île?"

The priest removes his stiff white collar and places it on the kitchen table. "Two years this month. I came here right after I was ordained. I wanted to go on the foreign missions to Africa, but they sent me here instead."

190

"For a finite period?"

"For no longer than one more year, I hope."

"Do you worry about catching the fever?"

"I take precautions. 'Tis a concern, however."

"Do you wear protection? Something to cover the face?"

"In the fever sheds, certainly. Sometimes in the infirmary, if I know I'm going to be there for more than a few minutes."

"I worried about that on the ship. Most of us had no protection at all. We lost many people during the voyage."

"We have funerals here every day, Diarmuid. Sometimes seven or eight of them. Will you have another drop?"

"Just a small one, thanks, Father. We have a long day ahead of us tomorrow, so I should get some rest." He doesn't want to stay on this wretched island any longer than necessary.

A S THEY CROSS THE FARMER'S YARD, Jerry and Cathal are followed by ganders snapping at their heels. "Like the dogs chasing after Little Eva in *Uncle Tom's Cabin*," says Cathal. The two of them laugh. They make their way through clumps of grass, broken branches, animal droppings, and a few old bicycle wheels and other bits of human-made refuse. Dead leaves crunch underfoot.

When they reach the stone shell of the old Carrignacurra castle, built on the brow of a hill near the banks of the River Lee, they can feel the centuries melting away like spring snowflakes. What's left of the moss-covered castle stands five storeys high.

"Can you believe how much of it is still standing?" says Cathal. "More than five centuries old."

Jerry snaps pictures. Colour and black-and-white with his Nikon FG. "They should spruce up this place, and open it to tourists," he says. "People from Calgary and Edmonton would love to come here, sip glasses of mead, and listen to music on the fiddle and harp."

"Ye Yanks are always thinking of the almighty dollar."

"Canadian, Cathal. Not as crass as the Yanks. So, this is where our O'Leary ancestors once sought refuge from the forces of the Crown?"

"The very place. Carrignacurra, the rock of the weir. There used to be an eel weir here back in the day."

"What else do we know about the castle?"

"Only that the last of the O'Learys lost it during the civil wars of the 1640s. I'm not sure who owns it now. However, look at this. See the letters 'A.L.' on the wall here? That suggests the builder was a clan member named Art or perhaps Auliffe O'Leary."

"Auliffe?"

"Still a common first name around this part of West Cork. Oddly anglicized, though, as Humphrey."

"Hard to see where that comes from."

THEY WALK BACK ACROSS THE FARMYARD to Jerry's rented Ford Fiesta. "What more can you tell me about our ancestor Diarmuid?" asks Jerry.

"I found out that his full name was Micheál Diarmuid de Búrca. However, because he already had an older brother named Micheál, he was called Diarmuid."

"Interesting. What more?"

"As well as being the youngest, he was also Máire Bhuí's favourite because he was a poet, like herself," says Cathal. "Also, a schoolmaster. Margaret also says he was wild as a young man, but become more responsible as he matured."

"Margaret?"

"Our family historian, Margaret Cronin."

"And she says Diarmuid was wild. In what way?"

"Probably a bit of 'Lord, grant me chastity and continence, but not yet.'"

"Saint Augustine."

"Right. Then he went for the priesthood, but didn't have a strong vocation, it seems. So, he came back to Inchigeelagh and became a schoolmaster."

"How does she know all this?"

"From talking to the descendants. Margaret knows them well because she lives in the area. Over in East Cappagh, beyond Ballingeary. They've given her stories that have been passed down from generation to generation."

"You had to pay her for the information, I presume?"

"Not much. She charged me just two quid for phone calls and petrol."

"Did you find out anything about the marriage?"

"Only that his wife's name was Nell, that she came from Bantry, and was one of the Murphy clan."

"Anything about an out-of-wedlock pregnancy?"

"Not that I heard. Do you know something about this?"

"No, pure speculation on my part. Tell me what else you learned from Margaret."

"She said that Máire Bhuí and James rented farming properties in the Inchibeg and Inchimore townlands – all the Inches, as she put it – and they sub-let tenancy rights to their two oldest sons."

"Clearly, the parents were well off. I read about that in the little red book. At one point, they farmed 150 acres and had up to ten men working for them."

"Right. And then, of course, the famine brought their world crashing down," says Cathal. "The parents were evicted, some of the sons were evicted, and some of the daughters and their husbands lost their homes as well."

"What happened to them after they were evicted? Did they have to go on the roads begging?"

"Micheál, the third son, took in the parents. He also took in his brother Alec, who of course was our great-great-grandfather. It was around that time that Diarmuid went to Canada."

"And after that?"

"That's where the story ends. None of the descendants could give Margaret more information."

"The mystery endures. What's our next stop?"

"The Pass of Keimaneigh, of course. It's a few miles west of here. Did you get enough pictures of the castle?"

"Plenty, thanks. The castle builders of the 1450s knew how to make them last."

THERE'S LITTLE TRAFFIC on the mile-long line of road through the Pass. It looks as if it was gouged out of the mountain by a violent act of nature. The rocks rise on either side to a height of one hundred feet and vary in colour from grey to red. Holly, ivy, and various other evergreens grow in the crevices.

Jerry pulls over onto a grassy verge and feels a sense of Gothic gloom as he looks up at the crags hanging against the western sky. "This road is as narrow as a country lane, isn't it?"

"Yes, but wider than in 1822, when the battle was fought," says Cathal.

Jerry takes a few steps into the yellow furze and then turns back. He can see no straightforward way to get up to the top of the Pass, where he hopes some remains of old famine dwellings might still stand. "I think I need a burro for this mission, Cathal. Where would Máire Bhuí and the family have lived?"

"Somewhere up there, I'm sure. We do know she was able to watch the fighting from her front window. 'Praise be to Jesus that we didn't regret the attack/but commemorated the occasion with joy.'"

"Is that a line from her poem?"

"A rough translation," says Cathal. "Another translation says something about the fighters being thankful they didn't have to pay any penalty for their actions, and that they lived to make a joke of it."

"But they did pay the penalty, right? Again, this comes from the little red book. Some were sentenced to be hanged."

"The owner of your hotel, Jim Shaughnessy, can tell us more about that. Feel like a pint?"

"I'd love one, thanks. Is there a commemorative plaque of some kind? I'd like to take a picture."

"There's one that stands in tribute to Máire Bhuí herself. The local historical society is planning to put in another. It'll name all the people killed in the battle."

THE CASTLE HOTEL PUB IS THREE-QUARTERS EMPTY when Jerry and Cathal arrive. Jerry half expects it to look like one of those faux Irish pubs in Calgary with the vintage Guinness posters on the walls and Sinéad O'Connor songs playing on the sound system. Instead, he's surprised to see framed photos of Banksy's street art and hear Whitney Houston singing 'I Will Always Love You.' The New Ireland has gone all cosmopolitan.

Owner Shaughnessy has plenty of time to talk. "Did you know that Máire Bhuí's brother and three of her sons were involved in the battle?"

196

"I knew her oldest son, John, might have been executed," says Jerry. "Who were the other two?"

"One of them was the boy who went to America, I think."

"Diarmuid?"

"No, Diarmuid would have been just a small child. The one who went to America was named Richard. He and his brothers John and James, and Máire Bhuí's brother, Conor O'Leary, were all charged with the murder of a militia soldier, Private John Smith."

"I saw the reference to Smith in her poem. I didn't realize the family was involved in his killing."

"John went to the gallows after he was convicted. Conor was transported to Van Diemen's Land. Richard and James were reprieved, thanks to the intervention of Daniel O'Connell."

"Yes, I read about that too," says Jerry. "O'Connell had a family connection with the O'Learys because his aunt was married to Art O'Leary."

"Right," says Shaughnessy. "Although, I don't know how Art was related to Máire Bhuí."

"His wife wrote a memorable lament for him after Art was murdered," says Jerry.

"She made him a folk hero," says Shaughnessy. "That lament is still being sung today."

"Like the songs of Máire Bhuí," says Jerry. "What do you know about her son Diarmuid?"

"The youngest boy? Only that he went to America. I don't think he ever came back to Ireland."

"He went to Canada during the famine," says Jerry. "I've been trying to get information on him because he's a mystery."

"How long are you here in Macroom?"

"Another couple of days. I want to go back to Inchigeelagh to take pictures at the old graveyard where Máire Bhuí is buried. Also, to visit with a third cousin who lives over in Inchibeg."

"I'll see you in the bar here at seven o'clock tomorrow evening," says Shaughnessy. "I have a surprise for you."

THE SURPRISE IS A FOLKSINGER FROM Ballymakeera. She comes into the bar and sings all seven verses of 'The Battle of Keimaneigh' from memory. Without accompaniment, in the traditional *sean-nós* style. Impressive.

"Is that the actual melody Máire Bhuí composed?" asks Jerry.

The folksinger doesn't know.

Cathal nods. "'Twould be, I s'pose. I don't know if the melodies of her other songs survived because I've never heard any of them sung. However, this one was passed down from generation to generation with words and melody intact."

"Very powerful, isn't it? My Irish is pretty rusty now, but I can still understand some of the words."

"Sends shivers down yer spine, me lad."

Grosse Île, August 1847

IFTEEN PEOPLE ARE PRAYING in the chapel when Father Moylan says the Requiem Mass for Donncha. Diarmuid notices that three are in military uniform. He thinks they must be the soldiers who fire guns across the water whenever a passing ship fails to stop at the quarantine station. The other congregants seem to be in good health. They must be the staff or the medically-cleared immigrants waiting for the steamboat to take them to Quebec City.

The priest turns away from the altar and addresses the congregants. "We're gathered today to give thanks and praise to God for the life and work of Donncha Lynch. He was much loved by family, friends, and neighbours. He composed songs that brought happiness into people's lives during a time of sorrow and great despair."

Diarmuid is intrigued. How can the priest speak so knowingly of Donncha when yesterday he struggled to remember his name?

"We offer our heartfelt sympathy and our prayers for his cousin Diarmuid, here, and all his relations back in Ireland. His death leaves a void in their lives."

Diarmuid wears a loose white surplice borrowed from the chapel closet. He kneels on the altar step with head bowed. Prays that Canada will be good to him and Nell. Prays that his mother will remain in good health for a while longer. He fears he won't be able to go back for her funeral when the time comes. Asks God to bring peace to her for the time she has left on earth. Also, to have mercy on the soul of his late father. To have mercy on Donncha's soul. Everlasting peace.

Father Moylan couldn't provide a casket for Donncha's body. "Too many people have died here to make such a service possible." Donncha will be buried in the biscuit sack he came in.

Two men come up to Diarmuid after the service and offer to be pallbearers. "Sorry for your loss, Mr. de Búrca. We'll help you dig the grave. We have picks and shovels behind the infirmary."

The sun comes out, and a gentle breeze blows as Donncha is laid to rest. Mosquitoes and horseflies swarm the air. Diarmuid picks some yellow goldenrods and places them on the body before the helpers fill up the grave with earth. They give him a small white cross to place atop the grave. The seabirds squawk discordantly, as if mourning the dead. The priest fingers his rosary beads and says a silent prayer while the men are shovelling. He then takes his aspergillum and sprinkles holy water on the grave.

Diarmuid shakes hands with the priest. "Thank you, Father, for your kindness and hospitality. You serve an important ministry here on this island."

"I'll be here for at least another year, so please come back to visit me again. They don't normally allow visitors here, but they do grant permits to people who have business on the island. You will always, of course, be welcome to come here as me server."

Diarmuid takes a last look at Donncha's grave. "What will ye do when ye arrive in Quebec City?" asks the priest.

"Nell and I will travel from there down to Huntingdon to make contact with me cousin," says Diarmuid. "The Canadian government is giving us one hundred acres of freehold land to establish ourselves. I'll seek me cousin's advice on where we might find the best farming."

"I'll leave you here, then. God bless you, Diarmuid. May the wind be always at your back."

THE CAPTAIN IS IN HIS CABIN reviewing the ship's manifest "How many passengers do we have left on board?" he asks the first mate.

"About a hundred, sir."

"Not many."

"No, we lost about two hundred on the journey over."

"More than usual. And about another two hundred, I suppose, who will have to remain at the quarantine station here?"

"That's correct, sir."

"How about Burke? Is he still with us?"

"No, sir. The medical officer said he and his wife were showing symptoms of fever, so they have to stay here on the island."

"Good. Then it's full speed ahead for Quebec City." Then back across the ocean with a cargo of timber and cotton that will be much less trouble to deal with than a shipload of Irish rebels.

WHEN HE EMERGES FROM THE TREES, Diarmuid is surprised to see Nell down on the strand, standing by the lifeboat. On the ground beside her is the chest holding their belongings. What's she doing here? She's supposed to be on the ship.

He races down and grabs her arm. "What brings you here, macushla?"

She pulls back from him and puts a hand to her lips. "Didn't you want me here? That's what the first mate said. He said you were going to stay here another night. That you needed me to help you with something."

"I never said anything of the sort. Why did you bring the chest?"

"I don't know. The sailors put it in the boat before they rowed me over."

He looks over her shoulder and sees that the ship is starting to move. Slowly, in a southwesterly direction, along the river. The sound of the ship's horn blares across the water like the tuba section of a brass band. A giant flock of seabirds flies raucously upriver for a moment or two and then changes direction. Diarmuid picks up a rock and hurls it toward the ship. The bastards. They've abandoned them.

He puts his hands on her shoulders and gently turns her around. "Look over there."

She shakes her head in disbelief. "They're not waiting for us?"

He picks up another rock and flings it toward the ship. "The boors, the runts. I know what happened. The captain, or his dastardly first mate, told the crew we're on an extended mission of mercy here. They've left without us. A pox on both of them."

Tears begin to well up in her eyes. "What are we to do?"

He hugs her, takes her hand, and walks her over to a boulder where they can sit for a moment. "There are steamboats that come up here from Quebec City. 'Tis about thirty miles away. We'll go up to the rectory, just a short walk from here. Talk to Father Moylan and find out when the next steamer is due." Should he tell her the steamers don't have any regular schedule? He'll wait until tomorrow before mentioning that.

He starts to pull their chest across the rocks. "We'll probably be able to stay in one of the buildings where the healthier people stay while awaiting passage." He walks a few more steps and then stops dragging the chest. Who would steal it anyhow? It'll be all right if he leaves it on the strand until the steamer comes.

She performs a little pirouette on the strand. Stops, winces, and clutches her stomach.

"The pains aren't going away, are they?" he says. "First it was your back and now 'tis your belly."

"'Tis not a bother," she says. "A few little aches."

She stands still for a moment and listens to the lapping of the waves spreading across the sand. "'Tis quiet here, isn't it, Diarmuid? Calm and peaceful, but desolate."

"There's a heap of misery on this island, Nell. Some patients in the infirmary who may never get well. People in the fever sheds who certainly won't."

"But some of them will be able to leave here?"

"Of course, and we will too. "'Twill be a grand new life for us, macushla. We'll have our little farm, to begin with. Then I'll see if I can work locally as a schoolteacher. Me lack of French will be an obstacle, no doubt. However, if they need an English teacher, I can do that. I could also teach the children how to speak Irish."

She laughs. "Why would anyone want to learn Irish? 'Tis not spoken anywhere else in the world."

"No, but 'tis like Scottish Gaelic. I'm told there are places in Canada – Cape Breton Island, for instance – where 'tis still spoken. So, there may be a demand for it in Quebec."

She does another little pirouette, this time without wincing. "I'd like to work with children, too. I could teach them how to sew and sing, and all the different ways they can cook the lovely big praties growing in their gardens."

"'Tis all before us, macushla." He hopes this is true. She seems so happy when she talks about their future together.

Calgary, August 1992

HE SIX-O-CLOCK TELEVISION news has a story about a big slab of concrete falling off the side of Montreal's Olympic Stadium. One of the sports commentators calls it "the Big Uh-Oh!" Cute. Jerry is heating the remains of the vegetable lasagna he ordered for lunch in the *Herald* cafeteria. That's about as sophisticated as his food preparation ever gets. If it can't be done in two minutes in the microwave or four minutes in the pan, it doesn't appear on his table.

He's about to take his first bite when the phone rings. Another telemarketer? Always happens at suppertime. He thinks of letting it ring, but something tells him he should pick up.

"Hello, Mr. Burke. My name is Michael Taylor. We haven't met. I came across your name in the Alberta Family Histories Society quarterly. I read that you're researching your ancestor, Máire Bhuí Ní Laoire."

The caller is clearly not from Ireland. He pronounces Máire Bhuí's name like someone who tried to learn it phonetically: Maura Bwee Nee Leary.

"I was wondering if we might get together for coffee or a drink. I'm descended from Maura Bwee's family as well, so we must be cousins."

A cousin? In Alberta? Is this another dream?

"Where do you live, Mr. Taylor? I don't recall hearing your name before."

"Michael, please. Here in Calgary. You mightn't have heard my name because I haven't been active in the Society during the past year. May I call you Gerald?"

"Jerry."

"Well, Jerry, I haven't been active, as I said, because I had a few health issues to deal with. Now, however, I'm becoming more involved. What part of the city do you live in?"

"Sunnyside. I'm in the Sunnyhill housing co-op." Because he doesn't want to deal with the hassle of mortgage payments or home repairs. Nor does he want to deal with the compromises involved in living with someone else.

"What a coincidence. I live in Sunnyside too."

"How are you descended from Máire Bhuí, Michael?"

"My grandfather's maternal grandfather was a nephew of – how did you pronounce her name?"

"Let's call her Mary O'Leary. Much easier."

"Well, Mary O'Leary then. She had a nephew named Pádraig O'Leary who came to Canada and settled in Quebec."

"During the famine?"

"No, before that, in the 1830s. He had a tiny farm in County Cork and thought he would do better in Canada. Came over when the Irish still had dreams to dream and songs to sing."

"The story of every immigrant. We always think we can do better somewhere else," says Jerry. "Emigration, the eternal solution. We migrate with the instincts of wild geese."

"When did your people come over?" asks Taylor.

"It was only me. I was in my early twenties. A buddy and I decided to quit our dead-end jobs in the civil service and try our luck in Canada."

"I'd love to hear more about that. And what's your connection to … um … Mary O'Leary?"

"My paternal grandfather's grandfather was Mary's son, Alec Burke."

"What do you know about him?"

"About Alec? Only that he was a farm labourer. Like most of his male siblings. And that he had many children. Like most of his Catholic siblings."

"What do you know about his youngest brother?"

"Diarmuid? Ah, that's the big unanswered question. I know he emigrated to Canada in the 1840s. However, the trail goes cold after that. I'm guessing he paid for his passage by selling his tenant rights. After that, who knows?"

"I have something about him that I think you'll find interesting."

"Well then, let's get together and talk. Do you know the Tullamore?" says Jerry.

"Of course. Best patio in town."

"Let's meet there on Monday or Tuesday evening, if that will work for you. I'll be the tall guy with the wispy brown moustache and the slicked-back hair. Wearing a black leather jacket and carrying a copy of the *Herald*."

207

What will this guy – this newfound cousin – have to say about Diarmuid? Can a solution to the century-old mystery be imminent? Jerry doesn't want to raise his hopes. He's been disappointed before.

Grosse Île, August 1847

FTER A WEEK ON THE ISLAND, Diarmuid and Nell are still waiting for a steamer to take them to Quebec City. One was supposed to arrive two days ago but never did. No explanation given. "It sometimes happens," said Father Moylan. "The schedule changes at the last minute and people are stranded." In the meantime, the best Diarmuid and Nell have been able to find for accommodation is a draughty old wooden shed. With holes in the walls and a leaky roof, it offers little comfort. Nothing was available in the buildings for the medically-cleared immigrants. Father Moylan's modest home could accommodate only one guest at a time, so no possibility for them there either.

After a night of heavy rain, Nell awakes shivering, Diarmuid hugs her close and tries to keep her warm. He tries not to think the worst. Can she have caught the fever? Oh God, please don't let this happen to her. We didn't come to Canada to have our journey end like this.

"The pains are terrible," she says. "All over me body." Her shivering turns to perspiring. A headache hammers a dart into her right eye. She says she feels as if a wild animal has been let loose inside her. Can't stand up. Can barely sit up.

Diarmuid reaches down and lifts her from the straw bed. "I'll carry you to the infirmary, macushla. The doctors will have some medicine for you."

He discovers there's no vacant bed in the infirmary. Frustration. However, there is one empty chair. Diarmuid sits on it and holds Nell in his arms like *The Pietà*. He waits three hours for Dr. Douglas to

209

finish with the other patients. "She presents like she might have the beginnings of the fever," says the doctor. "But it might also be influenza. It's hard to tell sometimes. I'll give you something that should make her feel better."

THE MEDICINE PROVIDES NO RELIEF. All through the night, Nell tosses, turns, gasps for breath, and then becomes delirious. Diarmuid rushes her back to the infirmary. This time, he's thankful to discover, there's a gurney available.

"Is there something else you can give her?"

"I'm afraid our pharmacy supplies have run out," says Dr. Douglas. "We won't receive more until the steamer arrives."

Diarmuid's heart is beating out of his chest. "This came on without warning. How can it be?"

The doctor holds her wrist and looks at his pocket watch. "She must have had a touch of the fever when she left the ship." He takes a device that looks like an ear trumpet and listens to her chest.

"But you cleared us both for travel. You said we wouldn't have to be in quarantine. This was not supposed to happen."

"You didn't have symptoms. There was no reason for us to detain you here."

Nell opens her eyes. "Sing me a song, Diarmuid."

"Of course, macushla." He begins: "In brightness and in splendour she is the stately maid ..."

"Is that one of yours?"

"No, 'tis from me mother's poem, 'By the River of Glenageary.'"

"Sing me one of yours, Diarmuid. Sing 'On a Lovely Sunny Morning.'" She smiles and closes her eyes.

It's the song he had started composing for her just before he asked her to marry him. "Am I not too young?" she had asked. "I've just turned eighteen." Diarmuid had smiled and said, "That's how old me mother was when she ran away with me father."

"As I lay on me soft bed/I heard the voices of the birds," he begins. "I thought to meself that I should go and let out the stock to graze ..."

Nell is still smiling when he finishes the song. She is not opening her eyes, however. She stiffens, then lies still as a statue. Diarmuid fears the worst.

"She has passed, I'm afraid," confirms the doctor.

Diarmuid breaks down in tears and drops to his knees. "Oh me God, no." He can't believe it happened so fast. Her energy, her spirit, her youth, her capacity for love, the songs she carried in her head – all gone in an instant. Is this punishment for his sins? Has God condemned him for planning Barry's death and the deaths of the other land agents? He kisses her eyes and hugs her tightly for several minutes.

"One more thing you should know," says the doctor. "She was pregnant."

"I didn't know," says Diarmuid. He sobs into his hands and then slowly starts to recite the prayer for the dead. "May she rejoice in Your kingdom, where all our tears are wiped away."

AFTER HE LEAVES THE INFIRMARY, Diarmuid heads for Father Moylan's rectory to talk about funeral arrangements. Another priest approaches. Diarmuid doesn't recognize him at first, then realizes it's Father Mathew Creedon, one of his former teachers from the Maynooth seminary.

"What a surprise to see you again, Father, after all these years. What brings you here to Grosse Île?"

"'Tis lovely to see you too, Diarmuid. Sure, I went on the foreign missions to Quebec after I finished me last term at home. Your good wife is here with you?"

"She was, Father, but sadly, she just passed."

"Oh, you poor soul, God love you. What was her name?

"Her name was Noreen, Father, but we all called her Nell. We were married just before we left Inchigeelagh."

"Yes, the cabin boy from the Sir Henry Pottinger told me about ye when I went to meet the ship at Quebec City. He didn't know yere names, but said you and your wife had been left behind here even though ye weren't sick on the ship. I went to the bishop then and asked for permission to come and see how ye were."

"When did you arrive, Father?"

"I came in on the steamer about an hour ago."

"We'd been waiting a week for that boat. I wish you could have seen me beloved Nell before she passed away."

"I'm sure she must have been a lovely girl, Diarmuid. Her memory should be your inspiration to do God's work here on the island."

"But what can I do here, Father? I don't think I can be of any help."

212

"Of course you can, Diarmuid. Irish people are dying on this island every day and there aren't enough helpers to bring them food and water. You could be one of those helpers."

"But I don't understand, Father. Why isn't the Canadian government providing the necessary help?"

"Because the government has more to worry about than a few thousand Irish immigrants dying on its doorstep."

"If I'm to help, Father, I should go first to Quebec City to see how our people are faring. We were promised ten shillings a head to be paid by the Duke of Devonshire's agent at Quebec, together with a deed from the Canadian government for one hundred acres of free land."

"I'm afraid that's all in your dreams, Diarmuid. The Duke of Devonshire has no agent in Quebec City. Nor is there any free land. That was a ruse they used to get ye out of Ireland. The Duke washed his hands of ye after he paid for your passage."

"God help us, I worried about that when I put me name down at the registration centre. Yet Father Holland kept assuring me everything would be all right. He told me His Grace was an honourable man."

"'Tis too late to be concerned about that now, Diarmuid. God has guided you to Grosse Île, and this is where you must begin your work in Canada."

T HEY MEET AT THE TULLAMORE on one of those golden days at summer's end when Calgarians hope that autumn will extend the warmth and sunshine for a few more weeks. Taylor is a well-preserved man of sixty-nine with the gaunt look of a person who has recently lost weight, and the patchy dull hair of someone who could be undergoing chemotherapy. He and Jerry sit outside on the pub's upstairs patio, drinking pints of Guinness.

"Here's the two-minute biography," says Taylor. "I grew up on a farm near Pincher Creek. Left at age eighteen to work as a roughneck in Turner Valley. Worked my way up to field superintendent for Imperial Oil. Moved to Calgary. Put on a suit. Attended meetings. Drank coffee. Read the newspapers. How am I doing?"

"You're doing fine."

"The office job was okay for a few years. Money was fairly good. However, when they came and offered me a severance package, I was ready to go. That was ten years ago."

"What have you been doing since?"

"At first I didn't know what to do. I had no retirement plan. No hobbies. Couldn't see myself as the volunteering type. I monitored drama courses at the university. Also took art classes. Now I'm learning how to do large-format film photography, and working on the family history."

"Do you have family yourself? A wife? Children?"

"Just a brother who lives in Pincher Creek. I never married. Never met the right person."

"I never married either. Couldn't make that commitment. I do have a girlfriend in Edmonton, however." His rock, his support system, his muse.

"How about your work? How long have you been with the *Herald*?"

"Eighteen years," says Jerry. "Before that, I worked at newspapers in British Columbia for six years. Before that, I worked as a professional musician."

"Interesting. What instrument?"

"Piano and guitar. I formed a duo with the guy who came to Canada with me. We started in Vancouver, called ourselves Ramblers Two, moved down east, toured Ontario and the Maritimes, and made a couple of recordings for RCA."

"Irish music, I presume?"

"At the start, yes. Then we began writing our own songs, mostly parodies. We wrote one about LBJ, 'the swingin' leader of the USA.' We wrote another about the Queen's visit to Expo Montreal in 1967."

"Sounds like fun. How long did you do that for?"

"Full-time, on and off, for about a year. Then we went our separate ways. I went back to Vancouver to go to journalism school, and Tom went back to Ireland to become a scientist."

"Is that where he is now?"

"Yes, he has a teaching job at the Dublin Institute of Technology. I still see him every few years."

"Did you ever think of going back?"

"Not recently. I did when my mother died in 1977. Felt guilty because I hadn't been back to visit her much after I came to Canada.

215

However, my father talked me out of it. Said I had a great life in Canada, with a terrific job I clearly liked. Said it would be a shame to give it all up."

"Your father sounds like a sensible man."

"A practical man, that's for sure. He's been that way since he joined the Irish civil service in the thirties. He could have stayed working for the British, but the new Irish government was offering more money so he jumped."

"Was he British, then?"

"Technically, yes, because Ireland didn't leave the Commonwealth until 1949."

"Ah, I didn't realize that."

"You mentioned that you had something to tell me about Máire Bhuí's youngest son."

"Yes. Look at this."

Taylor pulls a newspaper page from his briefcase. The headline says, "Fact and Fiction Blur in Tale of Irish Famine." "Do you read the *Gazette*?"

"We have it in the *Herald* library because it's one of our sister papers," says Jerry. "But I rarely look at it."

"This is a story you should read," says Taylor. "I have some information to add that you'll find of interest."

"It looks long. Maybe I can borrow it to read later? However, I'm intrigued. Can you give me a quick summary?"

"Sure. It's about a Scottish Protestant who came to Canada in the 1850s, started a weekly newspaper in rural Quebec, and did most of the writing for the paper because he didn't have the money for a reporter."

"Must have been a small paper."

"I've never seen a copy," says Taylor. "But I do know it was big enough to contain some of his fiction as well as the news of the week."

"Short stories?"

"Short stories, romances, even novels that he serialized in regular instalments."

"Like Charles Dickens, eh?"

"Like Dickens without the talent." Taylor laughs. "One of these novels, I guess you'd call it a novella, was about the Irish famine immigrants who landed at Grosse Île in 1847."

"Wonder why he chose that as a subject? It's not something you'd expect a Scotsman to be writing about."

"He had a useful source for it. A journal that one of the famine immigrants kept during the voyage."

"So, he read the journal and was inspired to turn it into a novella?"

"He wouldn't have read it," says Taylor. "It was written in Gaelic. He would have had to use a translation."

"Oh, I see. And then he turned it into fiction? Why wouldn't he have published it as a factual account?"

"Maybe he didn't think the writing was strong enough after the translation," says Taylor. "Found it easier just to use the translation as the source and put his own stamp on it."

"When did he do this?"

"Let me see here, it would have been in 1895."

"Almost fifty years after the famine," says Jerry. "What was the man's name? The newspaper guy, I mean."

"Sellar. Robert Sellar. He attributed the journal's authorship to an immigrant he named Gerald Keegan."

"So why is this in the news now, almost a century later? I guess I can wait to read about it in the *Gazette* later, but I'd prefer to hear it from you now."

"Because according to the *Gazette*, the chapters Sellar printed in his paper have now been collected in one volume and published as a book."

"In Canada?"

"All over, and here's the thing. It's being promoted as a work of nonfiction. In Ireland, it's on top of the bestsellers list. There's even talk of it being turned into a TV documentary series."

"Amazing. How did it go from being a novella to a work of nonfiction?"

"The editor of the book, a guy named Mangan, claims Keegan was a real person and that the journal is real too. However, he says the Canadian government suppressed it for 135 years because it was too graphic."

"Viewer discretion is advised," says Jerry. "So is he suggesting that what Sellar put in his newspaper was truth rather than fiction?"

"Exactly. "

"Translated from the Irish?"

"Indeed. But here's another twist, according to the *Gazette*. Two academics, one in Ireland and one in the States, have examined the book and branded it as fiction. They say there's no record of a man named Gerald Keegan being registered at the Grosse Île quarantine station at any time in the 1840s or 1850s."

"What does Mangan have to say about that?"

"He maintains that Sellar borrowed the journal from a local farmer, had it translated, and printed it verbatim in his newspaper."

"So he claims that what was first presented to the world as a novella, as fiction was, in fact, nonfiction?" says Jerry. "And now we've got a couple of academics saying it was fiction all along. Whom are we supposed to believe?"

"I know what I believe," says Taylor.

"What do you believe?"

"Let's put it this way. I have the original journal that Sellar used as the basis for the novella he published in his newspaper."

"So regardless of whether or not the published material was fiction or nonfiction, you're saying that Keegan *was* a real person?" says Jerry.

"His name wasn't Keegan. His name was Diarmuid Burke."

"You mean …?"

"Yes, our ancestor, Diarmuid Burke."

"Oh my God. Is this for real? Tell me more."

FATHER CREEDON AND DIARMUID are visiting the sick. "One of me regular pastoral duties," says the priest. Diarmuid is happy to help. He plans to do so until Father Creedon has to go back to Quebec City. At that point, he'll go with the chaplain, Father Moylan, on his rounds.

Diarmuid vaguely recognizes a familiar face in one of the fever sheds. It belongs to a young girl, standing next to a bed holding two people: a man and a boy.

She identifies herself as Mary O'Leary, the twelve-year-old daughter of Diarmuid's cousin, Timothy. Diarmuid didn't know that she and her family were going to emigrate. However, he's not surprised.

"When did ye arrive?" he asks.

"Today," says Mary. "Mammy passed on the ship, and Daddy and Seán are sick." She looks to be in good health, albeit pale and wan. Still infused with enough energy, however, to climb a tree or play hopscotch, were circumstances to allow.

Diarmuid looks down at the couple lying together in the bed. They don't recognize him, and he barely recognizes them. He fears they are near the end.

"You should go outside and get some fresh air," he says to the girl. "I'll stay here and watch over your daddy and brother."

She folds her arms across her chest and stands her ground. "I don't want to leave. I want to stay here with them."

"Then I'll step outside for some fresh air. I'll come back in a minute to see how ye are doing."

Father Creedon asks if Diarmuid had something to eat this morning before going with him on his rounds. Diarmuid shakes his head. "I was going to look for something in the quarantine building, but they were out of bread."

"Then you must come with me to Father Moylan's place to share a loaf and a jug of milk. You should never visit the sick on an empty stomach. Abstinence and disease go hand in hand."

When they return to the fever shed, they find Mary crying. "Daddy has gone to glory." Diarmuid bends down and puts his arms around her. She sobs into his chest. Father Creedon makes the sign of the cross, kisses his scapular, and says a prayer in Latin. The young boy appears to be still clinging to life, but Diarmuid doesn't think it will be for long.

The priest prays for several minutes and then makes the sign of the cross again. He removes the scapular from around his neck and puts it in his pocket. "May I talk to you outside for a minute"

"Of course, Father." He smiles at Mary, who has now stopped crying.

"I must return to Quebec City to tell the government about the conditions here," says the priest. "How many immigrants did we count on the island?"

Diarmuid does a quick mental calculation. "About a thousand."

"And there are thousands more on the ships waiting to land. How many of those did we count?"

"About forty ships. With each carrying as many as five or six hundred immigrants."

"I'll ask the bishop for permission to go down to Montreal to speak with the government ministers."

"While you are doing that, Father, I'll look after Mary there, and hope that her brother gets well. I fear, however, he does not have much longer."

"I think you are right, Diarmuid. The fever sheds are God's waiting rooms."

Diarmuid notices that the stewards are wearing damp cloths over their noses and mouths. He nudges the priest and whispers. "Should we be wearing protection as well?"

"Not for short visits. However, if it makes you feel safer, you might consider it."

SEVERAL DAYS LATER, Father Creedon returns from Quebec City. He meets Diarmuid in the infirmary. "The news is not good. Everyone I spoke to in government referred me to somebody else. After being passed from pillar to post, I tried to make an appointment with Mr. Macdonald, the new receiver general. However, he was absorbed in intrigues to keep his party in office."

Diarmuid nods. "The news is not good here, either. Poor Seán has now died, as we feared he would. Mary has left on the steamboat for Quebec City."

"Where will she go from there?"

"I gave her some money to continue on to Montreal and Huntingdon, but I don't know if it will be enough. Huntingdon is

222

where her uncle – me cousin Pádraig O'Leary – has a farm. I asked her to give him me best wishes."

"Would you come with me to Montreal, Diarmuid? I would like you to appear with me before a committee of inquiry appointed by the Legislative Assembly."

"But they won't listen to me, Father, if they didn't listen to you. Nobody cares about the sufferings of God's poor on this island."

"You'd be a powerful witness, Diarmuid. I'd like to have you by me side."

They walk over to the southwest corner of the island, sit on a rock, and watch the sun go down behind the hills. As darkness descends, Diarmuid starts to shiver and then perspire. He wonders if his own sun might be setting as well.

"I need to talk to you, Father, about matters that have been bothering me for a long time."

The priest looks away for a moment, hesitates, and then turns back to Diarmuid. "Did you want to begin by saying the Act of Contrition?"

PÁDRAIG O'LEARY IS HAVING DINNER at home with his wife after a day of threshing the corn. The door to the kitchen is open because it's hot outside. In walks young Mary O'Leary, who now looks gaunt and emaciated because she hasn't eaten in several days. Her dress is filthy and ragged. Her face, pockmarked with sadness.

She addresses the couple in Irish. "Mr. and Mrs. O'Leary?"

"The very same. What's your name, young girl? Do we know you?"

"I'm your niece, Uncle Pádraig. Me name is Mary O'Leary. Me father is your brother, Timothy."

"Lord save us, but isn't Timothy at home looking after the farm in Inchimore? What brings you over here by yourself, young girl?"

"We all came on the ship to Canada. The praties went bad at home, so Daddy and Mammy said we should go to Canada."

"Come over to the table and sit with us," says Pádraig. "So ye all came, did ye? Where are the rest of ye? Where are yere daddy and mammy?"

"They've gone to glory. Mammy passed on the ship, and Daddy and Seán passed after we got to the island." The girl bursts into tears.

"Lord save us. And how did you find your way here, young girl?"

"Shush, macushla, that's enough for now," says Pádraig's wife, Bríd. She wraps her arms around the crying girl. "You need some rest now, love, and then a bite to eat. You can tell us more later. Let me get you a cup of buttermilk."

The girl takes one sip of the buttermilk and vomits on the wooden floor.

Bríd takes a cloth from the cupboard to clean the floor. "Poor child, you haven't eaten today, have you? Come upstairs with me, love, and lie down on our bed. Deirdre's in her crib next to it, but she won't bother you at all because she's sleeping." She carries a cup of water while taking Mary up to their attic bedroom. Bríd then goes into the spare room to make up another bed for the girl to use later.

THE GIRL TELLS THE REST OF HER STORY the following morning while having breakfast. She eats a bowl of porridge and several slices of brown bread and butter. Pádraig and Bríd are relieved to see the colour come back to her cheeks.

"They told me in the village where to find your house. I had your address on a piece of paper. Some of them were able to read the Irish."

Pádraig smiles. "There are still a few of us here who have the *blas*."

The girl says that when the ship docked, she was met by a priest who spoke Irish. He gave her money to travel from Quebec City down to Montreal, and the name of a boarding house where she could stay. The landlady told her where to find a man who would take her on his horse and cart to Huntingdon.

"You're blessed that you found your way to us with all your family now passed," says Bríd.

"We had more family on the island. Daddy's cousin, Diarmuid de Búrca, was there too. Every day, he came to visit us at the place where Daddy and Seán passed. He asked me to give you his best wishes."

Pádraig's mouth falls open. "Lord save us, he would be Máire Bhuí's youngest son, wouldn't he? I didn't know he came to Canada. I'll have to go to the island tomorrow and see if I can find him."

"His wife passed on the island before we arrived there. We said prayers for her in the chapel."

"I didn't know he was married. Did they have children?"

Mary doesn't know.

THE FOLLOWING DAY, Pádraig leaves on a carriage for Montreal. Spends the night at a boarding house, and then takes the all-day steamer voyage to Quebec City. He stays there at a boarding house close to the Saint Lawrence River. The following morning, he asks the landlord where he can find the landing stage for the boat to Grosse Île.

"You don't want to go there. 'Tis full of suffering and death."

"I have to go there, to find me cousin."

"Your cousin is surely dead. You'll be dead too if you spend any time in that wretched place."

"I thank you for your concern, sir, but I must go."

The landlord shrugs. "Suit yourself then." He points down the road to where a steamer is moored. "That's the boat you'll be taking. God speed."

Pádraig slings over his shoulder the cloth bag holding his clothes, and he rushes down to the landing stage. A guard in black uniform holds up a hand to stop him from boarding.

"You need to have a permit."

"But I have to see me cousin."

"You can't see anyone without a permit."

226

A priest steps off the boat. "What's the name of your cousin?"

"Diarmuid de Búrca."

"I know him well. I'm a chaplain on the island. Me name is Father Liam Moylan. What's your name, me good man?"

"Pádraig O'Leary, Father."

"Are you Catholic?"

"I am, Father."

"Then, Pádraig, you can be me altar server today. I'll take you to the place where your cousin is staying."

WHEN THEY REACH THE ISLAND, Father Moylan introduces Pádraig to the medical superintendent. The three of them go to the fever shed where Diarmuid is now lying.

"Will I be able to take him home with me?"

"I'm afraid not," says Dr. Douglas. "He's failing now. Could be dead within a few hours."

Diarmuid is rambling, muttering, tossing around in the bed like a rowboat on a stormy sea. Pádraig can make out the occasional word. "Have to be on the next steamboat … start our own farm … be like Inchimore … grow praties again …"

He opens his eyes. "Are you the nurse?"

"I'm your cousin, Diarmuid. I'm Pádraig O'Leary. Our grandfather was Diarmuid Bhuí."

"Ah, Pádraig, I'm pleased to see you." He sounds more lucid now. "Can you help me outside because I don't want to die in here? I want to be near me beloved Nell. Her grave is just a few steps away from the door."

227

Diarmuid weighs little more than a house cat. Pádraig and Father Moylan carry him outside and place him on the grass near a little wooden cross with the word "Nell" cut into it.

"Go back now," says Diarmuid, "and bring me the small book I left under me bed. I want you to take it and keep it safe. It will tell you all about our journey."

It's the copybook with the stout cardboard covers and "Property of the National Board of Education" written in Irish on the back.

Diarmuid is nearing the end when Pádraig retrieves the journal from the fever shed. He is rambling again. "Barry, the bum-bailiff … worst of them all … have to burn his house down … no rest for the wicked … burn his house, and he burns in hell …" He turns quiet and still. Pádraig looks at him for several minutes, and then turns to Father Moylan.

"He smiles the smile of someone who has seen the angels or God Almighty Himself," says Pádraig. "I think Diarmuid has joined his wife in heaven."

The priest makes the sign of the cross. "Grant him eternal rest, O Lord, and may perpetual life shine on him forever." Pádraig wraps the body in a blanket, picks up a shovel lying nearby, and starts to dig. A couple of other men come over to help.

After they finish their work, the gravediggers take Pádraig to Quebec City in their small motorized boat. He knocks on the door of the same boarding house where he stayed before. Although it's late, after midnight, the landlord is still up. He stands in the doorway holding an oil lamp, peers at Pádraig and recognizes him.

"You were here before. Have you just come from the island?"

228

"I have."

"Then you can't come in. You might have brought the fever with you."

"I'll go back to the river and wash every part of me body."

"You'll have to leave all your clothes there, and the bag as well. I can't risk you infecting the other guests here. I have an old shirt and pants that I can give you when you come back."

"You're very kind, sir."

Pádraig goes down to the river, strips off his clothes, and washes himself from head to feet. When he gets back to the boarding house, *naked as the day I was born*, he is relieved to find the landlord's clothes, including the boots, fit him as if they were his own. "Let me pay you an extra dollar for your generosity, sir."

PÁDRAIG ARRIVES BACK IN HUNTINGDON two days later. He tells his wife about his trip to the island and says they shouldn't tell anyone else.

"Our neighbours don't need to know our business."

He puts the journal in the cabinet with the good china, and locks the cabinet door.

TAYLOR REACHES INTO HIS BRIEFCASE and puts a handwritten letter on the patio table. "I've something else to show you." The Tullamore server puts two pints on the table at the same time.

Jerry pushes his pint to one side and reaches for his notebook. "Before you do that, Michael, let me see if I've got the story straight. Do you mind if I take notes?"

"No problem."

"Old reporter's habit." Jerry pauses and thinks for a moment. "So, here we have a newspaper guy in Quebec who comes across an immigrant's journal. How did he acquire the journal?"

"My grandfather gave it to him. On loan."

"Ah. And how did your grandfather obtain it?"

"He got it from his grandfather."

"Okay, you'll have to start giving me names here. Your grandfather was …?"

"My namesake, Michael Joseph Taylor. He was living in Huntingdon then."

"And his grandfather was …?"

"His maternal grandfather, Pádraig O'Leary. Pádraig was the nephew of Maura Bwee that I told you about. The one who came to Canada in the 1830s."

Jerry nods and smiles. "You're improving with the pronunciation of her name. And how did Pádraig get the journal? We're still talking about the original journal of Diarmuid de Búrca, right? The one the newspaper guy claimed had been written by someone else?"

"By Gerald Keegan, that's right. Pádraig obtained the journal after his twelve-year-old niece, recently arrived from Ireland, showed up unexpectedly at his Huntingdon farm."

"And she brought the journal with her?"

"No, I don't think she would have known about it. However, she told Pádraig that she had met Diarmuid, our ancestor, when she and her family landed on Grosse Île, the Quebec quarantine station. Diarmuid was the one who gave her the money to go from there to Huntingdon."

"What about the rest of her family?"

"It's all in the letter. Her mother had died during the voyage, and her father and brother both died after they arrived at the island."

"And Diarmuid …?"

"Let's put it this way. Pádraig figured that Diarmuid had to be still on the island because otherwise he would have travelled to Huntingdon with the young girl."

"And brought his wife along as well?"

"Of course."

"Don't keep me in suspense, Michael. You like to do this, don't you? Why did Diarmuid remain on the island?"

"Pádraig went there to find out. And came back to Huntingdon with the journal. I won't tell you any more than that. You'll have to read it in the letter."

"I have a terrible feeling I know how this part of the story ended," says Jerry. "And you have the journal now?"

231

"Yes. A woman at the Irish Cultural Society is translating it for me. I should have it for you next week."

Jerry whoops for joy. "Yes! Finally. I can't wait to read what he wrote." After twenty-five years of wandering in the wilderness, has he arrived at the Promised Land? This could be the most encouraging development so far.

"You'll find it interesting, I'm sure."

"Just out of curiosity, Michael, how did your family end up here in Alberta?"

"My grandfather didn't want to work in the lumber mills in Huntingdon like his father. He came west on the new railway in 1883 to take up a homestead at Pincher Creek. My father, James Taylor, continued to farm in Pincher after my grandfather died."

"I look forward to reading this letter. And, of course, to reading the journal as well. However, before I take off, I'd like to know one thing, Michael. Why did the Quebec newspaper guy change the name from Diarmuid de Búrca to Gerald Keegan?"

"He changed pretty well everything in the journal. Including the place where Diarmuid came from. He changed it from County Cork to County Sligo. And the name of the ship. It was called the Sir Henry Pottinger, and this guy changed it to Naparima."

"Did your grandfather know he was going to turn the journal into fiction?"

"He found out after the fact and was angry about that. At the time, my grandfather had been given to understand it would be a literal translation."

"Then what happened to the journal?"

"My grandfather bequeathed it to my father and my father passed it on to me before he died in 1965."

"Your father wouldn't have been able to read it, I presume? Had he read the newspaper version?"

"No, but he knew from talking to my grandfather that the guy had turned the journal into fiction and said I should know the truth. My grandfather resented the fact that a Scottish Protestant with money in his pockets had stolen the voice and viewpoint of a poor Irish Catholic and used them for his own purposes."

"And the original, the 1847 journal, had never been translated?"

"In fact, it had. My father's grandmother, Deirdre, had arranged for it to be translated in the 1860s. She passed the translation on to her son, Peter, but he mislaid it."

"And Peter was …?"

"My grandfather's older brother, Peter Taylor."

"I'll need a computer to keep track of all this, Michael. Forgive me for being obtuse, but you'll have to take me through it one more time. Maybe start again from the beginning."

"Okay, let me give it to you as best I can. My great-great-grandfather was Pádraig O'Leary, the nephew of Maura Bwee. He emigrated to Canada in the 1830s and had a farm in Huntingdon. He went to Grosse Île in 1847 when he heard that Maura's son Diarmuid was there, and he brought Diarmuid's journal back with him to Huntingdon. Pádraig gave the journal to his daughter Deirdre, who had it translated. She married a lumber mill worker named Peter Taylor, and she gave the translation to their oldest son, also named Peter."

"Your grand-uncle. And he mislaid the translation?"

233

"So my grandfather said."

"Too bad. Did Deirdre give the original journal, as well as the translation, to Peter?"

"Probably. As the oldest son, he would have been first in line to receive the bequest."

"And that original document survived, thank goodness, because Peter gave it to his younger brother, your grandfather?"

"That's my understanding. Peter didn't have any children, so it would have made more sense for him to have the journal go to my grandfather and his children."

"Who wouldn't have been able to know what was in it because the translation had gone missing?"

"That's right."

"Was there a reason why your grandfather never had it translated again? Or your father, for that matter?"

"It wouldn't have been that easy for them. When you're living and working on a farm in Pincher Creek, there's not much time or opportunity to get someone to translate a document from old Irish into English."

"And, after more than twenty-five years, you're only having it translated now?"

"To be honest, I had forgotten all about it. I had stashed it away in a drawer. The *Gazette* story jogged my memory. When I read about the book being published, I realized I had unfinished business to take care of."

P ÁDRAIG O'LEARY UNLOCKS the china cabinet and
takes out the journal he's been safeguarding for twenty
years. "Come here to me, Deirdre," he says to his
daughter in the next room. "I've something to show you."

"What is it, Daddy?" She has been trying on her wedding dress
with help from her mother.

"Aren't you looking lovely this morning, me love. Peter Taylor is a
lucky man to have you."

"'Tis still tight around the waist, but Mammy is fixing that." The
dress ripples and flutters as she twirls around the dining room like a
debutante waltzing in a Paris ballroom.

"It's probably tight because your mammy was a slip of a girl when
we married. She always hoped we'd have a daughter one day to wear
it."

"I love it."

He hands her the journal. "You'll be moving with Peter to his
father's farm, I s'pose?"

"Yes, but he says he's going to leave the farm soon and apply for a
job in one of the new lumber mills. What's this book you're giving
me?"

"'Twas written by me late cousin, Diarmuid de Búrca, God rest his
soul. Before he passed, he asked me to keep it safe for him. I've had it
for many years and now 'tis your turn to keep it safe."

"Did I ever meet him?"

"No macushla, he passed when you were a baby. He was on one of those ships that came over from Ireland during the famine."

"Did you come on one of those ships?" She starts turning the pages of the journal.

"I did, but that was long before the famine. The ship that Diarmuid came on, it was one of what they called the coffin ships because so many people passed on them."

"Did he pass on the ship?"

"No, he passed in a place called Grosse Île. That was an island, a quarantine station, where the passengers landed after they first arrived in Canada. The ones who were well enough to travel farther continued on to Quebec City. The others stayed on the island."

"And you went to see him on the island?"

"I did, yes. Your cousin Mary, when she first came to us as a young girl, told me he was there."

"She was on the island, too? I don't remember her ever talking about that."

"'Twas incredibly sad for her. Her mother passed on the ship and her father – me brother Timothy – passed on the island. Her brother Seán passed on the island too."

"That must have been terrible for her. Terrible for you, too."

"It was dreadful. She lost all her family when she was just a young colleen. That's why she never talked about it. The memory was too painful. She mentioned it when she first came to us and then never spoke about it again."

"So, all those people who stayed on the island, they all passed?"

"Many of them did, yes. However, some of them also got well after treatment and were able to make a new life for themselves in Canada. Your cousin Mary was one of those lucky ones."

"Not so lucky if she lost all her family."

"True. However, life in Canada has been much better for her than it would have been if she'd stayed in Ireland. When the spuds went bad, everyone suffered."

She leafs through a few more pages. "This looks like a personal journal. Why did our cousin give it to you?"

"Because when someone writes something down, they want someone else to read it."

"How was he related to us?"

"His mother, Máire Bhuí Ní Laoire, was me father's sister."

"Why do you say her name in Irish?"

"Because that's what everyone called her. It translates as Yellow Mary O'Leary. She was a famous poetess in Ireland, and she only spoke Irish."

"Is any of her poetry in this journal?"

"A few lines here and there."

"Oh me goodness, I can't wait to see them."

"Yes, but I don't want you to look for them now. You wouldn't understand them anyhow. I want you to think about your wedding, and the grand life that awaits you." He gently places his hand over hers to stop her from turning more pages.

"Why are you giving the book to me now?"

"Because you are twenty-one years of age, macushla, and are about to be married. If you have children, and I pray to God you will, you must give the book to your eldest one day."

"Is all of it in Irish?"

"Yes. I could still remember what the words meant, but you'll need to have them translated."

"And you've read all of it?"

"Many times. Along with the lovely lines of poetry, there's a cloud of pain and sorrow darkening the pages of that book, macushla. After you've read it, those who are now unborn should read it too."

"Why do you say that?"

"I'll say this much and no more because I don't want to spoil your happy occasion. People should never forget how Irish people suffered and died in that terrible summer of 1847."

JERRY AND TOM RIDE THEIR RENTED BIKES westward along the Bow River pathway. They park and stop for an ice cream cone when they reach a little pop-up café near Edworthy Park. Grab an empty bench. Bask in the sun for a few moments. "Glad you thought of doing this," says Jerry. "I haven't been on a bike for so long." He feels heavy after one too many hamburger dinners at the Lido Café.

"I thought you rode all the time," says Tom. He has now lost most of his hair but looks fit and trim.

"I did in Dublin because I couldn't afford a car. Couldn't even afford a motorbike." He watches a seagull alight on the pathway, strut around in a pushy staccato, and then start pecking away at something stuck on the asphalt. What's the bird doing, so far away from the ocean? Must be attracted to whatever Calgarians put into the Spyhill dump.

"When were you last in Dublin? Do you still go every year?"

"Try to. Last time, however, I only went to Cork."

"When was that?"

"A week ago. I've been dealing with issues at work and needed to escape. I also wanted to do some family history sleuthing with my cousin, Cathal."

"How goes the quest to find your missing ancestor? You've been at this forever."

"Not much new from over there, although I did shoot some good pictures. However, I struck gold right here, if you can believe it. A man in Calgary phoned me up unexpectedly one day and identified himself as a distant cousin."

"Interesting. And is he related?"

"Indeed. We're both direct descendants of Máire Bhuí, which would make him my fifth cousin or something like that. And, get this. We both live in Sunnyside. A few blocks from one another."

"Quite the coincidence."

Jerry finishes his cone and stands up. "Did you want to ride some more?"

"No, I want to hear more about your ancestor. What did this Calgary cousin have to say to you?"

"He said that my ancestor, Diarmuid, kept a journal during his trip."

"Another scribe in the family, eh?"

"Funny, that's what my colleague Don Oberg said when I first told him about Máire Bhuí."

"Have you read the journal?"

"I hope to before long. The cousin here is having it translated."

Tom looks at his watch. "We should start heading back to that bike rental shop in Kensington."

"Do you have time for a coffee at the Roasterie?"

"Just a quick one. I need to get back to the Palliser to make some phone calls."

THEY SIT ON A BENCH outside the Roasterie, sipping from ceramic bowls of latte. "So how are things at the Institute of Technology?" Jerry asks.

"I enjoy the research and coming to conferences like the one here at U of C. But I have a new boss who's driving me crazy. Typical bureaucrat, always complaining that we're over budget. Never has a good word to say about our breakthroughs."

"I know the feeling. Can't remember the last time a boss at the *Herald* had anything good to say about my column."

"Do you ever think of going back home?"

"I get asked that all the time, Tom. My ears would burst if I had to listen to the roar of the Celtic Tiger every day."

"You should give it a try. Even for only a couple of years. I think you'd like the New Ireland."

"They say you can't go home again."

"I did. You could too. Nobody is holding you back."

"Carol might have something to say about that."

"Bring her with you."

"Then we'd both be out of work."

"You could freelance. Journalism is a transportable skill."

Jerry picks up the empty bowls. "I'll think about it."

ICHAEL TAYLOR IS, AS JERRY SUSPECTED, undergoing treatment for cancer. Colon cancer. He talks about his condition when they meet for drinks at the Tullamore.

"It runs in the family. Killed my father and paternal grandfather. The doc told me I had a one in six chance of being hit with it too. Said I should go for the colonoscopy every five years. However, the first one was so painful that I stopped going. Big mistake."

"It runs in my family too. Killed my mother when she was in her early sixties. Shall we go inside? I think we've had it for the patio weather this year." They head for two wingback chairs next to the fireplace and ask the server to turn down the music. "Bohemian Rhapsody" by Queen. Strange song to be playing in an Irish pub.

"How far along are you with the reading?" asks Taylor.

"I've finished Pádraig O'Leary's letter and am about halfway through the journal."

"So now you know what happened to the elusive Diarmuid."

"I had suspected he never made it off the island. Sad story."

"What do you think of the journal?"

"I can understand why moving into the workhouse would never have been an option for him. It was quite the Dickensian institution."

"Of course. Better to emigrate to Canada. In Ireland, he could see nothing down the road but bleak prospects."

"But he clearly had some guilt about leaving," says Jerry. "He was supposed to be his mother's successor. Her heir apparent as local poet laureate."

"What did you think about his rebel activities?"

"I was surprised that he wrote about his role in burning down the bailiff's house. Our ancestor was a confessed murderer, Michael."

"I wouldn't go that far, Jerry. He wasn't the one who pulled the trigger."

"Doesn't matter. He organized the raid on the house with the intent of burning the guy alive."

"It was a war, Jerry. The tenant farmers saw themselves as soldiers of destiny, with a mission to rid Ireland of the English oppressors."

"I know that's what he wrote in the journal, Michael, but I don't buy it. They weren't fighting an army; they were going out in the middle of the night and murdering people in their sleep. I think Diarmuid was racked with guilt because he knew this kind of killing was a mortal sin."

"He doesn't express any guilt in the journal, Jerry."

"No, but he doesn't offer any convincing defence of his actions either. I think that writing about the house burning was for him the equivalent of going to confession."

"Whatever you say. What did you think of his account of the journey over?"

"Ship of fools. Voyage of the damned. Cardboard villains. Helpless victims. Where's the hope? Cowed and starving Irish, unable to care for themselves. Travelling like ghosts across an ocean of misery."

"I had much the same reaction at first. Compassion fatigue sets in. However, there's a lesson to be learned from the serenity Nell shows in the face of Diarmuid's growing anger and frustration. The story of her sewing biscuit sacks into dresses is charming."

"Indeed, I've written about people like that, Michael. No self-pity, no anger, no raging at God for their troubles."

"Did you think it was a clever idea for Diarmuid to accept the bribe to go to Canada?"

"I accepted the bribe, and it worked out for me. So far. However, you've got a point. He had a job. Didn't always get his quarterly salary on time, but he did receive it eventually. I'm sure he could have negotiated a deal to pay the rent whenever his wages arrived."

"Do you think there might have been another agenda at work there? Ethnic cleansing?"

"That's a popular hypothesis, Michael. Some nationalists still believe the government managed the famine to prune a Catholic population that was growing too large. However, I think the government didn't want to disrupt the free-market flow of agricultural goods from Ireland to England. It's too simplistic to blame the famine on colonial villainy."

"Why do you think the landlords offered a financial incentive for their evicted tenants to leave the country?"

"Because, as a one-time payment, it was cheaper than subsidizing the living expenses of the tenants in the workhouse. The landlords saved on their taxes by exporting the tenants to North America like African slaves."

Taylor pulls from his briefcase a copybook with stout cardboard covers. On the back is written, in Irish, "Property of the National Board of Education." "I want you to have this, Jerry."

Jerry leafs through the handwritten document and shakes his head. "I can't take this from you, Michael. This is a family heirloom. You should be giving it to your brother or someone else in your family."

"You're in my family. You'll appreciate it more than my brother would."

"It's a cultural artefact. It should be in a museum, somewhere."

"Then give it to a museum. It's too late for me to be holding onto it."

Taylor reaches into his briefcase again. "I've one more document to give you. I received this from the Canadian Parks Service. The records from the old quarantine station at Grosse Île don't give much information, but at least they help bring closure."

A glance at the first names on the document tells Jerry why his earlier efforts to track down information on Diarmuid and Nell were unsuccessful:

Name:	Burke, Michael (Immigrant)
Sex:	M
Age:	31 Year(s)
Place of death:	Grosse Île Hospital
Ship:	Sir Henry Pottinger
Port of departure:	Cork, Ireland
Date of departure:	29 May 1847
Date of entry:	7 August 1847
Fiche No:	1586

Reference: Weekly returns of deaths in the
quarantine hospital at Grosse Île, *The Morning Chronicle* (Quebec), 7
September 1847

    Name: Burke, Noreen (Immigrant)

    Sex: F

    Age: 18 Year(s)

    Place of death: Grosse Île Hospital

    Ship: Sir Henry Pottinger

    Port of departure: Cork, Ireland

    Date of departure: 29 May 1847

    Date of entry: 7 August 1847

    Fiche No: 1580

    Reference: Weekly returns of deaths in the
quarantine hospital at Grosse Île, *The Morning Chronicle* (Quebec), 24
August 1847

Michael and Noreen, who knew? Now that he knows the location
of their final resting place, shouldn't he go to Grosse Île to say
goodbye to them? Perhaps.

J ERRY SIPS CABERNET SAUVIGNON with Carol in the back yard of her wartime bungalow in Riverdale. "You have a lovely little home here. Perfect for one person, or even two."

Once again, he has been given time off work while he continues to contemplate his future at the *Herald*. He managed to buy more time for himself by agreeing to take the desker training course. "Then I'll be in a better position to decide if that's what I want to do." However, he knows the deadline is looming. Webster expects him to say when he returns whether he will go on the desk or take the severance package.

"I bought the place for a song," she says. "They used to mine coal under here in the 1920s, and the ground still gives way from time to time. If you can put up with that occasional inconvenience, and the periodic flooding along the flats from the North Saskatchewan River, you're living in the most attractive, most inexpensive oasis in Edmonton. Much nicer, and cheaper, than Strathcona."

"I can't believe the warm weather you're still having here. It already feels like winter in Calgary."

Carol uncorks another bottle. "So, you've been granted another reprieve?"

"More like an extended stay of execution. The techies have now spent more than four months trying to make the newsroom transition from terminals to desktop computers, so I soldier on with the column. In the meantime, Webster tells me my severance will be upped to a year's salary if I decide to leave."

"That's much better than before. Are you going to take this package?"

"Still thinking about it. I'll make my final decision after I return from Grosse Île."

"Why are you going there?"

"To pay my last respects. Bring closure to the story of Diarmuid. I don't expect to find his grave there, but I do want to stand in the place where he stood when a new beginning was within reach. We had much in common, you know."

"Because you both were exiles? Because you both looked for the promise of a better life somewhere else?"

"Right. Plus, we both found ourselves in a place where we felt the need to write things down. To record the story before it was lost for all time."

"To bear witness."

"That's what he did, and that's what I've been doing. There's a strong spiritual connection there. I wish I'd known him."

"And he was a poet, too?"

"Indeed. He was the heir apparent until he left for Canada. He wrote a few lines in his journal, and you can see he had the gift. I certainly don't."

"I presume you still feel the same way about going on the desk at the *Herald*?"

"There are worse things in life, Carol. Oberg has agreed to give up his column, go on the desk when they finally fix the computer problem, and then rise every morning at five o'clock to work on his fiction. I might do the same. Work for a few hours on the Máire Bhuí manuscript and my revamping of the Diarmuid journal. Have breakfast and then head off to the *Herald* to edit copy and lay out pages."

"In your dreams, Jerry. Since when did you become an early morning person?"

"Good point. I wouldn't have the stamina to keep up that routine for more than a week."

"Let's go for a walk along the riverbank, sweetheart," she says. "Then we'll have a bite. There's a nice trail below the wooden steps at the end of the street."

As they walk hand in hand through the poplars and pines, Jerry thinks back to that long-ago summer evening in Dawson City when they first made love by the light of the moon.

"Do you remember that the sun didn't go down there until just before midnight and came up again shortly afterwards?" he says.

"In Dawson, mmm, yes. So long ago. How did you guys ever sleep?"

"Darkened blinds on the windows. Everyone had them."

"I wish I could have stayed there longer. However, as you may remember, our bus was leaving the next day for Whitehorse. Have you ever been back?"

"No, but I'd like to."

"Me, too."

"It probably hasn't changed much. I'll bet you there are still a few people singing 'Squaws Along the Yukon' in the Westminster Hotel lounge after they've had a few drinks."

"Oh my God, I forgot that you and Tom used to sing that song. Didn't you know it was racist?"

"I don't think we thought about that. We always got requests for it. The local Natives used to sing along to the chorus. In their own language."

"Oh, I want to go back to Dawson. I want you and I to go back."

"Do you remember what you said to me that night in the Westminster, when I came over to your table?

"What did I say?"

"You said, 'Are we going to make love tonight?'"

"No!"

"Yes! I remember it well. Nobody had ever said that to me before. You pursued me like a lion going after an antelope."

"I must have been drunk."

"I don't think you were. A little tipsy, maybe, but lucid and charming and lovely. And that was the beginning …"

She finishes the line: "Of a beautiful friendship."

"Right."

"Do you think we'll always remain friends?" she says.

"As long as we live in separate houses."

"In separate domiciles, you said once."

"In separate domiciles, yes. We can't live without one another, and we can't live with one another." He tells himself that life as a single man will make him better prepared for the loneliness of old age.

"Did you want to stop in for Chinese food?" she says. "There's a wonderful place not far from here called Riverdale Sunrise. It opened just a few months ago."

"Why don't we order takeout from there and then go back to enjoy some more of your ambrosial cabernet? My experience with Chinese restaurants is that they rarely stock fine wines. They want people to drink beer, not wine. If they have wine, it comes out of a box."

"Ambrosial?"

"My favourite new word. Elixir of life. Drink of the gods."

"Sounds like a plan. They do a yummy sweet and sour pork, you'll be glad to hear. Also, a delicious Szechuan beef."

As they enter the restaurant, she turns to him, smiles, and says: "Are we going to make love tonight?"

"Where did I hear that before?"

J ERRY ALIGHTS FROM THE FERRY that brought him here from Berthier-sur-Mer and steps onto hallowed ground. An island of mystery, history, and death. The final resting place for thousands of Irish immigrants who died of cholera, dysentery, and typhus. Some call it the scene of a holocaust. Jerry prefers to call it the scene of an unspeakable tragedy. Too late now to point fingers.

Will he find evidence of his ancestry here in this now strangely peaceful place? He doesn't expect to. Not in any meaningful sense, at any rate. He knows the doctors and their helpers were so overwhelmed by the hundreds of sick and dying arriving daily during that terrible summer of sorrow that they lost track of them within the first month. There likely will be no markers to show where Diarmuid and Nell are buried.

Still, however, it's crucial for him to be here. At the eastern end of the island, he can see the dilapidated remains of the old fever sheds where the terminally ill spent their last days. That is a closure of sorts.

He's the only visitor to the island on this day. Next week it will be closed for the season. Then he'll be back in Calgary contemplating his future.

He scrambles up a cliff to look at the most imposing monument on the island, a Celtic cross of grey granite erected by the Ancient Order of Hibernians in America. The English and French inscriptions refer to the thousands who ended their sorrowful pilgrimage here. The Irish inscription assigns blame: "The laws of foreign tyrants and an artificial famine."

A second monument, placed by the medical superintendent Dr. Douglas, downplays the size of the tragedy: "The mortal remains of 5,424 persons who found in America but a grave." Jerry believes the correct figure to be closer to twelve thousand.

Jerry has read in the *Globe and Mail* that there are plans in the works to turn the island into an immigration theme park. "Canada: Land of Hope and Welcome." Is this for real? What misguided civil servant dreamed that one up? The largest mass grave in Canada is to become a place to celebrate immigration? Our own Ellis Island? Not a smart idea.

One shocking set of statistics, obtained from the Alberta Family Histories Society, will stay with him forever. The Sir Henry Pottinger left Cork with five hundred passengers aboard. Two hundred and six died at sea. Two hundred more were dying of fever when they arrived at Grosse Île. Less than one hundred survived the voyage. The rest were doomed. There are no words.

A scattering of small white wooden crosses dots the furrowed brown and yellow landscape. Placed there by recent visitors, they look like a cluster of paper flags pinned to the collection box of a Capuchin missionary. A few have names written on them. Jerry arbitrarily chooses one of the unmarked crosses to represent Diarmuid and Nell. He stands for a few minutes in this valley of death and says a silent prayer for his ancestors. He has brought no wreath to place on their gravesite, so he picks some yellow goldenrods and places them on the uncut tufts of hair grass at the foot of the cross. "Goodbye, Diarmuid.

253

Goodbye, Nell." He makes the sign of the cross. "In the name of the Father, and of the Son, and of the Holy Ghost. May God grant you both eternal rest."

THE TWO MEN ARE HAVING their weekly drink at Tullamore, now sitting inside because the patio is closed for the season.

"I've received unwelcome news," says Taylor. "The oncologist says he doesn't expect me to live more than six months."

"Do doctors make prognostications like that?" says Jerry. "I didn't think they were allowed to."

"I'm happy he did. As Samuel Johnson said, when a man knows he's going to be hanged, it concentrates the mind wonderfully."

"How are you dealing with this news?"

"I have my church and my faith. We're lucky, you and I, that we have prayer and the sacraments to help us cope."

Jerry doesn't feel so lucky. Yes, he did tell Taylor that he played organ every Sunday at Holy Trinity. But Taylor doesn't know that Jerry does it for musical, not spiritual reasons. He only does the church gig to keep his chops up.

"You have a brother in Pincher Creek. Would you think of going to stay with him?"

"No, I have to stay close to the Tom Baker Cancer Centre."

"How's the treatment going there?"

"I'm at stage four," says Taylor. "There is no stage five. So now I'm talking to the folks at Bowview Manor hospice. Would you put me in the Passages column after I'm gone?"

"Let's not talk about that now, Michael."

"I'm serious. I'd consider it a great honour if you were to write about me."

"I may not be writing the column for much longer because of changes at the paper. However, I'll give it some thought. I find it tough to write about friends."

"You can say I was the guy who unravelled a 100-year-old literary subterfuge and gave the world the real famine journal of Diarmuid Burke. Speaking of the journal, where are you at in terms of doing something with it?"

"As you know, I've finished reading it. Now, I'm trying to figure out how to take the material and fashion it into something life-affirming."

"How would you do that? It's not exactly a life-affirming story."

"No, and that's the difficulty. It's an important historical document, of course, but the sense of tragic inevitability is overwhelming."

"You mean, people don't want to read about victims groping blindly and helplessly toward their doom?"

"Exactly. There must be a glimmer of hope for the future, some indication in the story that the tragedy could have been prevented. Even in the darkest Shakespearean tragedies, there are signs the deaths could have been avoided if the protagonist had taken a different path."

"And there's no such path here?"

"Not after they boarded the ship. There's only one path in this story, and it leads to the grave."

"How do you make that life-affirming?"

"By combining it with another story, perhaps. As it now stands, on its own, Diarmuid's journal is merely grist for the archives. The only people who will want to read it are researchers with a special interest in the Irish famine."

"So, is that what you'll do with it then? Give the journal to the Glenbow or University of Calgary?"

"I'll do that anyhow. However, I still want to see it reach a wider audience, and have to figure out how best I can do that. I told you I was working on a narrative nonfiction book about Máire Bhuí's life as a poet. If I incorporate a reworked version of Diarmuid's journal into the biographical part of that manuscript, that will flesh it out. By combining the two, I can produce a deeper study of Irish life during the famine years."

"I hope you can do that, Jerry. I thought I might write something for the Family Histories quarterly, but the chemo and radiation have left me without any energy."

"I also thought of doing a piece for the quarterly," says Jerry. "But I feared it wouldn't do justice to the journal because of the space limitations. There's one small glimmer of hope that came out of the Grosse Île tragedy, and I'd like to find a way of using that to give the story a happier ending."

"What's that?"

"As you know, there were more than two thousand orphaned Irish children left on the island after their parents died."

"I remember reading about that. Whatever happened to them?"

"An angel of mercy named Charles-Félix Cazeau, a priest from Montreal, arranged to have them adopted."

"Yes, that name rings a bell. They called him the priest to the Irish."

"He did something wonderful, Michael. He worked with a Catholic charity in Quebec to help these children. All of them found parents."

"That *is* a more positive ending."

"Not only that, but he persuaded the parents to let the children retain their Irish surnames."

"And that's why there are so many Ryans and MacCarthys now living in French-speaking Quebec?" says Taylor.

"You got it. They were able to preserve their identities."

"In a province where, even back then, preserving one's identity was of immense importance."

"That's how I think the story should end," says Jerry.

Dawson City, Yukon, August 1993

JERRY AND CAROL ARE REVISITING DAWSON CITY for the first time since they met in 1967. After taking in the evening's pub entertainment at the Westminster Hotel, they stroll along the wooden sidewalks to the cabin where he stayed that summer. He stops for a moment. Reaches down and touches the surface. Feels the cold. Permafrost must be rising, he thinks.

There's now a sign outside the cabin saying Robert Service once rented it. "I thought back then that Service's spirit still haunted the cabin," he says. "'It seems it's been here since the beginning/It seems it will be to the end.'"

"Too bad they won't allow people to stay there anymore."

"'Twould be nice." However, he'd prefer the comfort of a hotel room.

The pale moon warms the southern sky as they head back to the Westminster for a nightcap. She looks lovely in the moonlight. Chestnut brown hair dappled with flecks of grey.

The waiter brings them two glasses of the house merlot. "'Wine is from the gods a gift,'" says Jerry, raising his glass. She raises hers too, toasting a memory. "I was so sad to read Michael's obit in the *Journal*. Only seventy-one, what a shame."

"If I'd still been there, I would have asked them to let me resurrect the Passages column. Just this once, I would have said. Michael made

259

an important contribution. However, I suspect they would have said no."

She tilts her head and gives a slight smile. "Do you remember what else we talked about that night?"

He pretends he doesn't know what she's talking about. "That night?"

"That night when you and I met here. When I stroked your goatee, and you squeezed my thigh."

He leans in toward her and whispers. "And you asked if we were going to make love that night?"

She clasps hands to her chest and laughs. "I still play your old albums from time to time. Whenever I want to fall in love all over again."

"'Here you'll find all kinds of Yukon wildlife in their natural habitat,'" he says, gesturing toward the other drinking customers. "That's a line we used in our show." He and Tom had hoped some generous patron, flush with nuggets after a day's panning, would leave a nub or two in their tip jar. Never happened.

"I was impressed by the fact you still remembered my last name two hours after I told it to you," she says.

"How could I forget a last name like Dawson? I had to know if you had any connection to the town here."

"You were impressed when I said my great-grandfather's brother was a geologist who mapped this area in the 1880s."

"And you were impressed when I told you I had an ancestor who was a famous folk poet in Ireland."

"Why didn't you show me her poetry book that night?"

"I figured it would give me a good excuse to reconnect with you when I got back to Vancouver."

"And then we both went into journalism."

"It's been quite a ride, hasn't it?"

"How does it feel to be unemployed for, how long has it been now?"

"Eight months. Not bad. The severance package has given me plenty of breathing room."

"Have you been applying elsewhere?"

"Not formally," says Jerry. "I've made a few phone calls to friends. They tell me nobody is hiring."

"Why won't you let me inquire for you at the *Journal*? I'm still sure they can find a spot for you there. A couple of our senior reporters left in the past month, and an editor told me they would be filling those vacancies."

"Thanks, Carol, but I've pretty well made up my mind as to what my next step should be."

"And ...?"

"I've decided to move back to Ireland."

"No!"

"Reverse emigration, if you can believe it. After more than twenty-five years as an exile, I'm returning home."

"But I thought you said this was your home."

"It was. Certainly, I felt that way when I was doing the Passages column. But not anymore."

"I don't understand."

"I came here with a dream, with two dreams, in fact. One was to play music for a living, which I did for a while. The other was to write for a living, which I also did."

"But you can still write for a living."

"I can, and Canada has given me the tools to do that, for which I'll always be grateful. I didn't have those tools when I came here, and now I want to show the people in Ireland what I've learned."

"You could also show the people in Canada what you've learned."

"I know, Carol, but there's more to it than that. My father is getting on in years, and I'd like to stay closer to him than I did to my mother before she died. I also want to finish the work I've started on the Máire Bhuí poetry and biography project. I need to spend time looking at the transcripts of her poems in the archives at University College Cork. I also want to find out more about the Duke of Devonshire's clearances of *surplus* tenants from his estate at Inchigeelagh during the famine. You know what a profound effect Diarmuid de Búrca's famine journal left on me. I want to do something with that – find a way to combine the journal's words with the Máire Bhuí material – to bring his story to the attention of the wider world."

"I still think you can do most of that in Canada."

"Okay, here's the economic argument then."

"Is this going to be a lecture?"

He has thought this through. "The numbers are dire wherever you look. Newspapers are hurting because their top advertisers are bailing."

"Not in Edmonton, they're not. The *Journal* is not suffering."

262

"Not now, maybe, but that will change. The *Herald* is no longer spending the kind of money it did in the 1980s. On travel, for example. Our television guy used to go to L.A. twice a year to cover the network spring and fall launches. Now, he must get a papal dispensation to go to Banff for the TV festival. I'm sure it's the same at the *Journal*."

"The writers may not be travelling as much, but they still have their jobs."

"In the newsroom they do, but that could change, Carol. Look what happened to the composing room people. The company brought in these new computers, and their jobs became redundant. That's how the industry works. Out with the old, in with the new, and to hell with the consequences."

"They won't be replacing reporters with computers."

"No, but they'll be eliminating more beats, and that will shrink the reporting pool. The *Herald* doesn't cover labour any more. Nor does it cover Native affairs."

"What makes you think things will be any better back in Ireland?"

"The Irish economy has been doing well because of the EU transfer payments. I figure that if the Canadian economy is going to be in the dumper for a while, I should try my luck back home."

"But didn't you tell me only last year that you thought the roar of the Celtic Tiger would make you deaf?"

"That was then, this is now."

"I'll be so lonesome," she says.

"I'll write. I'll phone."

"It won't be the same."

263

"I'll come back for visits. And you'll come over to see me, won't you?"

She takes a tissue from her purse, dabs her eyes, and blows her nose. "It still won't be the same. Let's drink up now and go to our room."

"One more thing. I haven't mentioned this to you before, Carol, but I need to say it now. There's a part of me that has always felt I became a traitor to the Irish State – a deserter if you will – when I left my post and came to Canada. I had a decent job over there. I could have stayed. My siblings still accuse me of abandoning them."

"But then you became a Canadian citizen and lived here for as long as you lived in Ireland. So, do you now feel the same way about leaving Canada?"

"I never became a Canadian citizen."

"But I thought you …"

"I could never swear allegiance to the Queen."

Should he tell her he plans to meet with the Gardaí after he returns to Ireland? That he's been keeping something secret from her since they first met? Maybe not yet.

He looks out the window at the blue-green luminescence of the Northern Lights bathing the horizon in a mystical glow. Above them glimmers a proliferation of stars reaching deep into the void. They penetrate the cosmos like a million planetary explorers, extending into places unknown. He feels a shiver of awe and loneliness. "The love of one's country is a terrible thing."

"Why do you say that?"

264

"It's a line from a traditional folksong I learned when I was in the civil service. I used to sing it with Tom in Dublin, and again when we first came to Canada."

He now understands it better.

D ear Dad:

Sorry for the delay in responding to your Christmas letter. I've been distracted recently, as I'll explain in a minute.

Congratulations on recovering your old typewriting skills. I'm sure it's like riding a bike. Now that you've regained the touch, you'll never want to go back to longhand again. Typed correspondence used to seem impersonal to me. However, I've always liked it for the efficiency and speed, not to mention the legibility. Glad you're having fun with your new computer.

I haven't been doing much typing recently. That's because it's been over a year now – 14 months, to be precise – since I left the *Herald*. I didn't tell you about it at the time because I didn't want you to be worried and I hadn't yet decided what my next move would be.

Now I've decided. Hold onto your hat, Dad, because this will come as a surprise. My next move is back to Ireland. Yes, I'm coming home.

I've had plenty of time to think about this. The *Herald* gave me a generous severance package, which meant I didn't have to go looking for another job right away. When I did start searching, I discovered that the Canadian media landscape is bleak. Long gone are the days when you could walk across the street to land another job.

I'll tell you more about this when I see you. I expect it will take me about six weeks to finish wrapping up things in Calgary. I've cashed in my co-op shares and am now selling (and giving away) my furniture. That means I should be heading homeward sometime around the middle of April. If I can stay with you for a couple of weeks, I would like that. I will look for a flat in Dundrum or Rathfarnham because I've always been partial to the south side and would like to re-establish myself there in the first instance.

How is life as you approach your 76th? I hope the ticker problem isn't keeping you away from the golf club. Sounds like your "alphabetical" journey through the works of the world's great novelists is leading you into interesting places. You must be through with the Dickens canon by now and into the quirky domain of J.P. Donleavy and the sleuthing fiction of Arthur Conan Doyle. I want to be at the place that you've reached!

Keep well. I'll phone you in a few weeks to let you know my travel plans.

Love,

Jeremiah

JERRY STOPS OFF AT THE GPO to post a letter to Carol before heading over to the Pearse Street Garda station to confess. He looks at the Oliver Sheppard statue of Cú Chulainn and recalls Yeats's lines:

"When Pearse summoned Cú Chulainn to his side/What stalked through the Post Office? What intellect, what calculation, number, measurement, replied?"

The uniformed police sergeant opens a file with the words "Nelson's Pillar" stamped on the front. He puts a yellow legal pad on the table and starts taking notes. "Why did you decide to come forward now?" he asks Jerry.

"Because it's the thirtieth anniversary of the bombing and the eightieth anniversary of the Easter Rising. I wanted to clear my conscience."

Jerry looks around the sparsely furnished interview room and wonders where they put the security video camera. There must be a video camera, right? Isn't that how the cops get their evidence so they can prove to the judge that the accused made a full confession? Is the camera located behind that portrait of Dev hanging on the wall behind the sergeant? Jerry recalls with a smile that Dev, the normally humourless Irish president Éamon de Valera, supposedly phoned *The Irish Press* with a suggested headline for the story after Nelson was dispatched to kingdom come: "British Admiral Leaves Dublin by Air."

"Would you like to have a solicitor present, Mr. Burke?" asks the sergeant. He taps on the table with his Bic ballpoint pen.

"Not today. I want to help you close this case." It was difficult for him to make this decision, but he's held his peace for too long.

"Do you mind if I bring in my supervisor to hear what you have to say?"

"Not at all."

The sergeant leaves the interview room and returns a few minutes later with another uniformed officer. "This is Inspector O'Leary. He may have a few questions for you after I finish." The inspector is carrying a copy of *The Irish Press* dated March 14, 1966. The front-page headline says, "The Big Bang: Army Blasts Pillar Stump." After the bombing, the army had been dispatched to demolish the jagged stump that survived the explosion. Jerry smiles as he recalls how the army messed up the job. Blew out the nearby shop windows, with dust-coated mannequins bearing witness.

"Where did the idea to blow it up come from?" asks the sergeant, reaching for a cigarette from the Players Navy Cut pack on the table. He pushes the pack toward Jerry, who shakes his head, pushes it back, and reaches for the water glass.

"We were having a drink in a bar and ..." says Jerry.

The sergeant interrupts. "Who was there with you?"

"I can't give you the names."

"Why not?"

"I don't want to implicate anyone else."

"Okay, we'll leave it at that for now. How many of you were there?"

"Five or six."

"If you can't give us their names, can you at least give us a general description of who they were? Members of the IRA? Republican sympathizers?"

"Sympathizers, certainly. One or two members of the IRA might have been there as well."

"Are you, were you a member?"

"No, a sympathizer."

"What else were you doing then? Were you a student or were you working?"

"I was doing both. Going to my job during the day and taking courses at the university in the evening."

"Where were you working?"

"I'd rather not say."

"Continue."

"We were having a drink, and one of my friends said it was terrible to see a statue of a British admiral still standing in O'Connell Street. He said we should blow it to smithereens, and we all agreed this would be a clever idea."

"But the Pillar had stood there for more than 150 years," says the sergeant. "Why then?"

"It was the fiftieth anniversary of the Rising, and they were marking it with nothing more than a few public functions and dinners. We thought we should commemorate it with something more spectacular."

"So, you decided to blow up the Pillar?"

"That was the plan. We codenamed it Operation Humpty Dumpty."

"What happened next?"

"One of the lads said he could build the bomb out of gelignite and ammonal. However, he couldn't make it at home because his young son would be asking questions and might tell his pals about it. So, we found an empty garage for him in Rathmines where he could put it together. We decided the explosion should take place during the early hours of March the first."

"But it didn't happen until March the eighth."

"That's correct. Liam did put the bomb there on February the 28th, but the timer malfunctioned, and the bomb failed to go off."

"Liam?"

"Sorry, I shouldn't have told you his first name. He did say he plans to go public with his story at some point, but he's not ready to do that yet."

"So, the bomb failed to go off?"

"Yes. Liam went back up the spiral staircase the following day, March the first. He cut the wires with nail clippers he had bought in the Clery's chemist department, put the bomb into his duffel bag, brought it back down the steps, and gave it to me."

"What did you do with it?"

"I drove it back to Rathmines so that Liam could put a new timer on it."

"What kind of a timer was it?"

"An ordinary alarm clock, like you'd have on your bedside table."

"Aside from taking the malfunctioning bomb over to Rathmines, what other role did you play in this operation?"

"I did all the driving, back and forth from Rathmines to the city centre."

"Driving Liam?"

"No, driving the bomb. He didn't want to bring it with him on the bus from Ranelagh. I picked up the bomb in Rathmines, met Liam at the number forty-four O'Connell Street stop, and he carried the bomb from there to the Pillar. It wasn't a big device, so he could easily carry it."

"Were you at all concerned that it could blow up while you were driving it?"

"No. The wires would have to be connected before it could explode."

"When Liam placed it in the Pillar, were you concerned it might cause injury or loss of life?"

"Not at that hour of the morning. It was set to go off at 1:32 AM, and Dublin shut down at 11:30 PM. The pubs would have closed by then, and the last buses would have been driven over to Busáras."

"Some people could still have been walking along O'Connell Street at that time."

"Highly unlikely, we thought."

"Where in the Pillar did he place the bomb?"

"As I understand it, about two-thirds of the way up, in the little window facing up the street towards Parnell Square."

"Not in the viewing platform at the top?"

"No, he told me there were about five or six people on the platform the first time he went in, so he didn't want to risk doing the final assembly there."

The sergeant stops taking notes and closes the file folder. "That's all the questions I have for the moment, Jerry. Inspector O'Leary may have more to ask you. Did you want to take a toilet break before we continue?"

"No, I'm good."

"I have one or two questions for you," says the inspector. "Did you accompany Liam into the Pillar when he was placing the bomb?"

"No, I didn't go in on either occasion. I did walk some of the way up O'Connell Street with him, but let him go into the Pillar by himself."

"Why was that?"

"I guess I figured that if anything went wrong, if the bomb exploded prematurely, that I didn't want to become a martyr to the cause."

"Understandable. Did you go into the Pillar with him when he was retrieving the malfunctioning bomb?"

"No, I waited for him out on the street."

"Did you wait out there each time he went in?"

"Not the first time, because he was going home on the bus afterwards. I did wait for him the second time, when he went in to retrieve the bomb, because I knew I'd have to take it back to Rathmines."

"And the third time?"

"No, because Liam said something about wanting to see an afternoon matinee at the Savoy after he placed the bomb with the new timer."

"And these visits to the Pillar, they would have taken place in the morning or afternoon, right?"

"During the afternoon, that's correct. We had to be there no later than about half-past two because the Pillar closed at three o'clock."

"Did Liam say anything to you after the second visit? When he went in to retrieve the malfunctioning bomb?"

"He said he shook hands with the caretaker and felt tempted to tell him he wouldn't have a job the following week."

"Amusing. I presume he kept the retrieved bomb hidden from the caretaker?"

"Of course. He put it in his duffel bag."

"And the caretaker didn't check bags?"

"I guess he didn't think there was anything of value to be stolen from the Pillar."

"Have you talked to anyone else about this during the past thirty years?"

"No. I lived in Canada for twenty-seven years and never mentioned it to anyone over there."

"How about over here?"

"No, aside from the others who were with me when we planned the bombing."

"Have you talked to them since you got back?"

"To one of them."

"Your friend Liam?"

"That's correct."

"Can you give me his last name?"

"I'd prefer not to. You'll be hearing from him at the appropriate time."

"Did you go to Canada by yourself?"

"I went with a friend. We used to play music together. He's back here now, teaching at the Institute of Technology."

"Was he one of the people who planned the bombing?"

"No, he wasn't involved."

"And you never told him about your involvement?"

"I never told anyone."

"Why not?"

"I didn't want to look back. When I moved to Canada, I wanted to leave my past life behind." Modifying his Christian name was the first step. He wanted to reinvent himself. Create a new persona in a place where he knew nobody, and nobody knew him.

"So, I'm curious to know," says the inspector, "why are you telling us about this now, after thirty years of silence?"

"Residual guilt. Wanting to settle outstanding accounts. That kind of thing."

"You realize you could go to jail for this if convicted under the Offences Against the State Act?"

"I thought there was a statute of limitations?"

"Not for an indictable offence like this, although judges have discretion in the case of excessively lengthy delays."

"Isn't thirty years considered a long delay?"

"That would be up to the judge to decide. We would argue that you were responsible for the delay."

"Then I'm prepared to answer for all the consequences of my decision."

"Do you have family here?"

"My father and two sisters."

"Did you tell them you would be coming here today?"

"My father's in the hospital, so he has enough to deal with already. I haven't told my sisters yet. They'll hear about it soon enough, I'm sure."

The two officers push back from the table and stand up. "We'll have to discuss this matter with the Director of Public Prosecutions before we can proceed further. Did you want to come back here next week? We should be able to tell you then what the next step will be."

"Should I bring my solicitor?"

"That will be up to you."

JERRY RETURNS TO THE PEARSE STREET Garda Station the following week. A lawyer named Joe Christle accompanies him. "We have good news, Mr. Burke," says the sergeant. "There will be no charges. You're free to go."

Jerry looks up at the portrait of Dev. He seemed so dour in the photo before. Now, he looks as if he's about to smile. A republican Mona Lisa. Avoided execution for treason in 1916 because he was born in America. Rose to become president of the republic. Like Mandela, he was. A revolutionary turned statesman.

"Can you tell us what charges you discussed?" says the lawyer.

"We looked at a number of them," says the sergeant. "Conspiracy to commit a crime against the State. Aiding and abetting. Causing damage to public property. Becoming an accessory before and after the fact. Charges like that."

"But you had no corroborating testimony?" says Christle. "Only the unsworn statement of my client?"

276

"That's correct," says the sergeant. "We see many people who confess to crimes they didn't commit. Publicity seekers who want to see their pictures on the telly."

Jerry doesn't say anything. He didn't break his silence after thirty years to be dismissed by the Gardaí as a liar or attention getter. He knows he had a valid reason for being involved in Operation Humpty Dumpty. Couldn't stand the thought of a British admiral occupying the spot that rightly belonged to Pearse, Connolly and the other rebel heroes of 1916.

Now, however, he acknowledges it was probably not the best idea to blow up the iconic granite column. In hindsight, it was an empty gesture. Few Dubliners – aside from Jerry and his republican friends – thought of the Pillar as a hated symbol of British imperialism on Irish sovereign soil. For most, it was just a part of Dublin in the rare old times. The city's focal point. The terminus for many of the city buses. Office workers ate their lunchtime sandwiches there. The rendezvous of choice for courting couples out on the town for an evening at the movies. "See you on Wednesday, then? Meet you at the Pillar."

Jerry wishes he could turn back the clock. Regardless of who stood on top of it, the Pillar gave Dublin a distinctive appearance. Endowed the city with a beacon for visitors as recognizable as the Eiffel Tower or the Empire State Building. After his friends blew it to smithereens, they left the city bereft. Diminished the city core. Reduced downtown Dublin to a mirror image of the abominations that passed for human shelter in Luton, Coventry, and Birmingham. If they had simply taken out Nelson instead of half the entire Pillar, they would have still left the city with a splendid pedestal for honouring a popular figure from

277

Irish rather than English history. The Pillar's undistinguished replacement, "The Spire," was an inferior substitute.

Was there ever a justifiable reason for destroying the Pillar? Jerry recalls what the poet Louis MacNeice wrote twenty years before the bombing: "And Nelson on his Pillar/Watching his world collapse." Nelson had already witnessed the disintegration of his domain long before he was toppled from his perch.

Jerry looks at his lawyer and back at the sergeant, who is putting the "Nelson's Pillar" file back into its folder. "If there are to be no charges, then, do you now consider this matter closed?"

"Yes, unless someone else comes forward. Then we might take another look at the situation. In the meantime, you're free and clear."

Should he now go to confession? Cleanse his immortal soul? Do penance for his sins? He still has to answer to a higher authority. Maybe not yet.

He walks from the Garda station to the bus stop. He has bared his soul. He feels an uneasy sense of peace. Should he phone Carol in Edmonton? He'll think about it.

Author's Afterword

Much of *The Love of One's Country* is historically, geographically, and factually accurate. I wrote between the lines of narrative nonfiction to turn it into a work of fiction. Máire Bhuí Ní Laoire (Yellow Mary O'Leary) was a real-life Irish folk poet of the nineteenth century. She was also an ancestor of mine. Her son, Eilic (Alec) Burke, was my maternal grandmother's grandfather.

I had included translations of my ancestor's poems in my nonfiction biography, *Máire Bhuí Ní Laoire: A Poet of her People*, originally published in Ireland and republished in North America under the title, *Songs of an Irish Poet: The Mary O'Leary Story*. Some of the lines from those poems are featured in this novel. I also drew from what I know of Máire Bhuí's life and times. However, she didn't have an emigrant son named Diarmuid de Búrca. I created him to put a human face on the famine refugees who left Ireland on the coffin ships during the 1840s.

The famine refugee story takes as its point of departure the content of two diaries offering alleged first-person accounts by emigrants who sailed from Ireland to Canada in 1847. The first diary, published in Boston and London in 1848, was titled *The Ocean Plague* and credited to a cabin passenger named Robert Whyte. The second, serialized as in a Quebec newspaper in 1895, was attributed to a cabin passenger named Gerald Keegan. Both purported to be authentic accounts when first published, but proved suspect upon later examination.

The Whyte account appeared at first to be the more reliable source. The editors of a University of Virginia digital archive, *Irish Views of the Famine*, described a 1994 republication of the diary by Ireland's Mercier Press as "an authentic reproduction of the original text, rather than a dramatization" and thus a "relatively more trustworthy account." Mark McGowan, a University of Toronto history professor, begged to differ, however. The Whyte diary, he wrote, was "almost too good, and there are several problems that arise once it is placed under close scrutiny." McGowan concluded that *The Ocean Plague*, republished as *Robert Whyte's 1847 Famine Ship Diary*, was "weakly substantiated by fact, and historically perplexing." To that I would add that Whyte revealed a tin ear when he tried capturing the cadences of the Irish dialect.

The Keegan account was also republished in Ireland. In 1982, it appeared as a nonfiction book titled *The Voyage of the Naparima*. In 1991, it reappeared as a book titled *Famine Diary: Journey to a New World*. The Irish publishers claimed that both of these new editions were based on an authentic famine diary, but offered no convincing evidence that Keegan ever existed. Two scholars, James Jackson of Dublin's Trinity College and Jacqueline Kornblum of New York University, then worked independently to analyze the Keegan diary, and both concluded it was a hoax; the product of a Canadian editor's imagination. "It cannot be seen as a genuine historical document," wrote Jackson. "It must be considered historical fiction." When confronted with this accusation, the editor of the new editions, a retired Toronto teacher named James J. Mangan, acknowledged that his texts did, in fact, "contain fictionalized versions of Keegan's journal."

After reading the Keegan diary, I too remained unconvinced that an Irish person could have written it. The voice of Ireland didn't resonate in that text. It rang false to my Irish ears: "Beggin' yer pardon, Mrs. Finegan, 'tis a docthur he be, an' he is comin' down to see thim sick wid the favor ..." This blather is typical of what passed for Irish dialect in those sentimental Hollywood movies of the 1940s and 1950s starring such professional Oirishmen as Bing Crosby (*Top o' the Morning*) and James Cagney (*Shake Hands with the Devil*).

Another problem I had with the Keegan diary was that it got one crucial fact wrong. It said the cabin assigned to Keegan and his wife for their trans-Atlantic voyage was "a cubby-hole in the house on deck." If that was the case, they would have been travelling on a ship that doesn't appear in any of the existing nautical records. I have studied the architectural drawings of the Dunbrody, a barque that crossed the Atlantic from New Ross, County Wexford to Quebec several times during the 1840s. It didn't have any cabins, much less a house, on deck. Nor, from what I saw during a tour of the Jeanie Johnston Tall Ship replica in Dublin, or in the paintings of sailing ships on display in the Cobh Museum of County Cork, or in the exhibits in Dublin's Epic Irish Emigration Museum, were there any other famine ships that had passenger accommodations up top. The only famine ship that had a cabin on the deck was one concocted in the mind of Robert Sellar, the *Canadian Gleaner* newspaper editor who first published in 1895 what purported to be the Keegan journal.

That said, when I looked beyond the historical inaccuracies, the phoney dialect, and the suspect provenance of the two diaries – both of which were edited for republication by Toronto's James J. Mangan – I saw a story that asked to be told again. In writing *The Love of One's Country*, I tried to imagine what it must have been like for an educated young Irishman to leave family, friends, and students behind to cross the Atlantic on a disease-racked ship never meant for the transport of human cargo, in the hope of making a new life for himself in Canada. I took some of the situations described in the Whyte and Keegan diaries and framed them within the context of what I learned by visiting and exploring replicas of the famine ships recently built in Ireland, and by reading such memoirs and histories as David Thomson's *Woodbrook,* Peter Gray's *The Irish Famine* and Jim Rees's *Surplus People*. I then used my imagination and words to tell the story.

The story of Jerry Burke, my protagonist of modern times, follows the trajectory of my own life. This is the most autobiographical part of the novel. Like Jerry, I was a restless wanderer from Dublin who came to Canada in 1966, worked for a while as a travelling musician, drifted into journalism, and ended up as a staff writer and columnist with the *Calgary Herald.*

That's where the similarity ends. Much of what happens to Jerry Burke never occurred in my life. Many of the characters in this part of the book are either fictionalized versions or composites of real people, although I do feature cameo appearances by well-known figures from contemporary Irish and Canadian life. Many names are changed to protect the unsuspecting. If you want to know who some of the real people are, you may find them in the pages of my nonfiction book of memoirs, *Leaving Dublin: Writing My Way from Ireland to Canada.*

NOTE: You will have noticed that in some parts of this book, I call them famine "emigrants" and in other places, I use the word "immigrants." This was intentional. In Ireland, they were emigrants because they were leaving. In Canada, they became immigrants because they were arriving. I was an emigrant when I left and now, in Canada, am an immigrant turned citizen. I am proud to belong to both countries. Ireland made me, and Canada embraced me.

(Photo by Bob Blakey)

About the Author

BRIAN BRENNAN emigrated from Ireland to Canada the easy way, on an Aer Lingus Boeing 707 from Dublin to Montreal in November 1966. After working as a travelling musician for two years he became a newspaper reporter – and a Canadian citizen – in British Columbia. He left the news business in 1999 after spending twenty-five years as a staff columnist and features writer with the *Calgary Herald*. He lives and writes in Calgary. This is his sixteenth published book. For more information, visit his website at www.brianbrennan.ca There, among other things, you'll find a link to a Spotify playlist of the songs mentioned in this novel.

Acknowledgements

This story has evolved in sundry ways during the thirty years I've spent looking for the best way to tell it. It began life as a radio play where the Jerry character was going about his day-to-day business while the Diarmuid character was reading passages from his journal. That concept didn't work. I couldn't give the listener a sense what was going on in Diarmuid's head because I limited the telling of his story to a series of journal entries.

The first drafts of the novel had the same problem. While Jerry's story transported the reader from his unfulfilled life in Dublin to a more rewarding life in Canada, the journal entries sat flat on the page like piss on a plate. Turning the journal entries into an exchange of letters between Diarmuid and his mother didn't make things any better.

An accomplished American book doctor named Susan Sutliff Brown put me on the right track. "Forget the journal entries, forget the letters," she said. "They don't work in a novel. Tell this as Diarmuid's story with his personality (restless rebel leader with Catholic guilt) providing the vehicle for the readers to learn about the horrors of the Irish famine."

I read some of my new Diarmuid chapters to Susan during her intensive fiction workshop at a 2017 writers' conference in San Miguel de Allende, Mexico, and she gave me additional practical and constructive advice. I came home to Calgary, finished the novel, and gave it to my wife Zelda Brennan, my first reader, for reaction. She gave me useful and thought-provoking suggestions, along with support and encouragement. Additional suggestions and comments, all valuable and much appreciated, came from Michael Murphy, Arthur Kent, Peter McKenzie-Brown, David Scollard and Rose Scollard. For the final edit, I entrusted the manuscript to my friend and writing comrade Rona Altrows, who gave it the tough reading it needed for further polishing and improvement. Sincere thanks to all of you for giving strength and solace to a first novelist.

I would also like to thank graphic designer Sydney Barnes, who created the cover and included all the elements I requested, including an image of the little red book that plays a prominent role throughout the novel. *The Love of One's Country* is now a book that *can* be judged by its cover because Sydney created such an imaginative and complementary design.

B.B. August 2019

CPSIA information can be obtained
at www.ICGtesting.com
Printed in the USA
LVHW030130060919
630127LV00001B/21